# Brigid didn't let her finish the sentence

Her booted foot kicked high, thumping Skylar hard in the chest, knocking her backward once more until she slammed into the side of the desk. "The curious cat was killed, Skylar," she said.

"What's got into you?" Skylar wailed fearfully, struggling to keep her balance as she was forced against the desk.

"Never liked you," Brigid said again, leaping forward, her hands closing around Skylar's throat. "Nosy and arrogant because you know how to operate computers. That's not a talent, Skylar. That's barely even an ability."

"P-please," Skylar croaked as Brigid's grip tightened around her neck, "Miss Baptiste. I think something is very wrong with you…please try to…"

She could tell that Brigid wasn't listening, and she struggled vainly to loosen the grip of the taller woman. There was a dark, determined look in Brigid's narrowed eyes, a horrible joy in the set of her smiling jaw. Skylar thought that she knew what it was—bloodlust.

**Other titles in this series:**

# James Axler
# Outlanders®

## JANUS TRAP

A GOLD EAGLE BOOK FROM
# WORLDWIDE®

TORONTO • NEW YORK • LONDON
AMSTERDAM • PARIS • SYDNEY • HAMBURG
STOCKHOLM • ATHENS • TOKYO • MILAN
MADRID • WARSAW • BUDAPEST • AUCKLAND

Recycling programs
for this product may
not exist in your area.

First edition August 2009

ISBN-13: 978-0-373-63863-5

JANUS TRAP

Copyright © 2009 by Worldwide Library.

Special thanks to Rik Hoskin for his contribution to this work.

**Printed in U.S.A.**

I turn and turn in my cell like a fly that doesn't know where to die.

—Antonio Gramsci, 1891–1937.

## The Road to Outlands—
## From Secret Government Files to the Future

Almost two hundred years after the global holocaust, Kane, a former Magistrate of Cobaltville, often thought the world had been lucky to survive at all after a nuclear device detonated in the Russian embassy in Washington, D.C. The aftermath—forever known as skydark—reshaped continents and turned civilization into ashes.

Nearly depopulated, America became the Deathlands—poisoned by radiation, home to chaos and mutated life forms. Feudal rule reappeared in the form of baronies, while remote outposts clung to a brutish existence.

What eventually helped shape this wasteland were the redoubts, the secret preholocaust military installations with stores of weapons, and the home of gateways, the locational matter-transfer facilities. Some of the redoubts hid clues that had once fed wild theories of government cover-ups and alien visitations.

Rearmed from redoubt stockpiles, the barons consolidated their power and reclaimed technology for the villes. Their power, supported by some invisible authority, extended beyond their fortified walls to what was now called the Outlands. It was here that the rootstock of humanity survived, living with hellzones and chemical storms, hounded by Magistrates.

In the villes, rigid laws were enforced—to atone for the sins of the past and prepare the way for a better future. That was the barons' public credo and their right-to-rule.

Kane, along with friend and fellow Magistrate Grant, had upheld that claim until a fateful Outlands expedition. A displaced piece of technology…a question to a keeper of the archives…a vague clue about alien masters—and their world shifted radically. Suddenly, Brigid Baptiste, the archivist, faced summary execution, and Grant a quick termination. For

Kane there was forgiveness if he pledged his unquestioning allegiance to Baron Cobalt and his unknown masters and abandoned his friends.

But that allegiance would make him support a mysterious and alien power and deny loyalty and friends. Then what else was there?

Kane had been brought up solely to serve the ville. Brigid's only link with her family was her mother's red-gold hair, green eyes and supple form. Grant's clues to his lineage were his ebony skin and powerful physique. But Domi, she of the white hair, was an Outlander pressed into sexual servitude in Cobaltville. She at least knew her roots and was a reminder to the exiles that the outcasts belonged in the human family.

Parents, friends, community—the very rootedness of humanity was denied. With no continuity, there was no forward momentum to the future. And that was the crux—when Kane began to wonder if there *was* a future.

For Kane, it wouldn't do. So the only way was out—way, way out.

After their escape, they found shelter at the forgotten Cerberus redoubt headed by Lakesh, a scientist, Cobaltville's head archivist, and secret opponent of the barons.

With their past turned into a lie, their future threatened, only one thing was left to give meaning to the outcasts. The hunger for freedom, the will to resist the hostile influences. And perhaps, by opposing, end them.

# Prologue

In a broken air vent, in a hidden bunker beneath the Caucasus Mountains, a woman dressed in strips of material was waking up.

Almost two days before, when she had awakened to find herself beaten and bloody on the floor of the bunk room, Cloud Singer had immediately engaged the implant at the base of her neck and tried to dreamslice. But, to her horror, nothing had happened, no jump, no transferral, nothing.

She had strained her ears, listening for a trace of the singing bull roarer, its promising salvation, but all had been silent. Then, as she listened, she had heard voices, people in the underground complex, walking along the corridor, and the beam of their flashlight danced in the open doorway.

She had moved quickly, despite the pain from all over her body, clambering into the broken vent on the wall of the bunk room, the one that Kane had shot to pieces. Inside, she had hidden herself from sight while her enemies went about their cleanup operation, sweeping the bunker for stragglers, but failing to find her.

And she had tried, periodically, to dreamslice, to step out of Realworld and into the Dreaming, but nothing had happened.

Tucked there, in the absolute darkness, beside the room full of skeletons, she had slowed her breathing and willed herself into a healing coma, her heart beating at an eighth of its usual pace.

Almost two days later, conscious once more, she found herself alone.

Cloud Singer blinked, bringing her electrochemical polymer lenses to life on the nictitating membranes that slotted over her eyes, granting her night vision in the pitch-dark bunker.

On silent feet, she walked from the bunk room, checking each doorway in turn, confirming her suspicion that she was totally alone in the complex. Alone except for the corpse of Neverwalk, a bloody ruin where his neck had been.

With none of her strike team left, no access to the Dreaming, Cloud Singer was utterly alone.

Alone but *alive*.

# Chapter 1

*Several months later*

The whole of Cerberus redoubt was in pieces, or so it seemed when Donald Bry walked into the operations room.

Bry's breath caught in his throat as he saw exposed wiring and circuitry littering the surfaces of the three desks farthest from the door. He held two mugs of freshly brewed coffee, and as he took a step closer, the petite-framed Skylar Hitch popped up from beneath one of the desks, so close that she almost knocked the mugs out of his hands.

Hitch was a timid woman in her twenties who stood a mere five feet tall. Her light coffee-colored skin was smooth and flawless, while her hazel eyes seemed alive with intelligence. This day, she had tied her glossy black hair back in an abbreviated ponytail that brushed against her nape as she turned her head. Like the other personnel in the operations room, Skylar wore a white bodysuit with a vertical zipper. She laughed nervously as she saw Bry standing before her.

"My goodness, I'm sorry, Donald," she said, looking away from him in discomfort. "I almost knocked you flying."

Although only a small man himself, Bry doubted whether Skylar Hitch would actually be able to knock him flying, even catching him unawares like that. He was a round-shouldered man with an unruly mop of curly, copper-colored hair. A well-trusted member of the Cerberus team, Bry acted as deputy leader for the facility. He wore his customary expression of consternation as though always unable to find the answer to a pressing problem.

The operations room itself was large and high ceilinged. There were two aisles of computer terminals, and a huge Mercator-relief map stretched the length of the wall over the entry. The map was dotted with lights of different colors that played across it like old-fashioned flight paths.

In the corner of the room where Hitch worked at the dismantled computers, far away from the main door, a small chamber was set inside a larger anteroom, its transparent walls made of smoked armaglass. This was the mat-trans unit and, back when the redoubt had originally been established, it had formed the centerpiece of the whole military-funded operation.

Coffee sloshed about in the mugs Bry held as he gestured to the mess of wiring and circuitry. "What is going on here, Skylar? I left you alone for fifteen minutes…"

"I've located our problem." Skylar smiled. "The motherboards are overheating, and it's causing the system to crash."

Bry looked at her, astonished. Though timid and bookish, Hitch was a computer expert who sometimes gave the impression that she actually thought in computer language, she was so in tune with the machinery in the Cerberus redoubt. Over the past week, there had been several instances when the computers in the ops area froze, shut down or provided streams of gobbledygook on their monitors. Bry had genuine concerns that a virus was attacking their computers—a group in Australia had hacked into their system and fed the Cerberus machines false data only a few months ago—but he had been unable to find any obvious coding glitches.

Skylar Hitch was one of a number of IT experts who were on call for such problems, and she and Bry had spent the early morning running a series of system checks trying to diagnose the glitch. He had left her for a quarter of an hour while he used the bathroom and grabbed some strong coffee from the facility canteen, trusting Skylar to continue the diagnosis alone. The last thing he had expected to find on his return was three computers stripped down to their component parts.

"These computers are years old," Skylar explained. "They're just wearing out."

Bry shook his head and sighed. "We're all wearing out," he grumbled, finishing his statement with a sip of hot coffee.

Skylar rolled a two-inch-long screwdriver across her fingers, a nervous tic. "I can keep replacing bits piecemeal," she told Bry, "but ultimately we should probably look at updating or renewing the whole system."

Bry nodded. "Replace what you can, Skylar," he told her as he placed the mugs on the desk and offered to give her a hand.

Around them, the morning shift personnel filed in to begin their designated tasks, working the monitoring system and tracking the various field teams, all of them ignoring the disruption going on beside them.

ELSEWHERE IN THE VAST complex, Grant lay in bed in a darkened room, head resting against his upturned hand, admiring the beautiful woman lying next to him. He was a huge, muscular man, and he seemed like a coiled spring even as he lay peacefully watching his sleeping companion. Grant had skin like polished mahogany and his dark hair was cropped close to his scalp. A drooping, gunslinger's mustache brushed across his upper lip, and the dark shadow of stubble was just starting to appear upon his chin. Grant was an ex-Magistrate from Cobaltville, whose labyrinthine life's journey had brought him here to the Cerberus redoubt.

The woman beside Grant seemed tiny in comparison to the ex-Mag, but her slight frame was that of an athlete, her belly flat, tight knots of muscle visible on her arms and legs. Shizuka was a warrior born, but unlike Grant, her skin was a golden color accented with peach and milk, and her closed eyes showed the pleasing almond curve of her Oriental ancestry. She had full, petaled lips beneath a small stub nose, and her fine blue-black hair was cut so that it brushed the tops of her shoulders. Shizuka was a woman of astonishing beauty, and Grant knew that he would never, even for a second, take her for granted.

As he silently watched Shizuka, the woman's eyes fluttered open. After a moment she turned to face him, a smile on her lips. "What are you doing?" she queried, her voice barely more than a whisper.

"Just thinking about how beautiful you are," Grant told her.

Shizuka blushed, her smile growing wider. "What are you after, Grant-*san?*" she asked.

One of Grant's mighty hands reached forward and, with infinite gentleness, brushed her dark hair from her face. "Nothing you don't want to give, Shizuka," he assured her, leaning across the bed to kiss her fully on the mouth.

Shizuka's golden arms reached around and pulled the huge man closer, kissing him back with the same ferocious passion that she showed for battle.

SEVERAL FLOORS BELOW, in a long room at the end of a corridor that ran the length of the subbasement, two people stood side by side, blasting shot after shot from the guns in their hands as though their very lives depended on it. Four large speakers placed strategically around the room were pumping out loud, guitar-led music, filling the room with the strains of a long-forgotten rock and roll band.

One of the shooters was a muscular man with dark hair and steely blue-gray eyes. Like Grant, Kane was an ex-Magistrate from Cobaltville whose life in recent years had been intrinsically tied to the well-being of the Cerberus operation. He was built like a wolf, firm muscles across the upper half of his body, powerful legs holding him in a rock-steady stance as he reeled off a stream of bullets at the multiple targets that hurtled toward him from all sides of the room. He was dressed in casual clothes, a dark T-shirt and combat pants, and his eyes shifted from one target to the next as they appeared at various positions along the length of the firing range. His Sin Eater handgun blasted a continuous stream of 9 mm bullets as each item appeared, each bullet finding its target, not a single shot wasted.

Standing beside him, Kane's companion was a tall woman with pale skin and dazzling red hair that fell in waves to almost halfway down her spine. The woman wore the standard white jumpsuit of the Cerberus redoubt's staff, and it hugged her so tightly as to accentuate the curves of her trim, athletic body. Her emerald eyes narrowed as she scanned the room for new targets, the bulky TP-9 pistol held before her in a two-handed grip. Brigid Baptiste was an archivist-turned-warrior who excelled in both disciplines.

There was a clatter off to the left, its sound masked by the loud, pumping music, and a target dropped from the rails that ran the length and breadth of the ceiling. Kane and Brigid shifted their weapons toward the target in unison, their movements liquid smooth. Kane's favored Sin Eater pistol spit bullets at the silhouette's chest, scoring a hit dead center of the heart, while Brigid's TP-9 semi-automatic pistol blasted a bullet through the silhouette's forehead, leaving a craterlike wound in the upper half of the card target.

With a whir, the devastated target whipped back up into the ceiling while two others dropped from the right-hand side of the room. With an astonishing economy of move-ment, Kane and Brigid turned and sighted the new targets. As ever, Kane took the one that was farthest from the previous target while Brigid cut the other to pieces with a stream of 9 mm rounds.

Suddenly, a spinning red light flashed overhead, and a honking noise cut into the guitar chords blasting from the speakers. Fifteen minutes had passed; the gruelling training session was over.

Kane stood there, his gun still raised for a few seconds, feeling the rise and fall of his chest as he brought his heart rate back to normal. After a moment, he turned to Brigid, openly admiring her as she steadied her own breathing, beads of sweat dripping down her nose, her red hair damp.

"You okay?" he asked, raising his voice to be heard over the saxophone solo that had interrupted the gritty voice of the singer from the wall speakers.

Brigid nodded, her eyes closed, a tentative smile on her lips. Then she turned to look at Kane, and her smile widened, showing two straight lines of perfect white teeth. "That was intense," she said, her voice rich and husky. "What the heck setting did you use?"

"I got Hitch to rig up something with a little extra kick just for me and Grant," Kane explained with a chuckle. "Too much for you, Baptiste?"

The redheaded woman checked the breech and holstered her semiautomatic at her hip before looking Kane directly in the eye. "I'll let you know when it's too much," she told him, a definite challenge in her tone.

Kane couldn't help but laugh at her bravado. "You know, you shape up pretty good for a bookworm," he said, chuckling and reaching for the control panel and powering down the target-practice program as it waited on its standby setting. A moment later, he cut the music and followed his beautiful companion through the exit door and into the changing area.

A quick shower and they would be ready to face the day.

THE ANCIENT MILITARY redoubt that served as the head-quarters of the Cerberus operation was located high in the Bitterroot Mountain Range in Montana, where it had remained largely forgotten or ignored for the two bleak centuries that followed the nukecaust of 2001. In the intervening years, a strange mythology had built up around the shadow-filled forests and seemingly bottom-less ravines of the mountains. The wilderness surrounding the tri-level concrete structure was virtually unpopulated; the nearest settlement was some miles away in the flat-lands beyond the mountains themselves, just a small band of Sioux and Cheyenne Indians led by a shaman named Sky Dog who had befriended several of the Cerberus warriors over the years.

The facility itself had not always been called Cerberus. Its official name was Redoubt Bravo, named, like all prewar redoubts, after a letter of the alphabet, as used in standard military radio communications. Redoubt Bravo had been dedicated to the monitoring and exploration of the newly developed matter-transfer network. However, somewhere in the mists of time, a young soldier had painted a vibrant rendition of the fabled, two-headed hound of Hades to guard the doors to the facility, like Cerberus guarding the gates to the underworld. The artist was long since dead, but his work had inspired the people who had taken over the facility to call it the Cerberus redoubt.

Hidden within the rocky clefts of the mountains around the building, disguised beneath camouflage netting, con-cealed uplinks chattered continuously with two orbiting satellites to provide a steady stream of data for the Cer-berus operatives within. Accessing the ancient satellites had been a long process, involving much trial and error by many of the top scientists at the redoubt. The Cerberus crew could draw on live feeds from both a Vela-class reconnaissance satellite and the Keyhole communications satellite.

Despite its location high in the fresh air of the Bitterroot Mountains, the Cerberus facility was a self-contained unit. Its personnel had become accustomed to recirculated, filtered air as provided by vast air-conditioning units that continually churned and cleansed the facility's air.

The Cerberus operation had been founded and staffed by a cryogenically displaced scientist called Mohandas Lakesh Singh, who had dedicated the redoubt to the continued survival and freedom of humanity.

Kane, in his previous life as a Magistrate at Cobaltville, had come upon evidence of a vast conspiracy that threatened the autonomy of humankind. Kane had stumbled on the first clues to the existence of a hidden alien race called the Annunaki who had been dabbling in humankind's affairs for longer than anyone could comprehend. Appearing as gods to early man, the Annunaki had, from the shadows, guided the course of human history over the subsequent millennia, with an ultimate agenda of utter subjugation. Recently, the Annunaki royal family had revealed themselves on Earth once more, and Kane and his colleagues now found themselves in a deadly war of attrition against this seemingly unstoppable foe.

The Cerberus warriors were one of humanity's last bastions in the secret battle for the freedom of humankind.

GRANT'S THOUGHTS were suddenly interrupted by the buzzing of the transcomm at the side of his bed. He lay there another moment, just gazing up at the ceiling in the darkness as he felt Shizuka's lithe body stir beside him. Then, with a reluctant sigh, he leaned over and activated the button to answer the call.

After a moment, a man's face appeared in the tiny window display beside the little unit, smiling in a friendly manner. The man had dusky skin, an aquiline nose and a refined mouth. Lakesh appeared to be about fifty years of age, his sleek black hair displaying just the first hints of white at the temples and above the ears. In actuality, the expert physicist and cyberneticist was two hundred years older than that, having endured an extended period in suspended animation after the nukecaust in 2001. Until recently, Lakesh had physically appeared to be carrying every last one of his 250 years, until a would-be ally of the Cerberus exiles attempted to court their favor by reversing the aging process and giving the elderly scientist, literally, a new lease on life. However, in the months since that, Lakesh had become increasingly conscious that this miracle may not be all that it seemed, and he wondered whether this bountiful gift had hidden strings attached.

"Yeah, go," Grant said, looking into the screen where a tiny camera picked up his face and relayed the image to Lakesh up in the operations room.

"Grant," Lakesh began in his mellifluous voice, "did I wake you?"

Grant shook his head slightly as he felt Shizuka sidle behind him and wrap her arms around his wide chest, pulling herself close to him and nuzzling against his neck. "It's no problem, Lakesh. What's going on?"

"We've just heard from our contact in Tennessee," Lakesh explained. "The meeting's set up and, as we discussed a few days ago, I want you to attend with Kane and Brigid."

Grant nodded his acceptance. "The old crew back on the clock," Grant muttered with a reluctant smile. "When do we leave?"

"The meeting's set for 10:00 a.m., local time," Lakesh said. "You jump in forty minutes."

"No problem. I'll see you there," he vowed as he hit the button to cut the communication.

Behind him, Shizuka tightened her grip on his chest, grinding her hips against him. "Do you really have to rush off so soon, Grant-*san?*" she asked.

Grant turned his head to look over his shoulder. "Sorry, darling," he said, "but it's a simple pickup. It won't take more than a few hours."

Still holding him tightly, Shizuka kissed Grant beneath his ear. "I'll wait right here," she whispered.

After a moment, Grant extricated himself from the woman's grip and made his way to the tiny bathroom cubicle attached to the room. Shizuka watched from the bed as Grant flicked the motion-sensor light switch to the cubicle and began running the water for the little shower stall within. After a moment, Shizuka pulled herself from the bed and, naked, padded silently across the room to join Grant in the shower.

WHEN HE ARRIVED at the operations room thirty-five minutes later, washed and shaved, Grant found the large room a hive of activity. Lakesh had spread a series of papers across his desk that included several maps of the area around the recently destroyed ville of Beausoleil, Tennessee. Beside him, the red-haired Brigid Baptiste was glancing over the papers as Lakesh pointed out specific items of interest. Brigid was dressed in a shadow suit now, a one-piece black body stocking that appeared to be so thin as to be a second skin, and yet the fabric had remarkable properties. The shadow suit worked as a self-contained, self-regulated environment, and the weave was strong enough to deflect a knife blow or other blunt trauma but could not redistribute kinetic shock.

Off to one side of the room, Grant's longtime partner, Kane, rested against a desk as he spoke with Cerberus physician Reba DeFore. DeFore was a stocky but curvaceous woman with long ash-blond hair that she had tied up in an elaborately braided knot atop her head. Grant couldn't hear the details of their conversation, but he could see Reba count off items on her fingers. Grant watched as Kane copied her, his brow furrowed as he tried to remember each item that she had told him. Like Brigid, Kane was dressed in one of the remarkable shadow suits, as was Grant himself. Kane had added a thick belt with a heavy copper buckle to the suit, along with a pair of combat boots, and on the man's right wrist Grant could see the familiar pressure-sensitive holster containing a Sin Eater handgun.

Grant had added his favored long black duster over his own shadow suit, its dark Kevlar weave reaching past his knees. Like Kane, he wore the familiar weight of the Sin Eater pistol at his right wrist, tucked out of sight, just a little bulge beneath the sleeve. The weapon was a legacy from their days as Magistrates in Cobaltville, a position that Grant had held for almost two decades prior to his exile at the Cerberus redoubt. Kane had been his partner in Cobaltville, and the pair of them had defected together, along with archivist Brigid Baptiste, after stumbling upon the first hints of the Annunaki conspiracy.

Crouched at a desk beside the anteroom that held the mat-trans unit, Donald Bry and one of his technical team, a petite, coffee-skinned woman whom Grant had seen around a few times, were working through a bunch of wiring amid what looked like the remains of a half-dozen computer terminals.

Catching Lakesh's attention, Grant pointed to the tangle of wiring. "Trouble with the mat-trans?" he asked.

"No, thank goodness," Lakesh replied. "Just general problems with the old computers. Emphasis on *old*."

"Happens to us all," Grant said amiably as he joined Lakesh and Brigid at their desk to look over the paperwork that had been assembled for the mission.

Ten minutes later, Grant, Brigid and Kane were standing within the mat-trans chamber, ready to blast themselves through the ether in an instantaneous transition from Montana to Tennessee.

# Chapter 2

It took the blink of an eye to strip them down to their component atoms and fling the essence of their very beings across the country. And yet, no matter how many times he experienced it, Kane swore that he would never really get used to traveling by mat-trans.

Kane had added a denim jacket, a washed-out black turned gray, over his shadow suit. He stood in the Tennessee mat-trans chamber, its standard tiled floor and ceiling with the familiar, smoked armaglass walls all around. The armaglass here was tinted an odd color, and Kane knew from the color alone that he had not been here before. With the typical paranoia of the prenukecaust military mind, the mat-trans network, now over two hundred years old, used a simple color-coding system to establish location without any explicit indicators.

There were mat-trans units hidden in ancient military bases scattered across the old United States of America, with many others worldwide, including similar units developed by comparable military groups for other nations: The mat-trans units digitized an individual and thrust him or her across quantum space to a chamber at a programmed destination. In the intervening two centuries since their development, the network had remained largely undiscovered, with only a small number of people aware of these hidden gateways scattered across the globe.

Kane and the other Cerberus operatives considered the mat-trans a useful part of their arsenal, although traveling by it was still a disorienting and alien experience to the human body.

As his roiling stomach settled from the instantaneous journey, Kane glanced left and right, checking that his two colleagues had passed through the mat-trans gateway intact.

Grant stood to Kane's left, his dark skin shining with beads of sweat. While he had grown more used to travel by mat-trans, the man still had a deep-rooted dislike for the transportation method. All muscle, Grant was an ominous presence on any mission.

To Kane's right stood Brigid Baptiste. Brigid had put a loose-fitting suede jacket over her clinging shadow suit, and the scuffed, shabby-looking jacket gave her ample freedom of movement. Her ankle boots were a matching brown to the jacket, and she wore her compact TP-9 pistol in a low-slung hip holster. A pockmarked leather satchel, also brown, was hanging at her opposite hip, its strap slung across her body, cutting a line between her breasts.

Tensing his wrist tendons, Kane drew the Sin Eater blaster into his hand, the compact weapon opening up to its full size in a half second. Less than fourteen inches in length when fully extended, the 9 mm Sin Eater folded in on itself to be stored in the holster just above Kane's wrist. The holster reacted to a specific tensing of the wrist tendons, powering the pistol automatically into the user's hand where, if the index finger was crooked at the time, the weapon would begin firing automatically. The trigger had no guard—as the official sidearm of the Magistrate Division, the need for such safety features had been considered redundant; a Magistrate could never be wrong.

Though schooled in the use of numerous different weapon types, from combat blades to Dragon missile launchers, both Kane and Grant still felt especially comfortable with the Sin Eater in hand. It was an old friend, a natural weight to their movements, like wearing a comfortable and familiar wristwatch.

Kane's partners drew their own weapons as the trio exited the armaglass room and made their way to the corridor at a slow, wary pace. As they entered the corridor, banks of overhead lights stuttered into operation, bathing its walls in their brilliant glow. Although they had traveled here on what was ostensibly a peace mission, they had too much experience to enter any new situation unarmed.

They proceeded through the windowless military bunker at a steady pace. Although the facility was deserted, the lights came on automatically as they found their way along the corridors toward the exit. A bank of powerful generators located in the underground complex had begun channeling power through the redoubt automatically as soon as the old sensor units had detected that the mat-trans had been activated; it was standard protocol for these old military facilities.

Brigid took the lead as they jogged to a staircase and up into the main reception hall of the redoubt. Brigid Baptiste was blessed with an eidetic—or photographic—memory, and she had scrutinized the plans of this facility in preparation for their mat-trans jump here. Now she could recall every detail of its construction from those blueprints merely by calling them to mind.

In less than three minutes, the group stood shoulder to shoulder at a huge door leading to the outside world.

"Everyone ready?" Kane asked, his voice echoing in the empty, gray-walled reception chamber of the redoubt. To one side, a dusty old desk stood behind a pane of armaglass with a grille in its center. A computer sat atop the desk, long since inactive, its monitor stained with the greasy black charring of smoke.

Brigid nodded while Grant just put a finger to his nose in silent acknowledgment of Kane's question. Brigid typed the code into the old push-button pad to unlock the door. They heard the magnetic lock click, and Grant, having holstered his Sin Eater, worked the large lever on the front of the huge door to move the heavy slab of metal on its ancient rollers. The door creaked a little, juddering on the tracks after so many years locked in one position. But with a little effort, Grant got it moving enough that a three-foot-wide gap appeared at the far right side.

Kane stepped forward, gun held in the ready position, his old point-man sense alert as he peered through the gap and into the Tennessee morning sunshine. "Welcome to Beausoleil, people," he announced. "Let's try to keep things friendly out there." With that, Kane edged sideways and made his way out of the redoubt and up the dirt bank that he found immediately outside.

They had journeyed to Tennessee at the request of Reba DeFore on what could loosely be described as a mercy mission. During her recent inventory, Reba had noticed that supplies of their standard immunization boosters were falling low. With the devastating radiation storms that had accompanied the nukecaust, the whole landscape had become a near-lethal hot zone. Even now, more than two hundred years after the last bomb had been dropped, there were still dangerous pollutants in the air and pockets of radiation scattered across the globe. While the atmosphere was far cleaner than it had been, the use of immunization boosters remained standard procedure for anyone involved in fieldwork.

Many of the medications in use by Cerberus had actually been produced in the villes of the nine barons who had ruled over America until very recently. Black marketers with connections to the villes remained a convenient source of immunization boosters when necessity demanded it.

A few months earlier, the barony of Beausoleil in the Tennessee River Valley had fallen in a devastating air attack orchestrated by Lilitu, a would-be goddess whose ambition was matched only by her unquenchable blood thirst. Beausoleil had been razed, leaving a vast number of refugees and a blossoming secondary market in salvage. Just a few weeks earlier, Kane, Grant and Brigid had been involved in tracking genetic material that had been stolen from its ashes and had fallen into the hands of a criminal gang on the Pacific coast.

Now, once more, the three Cerberus warriors found themselves tracking down material taken from the devastated ville, only this time it promised to be a far simpler mission—or so the Cerberus desk jockeys would have them believe.

Brigid glanced up at the sun and checked her wrist

chron before pointing to her right up the bank of the muddy slope. There were shallow puddles all around, and the air smelled fresh and crisp. It had been raining here less than an hour before, she concluded.

"Ohio's people said she'd meet us about two klicks to the north," Brigid explained as she strode up the muddy incline and made her way toward a rusty chain-link iron fence that surrounded the redoubt's hidden entrance.

"Lead on, Baptiste," Kane muttered as he watched the beautiful woman duck through a gap in the fence and make her way across the puddle-dotted fields beyond.

Kane and Grant followed, their boots sinking into the sodden ground as they trekked toward the fence.

Grant pulled at the gap in the fence, lifting the chain link a little to provide Kane with more clearance. "She knows what she's doing," he reminded his friend.

"I know," Kane allowed. "I just don't like dealing with these bandit types. It never ends well."

Grant agreed as he pulled himself through the gap in the fence after Kane. They found themselves on a grassy hill that sloped gently toward the distant Tennessee River.

"Way I see it, what it really comes down to is you can't trust anyone," Grant said. "First rule of survival."

Kane glanced at him, the trace of a sarcastic smile crossing his lips. "You're still thinking like a Magistrate." He laughed.

"It's kept me alive so far," Grant retorted.

Kane snorted. "That and having me at your back."

Grant shook his head in mock disbelief as the pair of ex-Mags made their way across the soft, muddy ground after the svelte figure of Brigid Baptiste.

OHIO BLUE WAS a tall, slender woman in her midthirties with thick, long blond hair that was styled to fall over her right eye. She wore a shimmering sapphire dress that reached almost to her ankles, with an enticing slit revealing almost the entire length of her left leg. She sat, legs crossed, on a crimson-cushioned recliner set in the middle of a vast boathouse located on the banks of the Tennessee, in an area that had once been called Knoxville. Surrounding Ohio Blue and the recliner were approximately fifty large crates and twenty well-armed guards.

The boathouse was solid on three sides, while the fourth was open to the mighty river itself. There was a sunken area in the large structure where boats could be docked, with the dark river waters lapping against the sides with a constant swishing that echoed throughout the vast, high-ceilinged building.

With a graceful shrug, Ohio swept her luxuriant hair over her shoulders and stood up, offering her hand to Brigid. The hand was sheathed in a silk glove that stretched all the way past the elbow in a shade of blue that precisely matched the color of her shimmering dress. "You must be Miss Baptist," Blue said, her voice wonderfully musical.

"Baptiste," Brigid corrected as she clutched the woman's gloved hand and briefly shook it.

Kane and Grant stood a few paces behind Brigid, flanking her with arms crossed, their Sin Eaters hidden once more in their wrist holsters. Ohio Blue swept her hand casually toward them, a smile playing across lips that were painted an ice blue to match the highlights of her sapphire dress as it caught the light with the movements of her curvaceous figure. "A pair of handsome things," she said, matter-of-factly. "Companions or employees?"

"A little of both." Brigid smiled. The art of the deal was in making the other party comfortable, and Brigid knew that she had better make this black marketer happy. If Reba DeFore's estimates were correct, the Cerberus personnel would be needing these shots before the month was out.

Kane and Grant took up positions to the sides of the open area of the boathouse as Ohio Blue sat back down on her crimson-cushioned recliner. The blond-haired woman patted the cushion with her hand, encouraging Brigid to join her. "Let's talk business, Miss Baptiste," she drawled. "I understand that you're in the market for some pharmaceuticals."

"That's right," Brigid replied, resting herself at the edge of the couch beside the stunning woman. "I'm looking for some specific jabs, the kind of stuff they were producing in Beausoleil before the…" She trailed off, her hands open to indicate that she didn't have the words to describe it.

"A terrible thing," Ohio agreed. "Truly, truly terrible. My brother died in the attack."

"I'm sorry," Brigid lamented.

"No matter," the slender blonde continued. "Many a good business opportunity has come out of that disaster, as I'm sure you're aware."

As Baptiste continued to talk with the trader, Kane and Grant warily scanned the vast room. The place smelled damp. There was green mold scabbing over the walls and the wooden floor planks, and the lighting was inadequate for such a large room. There were several broken windows high in the walls of the building, and the whole place felt cold and dank. Guards patrolled all around, armed with subguns, heavy rifles and pistols. When he looked up, Kane spotted half a dozen more guards walking across the tops of the highest crates, and two more just standing up there, their blasters trained on the negotiating parties below. He turned to Grant, caught the man's eye and mouthed the words, "We are *very* outnumbered."

In response, Grant just nodded and beamed a bright smile. Kane knew what that meant—they were here now, and there wasn't a lot they could do about it.

The discussions seemed to be going well between Ohio Blue and Brigid Baptiste, until Brigid opened up her satchel and showed the trader its contents.

"What is this?" Ohio said, clearly affronted. "Some kind of joke?"

"Fifty gold coins," Brigid stated, trying to remain calm. "Exactly as requested in your communiqué."

Blue held one of the ancient coins before her visible blue eye and, for a moment, Brigid half expected her to bite down on it like an olden-day pirate testing if a gold piece was genuine.

"We've traveled quite some distance to obtain this merchandise," Brigid prompted.

Blue looked at the gold coin for another half minute before finally flipping it back into Brigid's satchel. "I need more," she said.

Brigid was incredulous. "You're upping the price?" she said. "But all I brought was fifty pieces."

"Seventy," Ohio declared, her lone blue eye staring at Brigid.

Brigid sighed, considering her options quickly. "What if I take less?" she suggested. "What does fifty get me?"

Ohio Blue smiled tightly. "Nothing. Deal's off."

"Wait," Brigid instructed. "I can get seventy. I just don't have it here."

A wicked smile crossed Ohio's thin blue lips. "Perhaps," she said, gazing openly at Grant, "we can work out a trade?"

Brigid followed the woman's eye line, watching Grant as the huge ex-Mag stood with his broad back to them, checking their surroundings. "What kind of trade?" she asked, her tone dubious.

"One can always use more…employees," Ohio said, her tone dripping with meaning.

"Grant's not for sale," Brigid stated firmly.

Ohio Blue's gloved hands turned inward, held open before her as though such a suggestion were beneath her. "I'm not talking about a sale, Miss Baptiste," she said. "I'm not a barbarian. A simple trade is all. Your impressive friend there for the items you wish to acquire."

Brigid appeared to be giving the matter some serious consideration before she finally shook her head, her red tresses flowing back and forth with the movement. "I'm afraid I can't let Grant go right now," she explained sadly.

"In which case," Ohio told her, standing up from the couch, "you'll be leaving empty-handed."

After a moment, Brigid stood, too, and turned to offer the woman her hand once more. "It was nice meeting you, Miss Blue," she said, a tight, businesslike smile on her face. "Seventy coins. My people will be in touch to organize another meeting."

Blue nodded her agreement, and Brigid walked back through the makeshift alleyways of stacked crates with Kane and Grant falling into step behind her. The coins in the satchel chinked as it slapped against Brigid's leg with the roll of her hips.

"A swing and a miss," Grant muttered. "I could have stayed in bed."

Brigid turned to look at him, a mischievous smile on her lips. "You almost ended up in someone else's," she said quietly as they neared the door.

Just then, Kane flinched, an almost unconscious movement, and his arms swept forward in a blur, shoving Brigid to the floor and pulling Grant down to join them. "Down!" he shouted, but the word was obscured by the explosive sounds of gunfire coming from behind them.

"What the hell!" Grant snarled, scrambling to cover between the crates in a rapid crouch walk.

Kane rolled beside him, while Brigid ducked behind the stacked crates across from them, pulling the TP-9 from its holster. Kane and Grant powered the Sin Eaters into their hands as they backed up against the tall stacks of crates.

"This is crazy," Brigid hissed across the gap between them in a harsh whisper. "They had us outnumbered, could have killed us at any time. Why now?"

There were more gunshots, and a hailstorm of bullets drilled against the crates beside them. When the shooting stopped, Kane flicked his head out into the space between the crates, taking in the scene in a fraction of a second before ducking back behind cover as more bullets whizzed past.

"It's not us they're after," Kane told Brigid as he returned to cover. "I think someone's come to speak to your new friend."

"With bullets," Grant added, shaking his head. "Nice."

# Chapter 3

At the back of the cave, the assassin who moved like a ghost waited patiently as Decimal River's fingers played across the laptop's glowing keyboard. At the other side of the low-ceilinged cave, Cloud Singer's eyes flicked to the ghost woman, still wary of her despite all that had happened in the month since she had found her way back to the Original Tribe.

The woman, the assassin whose warrior name was Broken Ghost, had such an air of stillness about her, of utter calm despite the tenseness of the situation, that it made Cloud Singer uncomfortable. The woman's flesh seemed almost washed-out compared to the café-au-lait complexions of the other members of the tribe. Her braided black hair and dark eyes gave Broken Ghost a striking appearance unlike anyone else in the tribe. She had painted her face with subtle blends, adding the illusion of shadow, intensifying her cheekbones, making her sharp-angled face appear almost skeletal, and she had weaved bits of glass and small, sharp chips of rock into her thick hair. She wore a loose undershirt that left her lean arms bare, their tight, corded muscles visible. Her skirt was really just two strips of material—one in front and one in back—that dangled to her knees and left her firm legs unencumbered.

Cloud Singer looked down at her own body, perversely unable to stop comparing herself to the magnificent warrior. By contrast, Cloud Singer was just a girl. Sixteen years old, with all the energy and suppleness that that granted, but none of the raw power of the formidable woman at the back of the cave. She wore her warrior's garb, as she had done ever since returning home to the outback: a tight strip of material stretched across her small breasts like a bandage, with more strips across her groin and legs, wrapped around her arms and encasing her scarred knuckles. Once upon a time, those strips of material had been the pure white of the clouds for whom she sang. After the massacre in Georgia, of which she was the only survivor, the strips had been washed with the blood of a squealing boar while Cloud Singer slit its neck, squeezing its life out of it, until the material was dyed red. After that, despite protests from the elders of the tribe, Cloud Singer had refused to remove her warrior clothes, to the point of even bathing in them in the underground pool that the tribe used. Only alone, in her few moments of absolute solitude, had she stripped out of the strange uniform, and then only to be naked. Until the mission was complete, she would never wear anything other than her warrior's garb. She had promised that much to Neverwalk as he lay there, head lolled at that dreadful angle, the dried blood splashed all about him in the underground bunker in the Caucasus Mountains.

"They've used their slicer," Decimal River stated, his head turning right then left as he addressed the two women on opposite sides of the cave. He was a young man, just a few years older than Cloud Singer, and his left arm was decorated with tattoos of circuitry. He wore baggy shorts and a loose shirt, open to the waist. The shirt was dark with sweat, and clung to his dark skin where its folds touched him. His hair was braided, like Broken Ghost's, and his face showed a nasty scar from a burn across the left cheek, stopping just shy of his eye.

"Not slicer," Broken Ghost corrected, her voice low, eyes closed in meditation. "Mat-trans. They call it a mat-trans."

Decimal River pulled up a window of scrolling information on the laptop's screen, flicking his hand before the motion sensor to run quickly through the pages of information displayed there. "Fifty-seven minutes ago," he continued, "they activated the mat-trans, crossing from their home in the Montana mountains to...here." He pointed to a paper map that was stretched across the wall of the cave. The map showed North America, and a red cross marked the Bitterroot Mountains. His finger tapped at an area close to the bottom right, but it meant nothing to Cloud Singer.

Broken Ghost took a single pace forward, and she seemed suddenly much more imposing as Decimal River looked up at her from his seated position. "Prime the trap," she said, her words the barest whisper as they left her mouth.

Cloud Singer smiled. Soon the Original Tribe would get its due. Soon they would have their revenge on Cerberus and its accursed leader. And then Lakesh would die.


"IT'S ALWAYS THE SAME with these bottom-feeders," Kane growled as he mentally assessed the immediate area around the crates where the three Cerberus warriors had taken cover. The exit door was ten paces ahead of them, and there was certainly enough cover to escape the boat-house if they wanted to.

"What do you see out there, Kane?" Grant asked.

Another hail of bullets hammered into the crates beside them, splintering the wood and kicking up puffs of sawdust, and they heard the sounds of guards running all about them between the stacked crates.

"People in diving suits," Kane said. "Frogmen armed to the teeth. They were rushing in from the open dock."

Grant nodded toward the door to the boathouse. "You want to get out of here?"

Kane thought for a moment, glancing across at Brigid for confirmation. "Nah," he decided. "Let's go make friends, cause mayhem." With that, Kane stood, reached up and pulled himself up the stack of crates beside him, clambering to the top in a series of quick, economical movements.

Raising the Sin Eater before him, Grant hunkered down and stalked off into the shadows, his black duster helping him blend into the darkness. Brigid took a different route toward the opposite side of the boathouse, weaving through the crates at a fast trot as bullets zipped all around, the TP-9 held high. As she ran, she rooted around in her satchel with her free hand, producing three small metallic spheres, like ball bearings, from its hidden depths.

As Kane pulled himself to the top of the stacked crates, he saw one of Ohio Blue's men up there stagger backward toward him, an oozing red stain across his chest where he had been riddled with bullets from below. The man cried as he misstepped, falling from the high stack and plummeting past Kane to the solid floor almost fifteen feet below. Across from him, on a nearby tower of crates, another guard was falling over his own feet, a gout of red gushing from a large wound in what was left of his skull. Whoever the newcomers were, they were well-trained,

Kane realized—it took some nice pinpoint work to take out the high guards so quickly.

He pulled himself over the lip of the crates and, keeping his body low, stalked across the towers as flashes of gunfire continued to light the floor below. The body of another security guard lay sprawled on his back close to the far side of the crate tower, a single red-rimmed wound between his staring eyes. In an automatic gesture, Kane's left hand reached down and closed the dead man's eyes as he passed.

Kane dropped, lying flat on his stomach, and crawled the last few yards to the edge of the tall tower. His head popped forward, and he peeked over the side as the gunfire continued below him. It looked as though a miniature war had erupted down there. In heavy helmets and diving gear, a dozen men were working as a team, using long-nosed pistols to take out Ohio Blue's guards as they approached the beautiful trader where she cowered behind her crimson recliner, bullets flying all around.

As Kane watched, the tall blond trader reached beneath the bullet-riddled recliner and produced a long-barreled revolver from its hiding place, taped to the underside of the couch. It was a Ruger Security Six, a silver six-shooter with enough stopping power to drill through a wag door. Blue hadn't been cowering, Kane realized; she was using the recliner as cover while she armed herself.

In a flash, Ohio Blue raised the Ruger, steadying the butt with her free hand, and blasted a shot at the lead frogman. The bullet took him full in the chest and the masked man staggered for a moment. Then, to Kane's surprise, the frogman shook his head and continued walking toward Ohio Blue, almost as though nothing had happened.

Ohio's guards were also having little success, and Kane now saw why. The divers were wearing bulletproof vests over their diving suits.

Ohio Blue continued firing at the lead frogman, her shots going wild as she started to panic. A moment later, the six-shooter was out of bullets, but it took several pulls of the trigger before the beautiful woman realized. She tossed aside the useless weapon and ducked behind her crimson recliner as bullets zipped all around her.

"We want her alive," one of the frogmen reminded his team as the group got closer.

On the crates above, Kane sighted down the length of his Sin Eater, slowing his breathing and focusing on the rearmost man in scuba gear. After a moment, Kane's finger stroked the trigger, unleashing a short burst. The 9 mm bullets raced to their target, hitting the diver's faceplate and shattering the strengthened plastic mask in an explosion of hard splinters.

Kane watched as the man ducked and clawed at the mask, his companions turning to look at him. From up there, Kane couldn't hear the man's howls over the sounds of gunfire, but he assured himself that his victim was cursing their unseen attacker even now. A grim smile crossed Kane's lips at the thought, and he pulled himself back from the edge of the crates, rolled to one side and made his way to a new location as a hail of bullets slapped against the edge of the uppermost crate.

On ground level between the towers of crates, Grant rushed back toward Ohio Blue, his dark eyes assessing the squad of men in scuba gear. Even as he watched, the rearmost man took Kane's bullet to his face and dropped to his knees, clawing at the shattered remains of his faceplate.

Placing his back flush to the crates, Grant scanned the area until he spotted Ohio Blue crouching behind her recliner, muzzle-flashes reflected in the sapphire blue of her dress. She was too far away and too out in the open for him to reach safely; he would need a distraction.

"Kane, Brigid," Grant whispered as he activated his Commtact, a top-of-the-line communication device that had been recovered from Redoubt Yankee years before. Commtacts featured sensor circuitry incorporating an analog-to-digital voice encoder that was subcutaneously embedded in the mastoid bone. Once the pintels made contact, transmissions were picked up by the auditory canals, and dermal sensors transmitted the electronic signals directly through the skull casing. Even a deaf user would still be able to hear normally, in a fashion, using the Commtact. The Commtact didn't need sound to be activated; it could pick up and interpret subvocalized speech if necessary, making it an ideal device for sneak work. Permanent usage of the Commtact involved a minor surgical procedure, something many of the Cerberus staff were understandably squeamish about, and so their use remained at field-test stage for now. However, the communication device was considered an essential tool for Kane and other field teams.

"The trader's in trouble," Grant explained. "I can't reach her. Any ideas?"

"Be careful," Kane instructed over the linked transmission. "They're wearing some kind of armor that deflects bullets."

Brigid's voice came over Grant's auditory receiver after a moment. "I'm just getting in position now," she said. "Going to give our guests a little light show."

Grant knew what that meant, and he pulled a pair of sunglasses from the inside pocket of his coat as Brigid spoke, following up by inserting tiny earplugs into his ears.

"Count us in, Baptiste," Kane said in a low voice over the Commtact as he got into place above them.

Brigid Baptiste was hunkered down in the shadows of the towering crates, close to one of the high walls of the boathouse. She had placed a pair of dark lenses over her own eyes and wore earplugs to muffle sound, just as Grant did. Her head was steady as she watched the group of frogmen swarming around the main area of the building, shooting the few remaining guards as they approached the recliner where Ohio Blue cowered. Swiftly, Brigid assessed the floorboards between her and her target—they were rough in places, and a little warped here and there with damp, but they were basically flat and smooth enough for her purpose.

She drew her arm back, rolling the three silver spheres in her hand for a moment, assessing their weight as she gave one last look at the scene. Then, her arm arced forward, low to the floor, and she released the three globes as her arm continued its fluid sweep ahead. Released, the tiny silver spheres rolled along the floorboards, bumping across the rough chinks in the wood as they rushed toward the recliner.

As the spheres rolled steadily across the floor, Brigid engaged her Commtact once again. "Three, two, one," she whispered, narrowing her eyes and turning her head away from what she knew was about to happen.

For a moment, nothing did. The three spheres rolled to the open area beside the recliner, their momentum dwindling. Two of the intruders in scuba gear had spotted them, and one shouted a query as he stepped ahead and placed his foot in the path of the first sphere. "What the fu—"

His words were lost in the explosion of sound and light that followed as the flash-bangs detonated.

Atop the crate tower, Kane surged forward, his Sin Eater held low. Even through the polymer lenses of his darkened glasses, the dazzling explosive burned into his retinas, and he blinked the pattern away as he leaped from the high crate and out into the open.

A moment later, Kane dropped into the open area of the boathouse, the Sin Eater blasting a lethal arc of 9 mm steel before him. He landed amid the frogmen with a heavy thump of boot soles against wooden floorboards, then swiftly recovered into a fighter's crouch as he began targeting the men in scuba gear. The sound of the Sin Eater seemed dulled by the ringing in his ears that the flash-bang had wrought, but his earplugs had helped protect him from the worst of it.

The flash-bang was a miniature explosive device, designed purely to shock and startle an opponent. The explosive was all sound and light, but the charge itself was so tiny as to be worthless as a demolition device. The flash-bang was standard equipment for Kane and his team, who often saw a benefit to using nonlethal force to restrain or completely halt an enemy.

The divers were all pulling at their masks in their sudden blindness, and several fired shots at random as they struggled to recover. To one side of the recliner, Ohio Blue was sitting on her backside, an enticing sweep of bare leg visible where her dress had fallen about her. Her blue-gloved hand was held over her eyes and her shoulders heaved as though she was crying.

Off to Kane's left, Brigid was securing the area, her TP-9 raised as she checked every nook and cranny before moving closer to the main action. A few of Ohio's guards were still alive, but they seemed to be wounded almost to a man. Tough to stand toe to toe with an enemy who could shrug off bullets, Kane realized.

Like a charging rhino, Grant joined Kane from his hiding place among the crates, fists swinging at the closest two frogmen as they staggered about blindly. His blows connected with solid finality, and the two men fell to the floor.

Kane turned to Grant and nodded his approval. "Not exactly subtle," he shouted to be heard over the earplugs he assumed that the other man still wore.

Pulling the handblaster from another frogman and throwing it aside, Grant lifted the man off his feet and tossed him against the nearest stack of crates with bone-jarring force. "Their vests shrug off bullets, right?" Grant explained. "What was I supposed to do?"

Kane aimed a stream of bullets at another frogman's head, blasting his faceplate to splinters. "Aim for the head?" he suggested.

Grant's leg kicked out, slamming into the gut of a blinded diver, knocking him backward with a shriek. "Sure. Now you tell me."

Brigid joined them then, looking around as Kane and Grant made short work of the final few intruders. She crouched beside Ohio Blue, placing a steadying arm around the woman's shoulders. "Can you hear me?" she shouted, close to the woman's left ear.

Ohio nodded, looking in the direction of Brigid's voice with vacant, bloodshot eyes.

"We're getting out of here," Brigid explained as she helped the trader to her feet.

There was a noise from the far end of the boathouse, and all three Cerberus warriors spun to see the front of the building—the wall where the exit door was located—cave in as a heavily armored vehicle crashed through it.

As the dust began to clear, the vehicle stood revealed. It was a square block on caterpillar tracks. Four abbreviated arms stretched out to either side of the vehicle, two on each side in a stack array, each containing three large missiles along its length. The muzzle of a gun stood out low in the rounded nose of the vehicle, swiveling left to right as it searched for a target.

Men swarmed in through the hole in the wall that had been created by the tank, armed with rifles, pistols and shotguns blasting the few remaining guards who were hidden among the crates.

"We're going to need another exit," Grant growled as he powered the Sin Eater back into his grip and, in unison with Kane, started taking shots at the approaching gunmen. The shots hit their targets but did nothing more than make the approaching gunmen slow for a moment. Like the frogmen, this team was wearing protective armor.

"Baptiste," Kane shouted over the furious sounds of gunfire all around, "you studied the maps—any ideas?"

Brigid looked around the boathouse, and her eyes stopped as she came to the sunken area that dominated its center. Letting go of the stunned trader at her side, Brigid dashed across to the safety rail that surrounded it and peered into the lower area. There, bobbing in the choppy waters of the Tennessee River, was a long powerboat, painted blue and shaped like a dart. *Perfect.*

Brigid turned back to Kane and Grant, calling them over. "Come quick and bring Ms. Blue," she instructed.

Bullets thudded all about them as Grant, Kane and Ohio Blue made their way toward the area where Brigid waited. Kane kicked over the recliner as he passed, using it for a shield while they retreated from the approaching gunmen.

At the far end of the boathouse, Kane could see the odd-looking tank trundling slowly forward, knocking against one of the towers of crates before shunting it aside.

"Oh, this had better be good," Kane muttered.

When Kane turned he saw that Ohio Blue was at Brigid's side, trotting down the short staircase that led to the sunken dock. Grant waited at the head of the stairs, blasting at targets with his Sin Eater, providing what cover he could for Kane.

"Keep moving," Kane told him as he passed.

Grant drilled a line of bullets into the edge of the lowest crate in a nearby stack. Under the relentless attack, the crate began to sag, its structural integrity ruined, and then the whole tower swayed for a few seconds before it slowly toppled to the floor of the vast boathouse, blocking the way for the approaching gunmen.

The two ex-Mags turned and rushed down the staircase, one after another, their heads kept low as bullets whizzed all about them. Ahead of them, Brigid stood beside Ohio Blue in the dart-shaped boat, swiftly assessing the vessel's dashboard controls.

Grant stepped into the boat with Kane just behind him.

A moment later, the boat roared away, engine howling as Brigid powered it out of the boathouse across the undulating waves. A wall of water cascaded around them as the boat turned sharply and arrowed down the choppy waters of the Tennessee. Behind them, gunmen in the boathouse were blasting shot after shot at the rapidly disappearing boat, but they were already out of range.

As Brigid manned the wheel, Ohio Blue rubbed at her face and looked at the three Cerberus teammates. "I can't thank you enough," she said breathlessly.

"Who were they?" Grant asked.

Ohio Blue shrugged her pale shoulders. "Competition?" she suggested, a note of query in her tone.

"See," Kane told her angrily, "this is what you get when you jack up the price at the last minute."

In reply, Ohio Blue just gave him a cold smile as the boat carved a path through the waves away from the boathouse. "I guess my brother's not quite as dead as I thought," she muttered to herself.

At the wheel, Brigid glanced across to the passengers before addressing the black marketer. "Do you have somewhere else we can go?"

Ohio Blue laughed, pushing her blond hair—now damp from the spray of the river—back over her shoulders. "That place was an empty shell, just for show," she said. "Do you think I'm foolish enough to invite interested parties to my stock?"

Kane's jaw was set firm as he looked at the woman. "I figure you just lost maybe twenty men back there," he said.

"Men can be replaced," she told him. "They were slow and stupid, so they died."

Kane's finger snapped up, jabbing toward Ohio's face in accusation. "You very nearly died, too, sister," he snapped.

"Ah, but you saved me, O handsome prince." Blue sighed. Her visible eyelid fluttered as though swooning, and she clutched her hands together before her breasts. She was mocking Kane and he knew it.

Brigid powered down the engine and the boat slowed to a crawl as she steered it toward the muddy bank. They were over a klick away from the boathouse already, and no one was chasing them as far as Brigid could tell—they didn't need to keep running. When Kane looked at her quizzically, she nodded toward the verdant slopes in the distance: the redoubt was nearby, its mat-trans unit their quickest way home.

Brigid spoke briefly to the trader before exiting the boat, with Grant leading the way. Kane was the last to leave, his senses on high alert once more in case they ran into further trouble on their way back.

"Well, it's been a blast," Kane told Ohio as he stepped up onto the edge of the boat, "but this is our stop."

"Ohh," Ohio drawled. "Leaving so soon? How will I ever take care of myself, O handsome prince?"

"You'll manage," Kane growled. "And I'm not your handsome prince."

A wide smile crossed Ohio Blue's cerulean lips then, that playful fire back in her visible blue eye. "But what else would I call you?" she challenged. "I never did learn your name."

"Kane," he told her as he stepped from the boat.

Ohio Blue reached out and pulled him back by the arm. Then she inclined her head, her mouth close to Kane's ear, and whispered, "I owe you, Kane. Tell Ms. Baptiste that she will get her meds, and at the original price."

Kane's steely blue-gray eyes looked at her and a lopsided grin crossed his mouth for a moment. "That's a very noble gesture," he acknowledged.

Ohio Blue looked at him through the drooping curtain of her damp blond bangs. "I remember who my friends are, Kane," she told him, squeezing his arm tightly for just a moment before letting him go.

In a few moments, Kane joined Grant and Brigid on the banks of the Tennessee as Ohio Blue powered the boat away. When he told them that they were getting the booster shots after all, Grant laughed.

"You do have a way with the ladies," Grant said, slapping his friend on the back.

Kane wasn't so sure. Friends like Ohio Blue almost always turned out to be more trouble than they were worth.

SHIZUKA SAT CROSS-LEGGED upon the ground on the empty plateau outside the entrance to the Cerberus redoubt. She had dressed in casual clothes, a loose-fitting cotton blouse in a pink so pale as to be almost white, black trousers and flat, open sandals. She sat there, breathing deeply as the midmorning sun played across the exposed skin of her arms, her throat and face, letting her mind fall silent with stillness.

Shizuka had brought two items with her that seemed, because she was dressed so casually, very much out of place: a *katana* blade, twenty-five inches of sharpened steel, held within a dark scabbard beautifully decorated with gold filigree, and a small wooden casket, just six inches by three, like a musical box. The sword and box rested on an open blanket that she had laid out on the dusty ground before sitting on it.

She had been thinking of Grant, that aching need to be in his company, to share nothing more important than the simplest of moments. But between his commitments to Cerberus and hers to the Tigers of Heaven at New Edo, the couple never quite seemed to have enough time together. Indeed, some of their most significant shared moments had been during the heat of raging battle. This day, for the first time in months, it seemed, Shizuka finally had a free day, the demands of her role as leader of the Tigers of Heaven quiet for once. And, with typical bad timing, Grant was required on a mission halfway across the country.

What had he said? A simple pickup, won't take long. Her breath slow and calm, Shizuka reached forward and flipped open the brass catch on the little wooden box. She would wait for Grant, so that they might yet spend the afternoon together, with no distractions but for each other.

Shizuka's delicate hands pushed open the lid and reached inside the box. Its contents had been placed carefully inside specific compartments, a masterpiece of simple design and economic use of space. There were sheets of thin rice paper, a soft square of cotton, a lightly chalked powder ball and a small bottle of oil. Along the front of the compartmentalized box rested a tiny brass hammer, held separate from the other items in the cleaning kit.

Shizuka reached forward, taking the sheathed *katana* from where it lay on the blanket. Gripping the hilt of the sword with her right hand, she pulled at the scabbard with her left, drawing the blade into the open where its polished steel surface reflected the rays of the sun. The graceful movement was automatic, an unconscious thing for her, practiced so many times as to be a part of her muscle memory, the weight of the sword like just another segment of her body. She looked at the blade for a moment, her eyes scanning its length, observing the grain of the steel, checking for flaws. Then, careful to hold the sharp edge of the blade away from her, Shizuka took a single sheet of the crackling, wafer-thin rice paper and began to slowly stroke the blade with it.

This was a necessary process, a chore that every samurai going back to the days of feudal Japan had performed to ensure that his *katana*—often referred to as the soul of the samurai—remained strong and clean, free from defects that might hinder a warrior in battle. But it was also a ritual, one that served to fill and calm Shizuka's mind as she awaited her lover's return.

As Shizuka sat there, the rice paper now discarded, tapping the length of the finely honed blade with the powder ball, she became aware that someone had approached and was standing behind her. She tilted the sword just slightly, looking in its reflective surface between the dustings of chalk, to see who it was who had come upon her with such stealth.

"Domi," she said calmly, a pleasant smile lifting her lips for a moment before she moved the sword back and continued tapping chalk along its length.

"Hi, Shizuka," Domi said breezily as she walked across the plateau to stand before the sitting woman. Shizuka thought that she could detect just the tiniest hint of disappointment in Domi's tone, where she had perhaps hoped to sneak up on the warrior woman unawares.

Domi cut a figure like no other. She was barely five feet tall, with a tiny, waiflike frame. An albino, Domi's skin was as white as the chalk that Shizuka used to dust her blade.

Her hair was also white, with the slightest variation in color, like paper turned to ash, and cut short in a pixie style that framed her face. It was within that face that Domi's most unearthly feature resided, however—her eyes, which were an angry, vibrant scarlet, like pools of blood, and seemed to burn into the soul of whomever she looked at.

Domi had appeared from the undergrowth around the plateau, dressed in a pair of denim shorts cut high to the leg, and a drab green abbreviated halter top that barely covered her small, pert breasts. Her skin and bare feet showed a few marks, where dirt had brushed against them, and Shizuka saw the bow and quiver of arrows strapped to Domi's back. The young woman had been out hunting, not for any real reason beyond the pleasure of the early-morning solitude and the thrill of the chase. Domi was a true child of the Outlands, often distinctly out of place around others—particularly the scientific types who dominated the Cerberus facility—and a born survivor. Like Kane, Grant and Brigid, Domi had joined the Cerberus operation via a disrupted life in Cobaltville, in her case, as a sex slave to the repulsive Guana Teague. Since then, she had become a highly valued member of the Cerberus crew.

"What you doing?" Domi asked, gesturing to the blanket spread across the ground. "Picnic?"

Shizuka smiled, shaking her head imperceptibly. "Only as food for the soul," she said, running another sheet of rice paper along the length of her *katana* to brush away the powder.

As Domi stood watching her, Shizuka reached for the bottle of oil and dribbled a few spots along the blade. Then she tilted the *katana* so that the oil ran along its length. With her free hand, Shizuka took the cotton square from the wooden box and began to clean the blade in a long, sweeping stroke along its length, following the lines of the grain of the steel.

"You want maybe some food for the stomach, too?" Domi asked. "'Cause I'm heading inside and I wouldn't outright *object* to company."

Shizuka waved her blade before her, feeling its familiar weight in her hand as it swept through the air. Looking up at Domi, she smiled. "That would be nice," she said, sheathing the *katana* and placing the contents back in the little wooden box.

THE THREE CERBERUS rebels made their way across the grassy swells back to the hidden redoubt. As they walked, the rain started once more, a cold, lancing drizzle on their faces that dimpled the surfaces of the puddles and turned the ground to slippery mud beneath their feet.

Making certain that they were not being observed or followed, Kane led the way through the gap in the chain-link iron fence and stood there for a moment, waiting as the others stepped through and followed. According to his wrist chron it was almost 1:30 p.m., local time; the back-and-forth of their little escapade had made it a three-hour-plus effort. Still, with the instantaneous transportation of the mat-trans, they would be back at Cerberus in a few minutes—plenty of time to catch the lunch shift at the canteen and grab themselves a proper meal.

Grant yanked back the heavy door just a little—he had left it slightly open when they had passed through earlier—

and rainwater had already pooled across the flat concrete flooring that stretched out into the lobby of the abandoned underground bunker.

"Do you have afternoon plans, Grant?" Brigid asked as he held the door for her.

He shrugged. "Shizuka," he said, the hint of a smile on his lips.

Brigid winced at that, feeling that she had somehow invaded her friend's privacy without meaning to.

Once Grant had closed and sealed the main door, they trekked through the silent corridors of the redoubt and found themselves back at the mat-trans room just three minutes after they had entered the complex. Kane checked the room briefly as they entered, assuring himself that no one had been there in their absence.

HALFWAY AROUND the world, in a cave that was hidden from the late-afternoon sun, Decimal River watched a blinking light flashing on his laptop screen. "They're inside," he announced, his eyes never leaving the screen.

"Activate the trap," Broken Ghost said, her voice a whisper just behind the man's tattooed shoulder.

Across from the ash-skinned assassin, Cloud Singer, the bloodred strips of cloth that she wore blending with the russet walls and dark shadows of the cave, felt a tiny shiver run up and down her spine in anticipation. To her irritation, the shiver reminded her of how it felt back when she could activate the implant, back when the dreamslicer still took the Original Tribe into the Dreaming World, before the Cerberus people had blocked their access with the master weapon, the Death Cry. Cloud Singer held her breath as she watched Decimal River's nimble fingers race across the keyboard of his portable computer.

Decimal River watched the numbers on his screen race toward zero as the mat-trans unit was activated in Tennessee.

"They've primed it," he said in a hushed voice. "Just a few seconds longer."

Beside him, her head jutting forward as she watched the countdown, Broken Ghost remained utterly expressionless. Her voice betrayed no emotion when the readout went to zero and she finally spoke.

"Close the trap."

# Chapter 4

"And could there be any particular significance to the name that you chose for the operation, Magistrate?" a man's voice, clear and sympathetic, was speaking close to his ear.

Kane opened his eyes and looked around carefully. He was stretched out on a leather couch in a small office, the walls of which were painted a reassuring, rich butterscotch. He turned, looking at the man who sat in a chair beside his head, peering over his regulation glasses at Kane, a notepad resting on his crossed legs.

"I'm sorry?" Kane asked, confused.

Beside him, the man thumbed back two sheets of his notepad, and Kane saw the tiny scrawl that covered each page. "Cerberus, you called it, the hound of Hades," the psychiatrist said, tapping the top of his pen against the notebook. "Do you think that has any particular significance?"

Magistrate Kane shook his head. "I don't really remember," he said. "What were we talking about?"

The psychiatrist offered a sympathetic smile. "Are you still perhaps confused after the gas attack? Magistrate Salvo told me that you were lucky to get out alive."

Kane closed his eyes, letting the words wash over him as he tried to remember. It had been a regular PPP—Pe-

destrian Pit Patrol—down in the Tartarus Pits, which sat
at the very bottom of Cobaltville, surrounding the Administrative Monolith. He and his partner, Grant, had been ac-
companying some newbie, couldn't remember the name,
checking ID chips and generally making their presence
known, when someone had launched a burning bottle of
something flammable—a molly—in their direction. It had
been a long time since the Pit dwellers had openly attacked
Magistrates like that, and the newbie had asked why they
had targeted them today.

"We're Mags," Kane had said, the regulation helmet
sitting low over his face, masking his features and adding
to his stern appearance. "That's reason enough."

There had been explosions and blasterfire, and a smok-
ing canister had almost exploded in his face. After that it
was all lost; he couldn't remember anything.

"How's the newbie?" Kane asked, recalling the rookie's
name at last. "McKinnon?"

The psychiatrist looked at him, his expression the well-
rehearsed mask of sympathy that every psychiatrist on
Cappa Level had been trained to employ in such situations.
"I'm afraid Magistrate McKinnon died," he said, holding
Kane's gaze.

As he lay back on the couch, Kane's eyes wandered
around the room once more. Despite the relative safety of
the surroundings, his point-man sense was alert. He felt as
if he was being watched, and not just by the psychiatrist
who sat patiently beside him. There, in the far corner of
the ceiling, a little black blister, no bigger than his hand,
contained a surveillance camera. You were never truly
alone in Cobaltville, he remembered.

"What about my partner?" he asked, still looking at the surveillance blister. "What about Grant?"

"He was still in surgery when you came in here," the shrink said. "Would you like me to go check?"

Something was wrong, Kane knew. Some instinct deep inside him felt unsettled. Maybe the gas attack had affected him, just as the psychiatrist had said. And what was this Cerberus that the man had been speaking about? The name seemed familiar and, even as he thought of it, an image flashed in his mind: a woman's face, her porcelain skin beautiful and clear, her hair a flowing tumble of red curls, her glowing eyes like twin emeralds reflecting flame.

"That's okay," Kane said, pushing himself up from the couch and smoothing back his dark hair, gathering his thoughts.

Beside him, the shrink checked his wrist chron. "We still have almost twenty minutes before the session is over, Magistrate Kane," he announced as Kane stood.

Kane looked at him, standing in the dark T-shirt and combat pants of an off-duty Mag, the muscles of his tanned arms flexing as feeling returned to them. He felt as though he had been sleeping and was only now awakening. "I think I'm going to skip out of this one," he explained. "You've been a great help. I'm better now."

The psychiatrist looked about to complain, but Kane stared through him before placing the dark-lensed glasses over his eyes, becoming an emotionless Magistrate once more. The whole culture of the Magistrate system was built upon intimidation; everything they did, the way they dressed, the way that they carried themselves—even when off duty—was designed to instill fear in the people around them. They were the last bastions of order in a world that had tipped close to utter chaos, and their authority was absolute, their judgment incontestable.

The psychiatrist stood up, and Kane could see the little beads of sweat forming on his brow as he peered into Kane's dark lenses. "Well, I wouldn't wish to waste any of your precious time, Magistrate," he said in a shaky voice, visibly cowering before the larger man.

"No," Kane agreed, shucking into his regulation black, ankle-length, Kevlar-weave overcoat, the familiar red shield of office attached to the lapel, "I'm sure you wouldn't. Good day to you, psychiatrist."

"G-good day to you," the shrink said, rushing in front of Kane to open the door to the office and let him out.

Kane walked along one of the corridors of Cappa Level. Above him, the grand structure of the Administrative Monolith towered high into the sky, brushing the clouds that languished across the Colorado plains. Off to the west, the sun was sinking, a rich orange ball as late afternoon turned to evening.

He thought back to the discussion he had been having with the shrink minutes before. "Cerberus, the hound of Hades," he muttered. "What the fuck does that mean?"

Before he had time to consider it further, Magistrate Kane found himself standing outside his apartment in the Residential Enclaves, and the aching in his limbs and gnawing at his stomach told him that he needed to get home, prepare some food and get a proper night's rest. He would check on Grant tomorrow; right now he was dead on his feet.

A SUDDEN JOLT OF PAIN and Grant was awake.

He tried to open his eyes, but they wouldn't open. He felt so lethargic and yet strangely he was utterly awake.

And the pain. The crazy pain.

It was so intense, so absolute, that it threatened to overwhelm him, consume him. He clenched his fists, holding on to his tenuous grip on wakefulness. Did his fists really clench? He couldn't tell, couldn't be sure. No matter now, what really counted was the pain. All that counted was the pain.

He calmed his mind, remembering the techniques they had taught him years before in Magistrate training. *A Magistrate is never ruffled, never swayed by emotion.*

The pain was in his right leg. High in the leg. A line of pain across the top of the leg, close to his groin.

And the left? The left leg? What did that feel? Was he trapped under something? He felt as though he may have blacked out and had lost his immediate short-term memories. Even in not remembering how this came about, he still recognized the symptom, the feeling of bewilderment.

The pain continued, a blazing sensation that felt so strong across the top of his right leg.

Pain equaled danger, which meant that Grant needed to be awake, needed to find out what the pain was, what was going on. To escape perhaps? To save himself? Perhaps even to save others.

He struggled once more to turn his head and open his eyes. I'm awake, he told himself, but I can't wake up.

It seemed impossible, but suddenly the pain became worse, went beyond absolute into a whole new level of agony that Grant had never even imagined existed. He felt the muscles of his mouth strain, stretching open, trying to scream, yet no sound would emerge.

And suddenly his eyes were open, assaulted by lights so bright that it stung to look. His vision blurred immediately, salty tears streaming across his eyes, rolling down his cheeks. He struggled, blinking the tears away where he couldn't move his hands to reach them, and he saw properly for the first time where he was.

Safe.

That was Grant's first thought when he realized where he lay. He was on his back, bright lights around him, people bustling about in the familiar, starched uniforms of the Cobaltville medical hub. Behind the lights it was hard to see. Everything was lost in comparative darkness, but he could smell the disinfectant, the antibacterial wash. He counted six—no, seven—people in the room with him, reduced to silhouettes by the overhead rig of fierce lights. As Grant watched, he began to discern their features, his eyes getting used to the bright halogen lighting. They were looking at him intensely, with concern and furrowed brows and much muttered, hasty discussion that he couldn't seem to make out. They were looking at him intensely, but not at his face. They were staring at his legs.

Grant tried to look down the length of his body, to see what had transfixed them, but he found that he couldn't move, couldn't make his body react.

The pain in his right leg burned and ached, but he could not see why, could not see what was going on.

Suddenly, one of the doctors, a middle-aged man with a shaved head and vibrant blue eyes, wearing a cotton mask over the bottom half of his features, leaped back from where he stood at the foot of the gurney, and Grant watched as a fountain of blood flew up and splashed over the doctor and the other people there.

The bald surgeon bit out a curse, and Grant saw something glinting in his hand, a whirring blade of some kind, attached to a wire that led to a socket in a portable machine.

Please, Grant thought, please let me know what is going on. And, once again, the salty tears blurred his vision until all he knew were the frantic voices and the sounds of the machines beeping steadily in the far distance.

"Doctor?" It was a woman's voice, softly spoken yet urgent. "Doctor, look. I think he's awake. The Magistrate is awake."

"In the name of the baron," said a man's voice, fearful but with anger bubbling beneath the surface, "where the hell is that anesthesiologist? He shouldn't be awake for this. Put him out, Elaine."

Tears swam across his vision, and Grant saw the blur of a woman dressed in white rushing closer to his face, the sound of her heels clattering on the hard tiled floor. She was reaching toward him, her hand a pinkish, blurred rectangle that smelled of antibacterial wash.

Suddenly something hard was pushed against Grant's face, wrapping itself around his mouth and nose, coiling and shaping itself as though it were alive. And the woman, the nurse, was pushing her hand against his forehead, holding him in place as though he could move.

"Upping feed level to 3.8," she said.

The sensation of pain in his leg was abating and, for just a second, the thick tears seemed to clear. Grant saw the nurse close to him, leaning over the gurney, her white uniform starched with perfectly creased lines down its edges. The uniform was unflattering, but Grant could see that she was a curvaceous woman, the tunic straining against the swell of her breasts. Above that, russet hair, her head turned away as she spoke to the chief surgeon, counting down in her clear voice, her frank concern clear in her tone.

She turned back then, looking at Grant, her hand still pushing at his forehead to hold him down. His eyes seemed to see only her smile for a moment, white and dazzling beneath the lights, with large, straight teeth; a photogenic smile. The canine teeth at the edges of her burned-umber lips were just visible as she spoke, her tone a soothing purr but the words lost.

Grant's vision swam and he looked at the nurse's face, trying to make sense of it. Two dark, watery eyes looking back at him, set deep in her face. Her beautiful, flawless teeth showing in her sweeping jaw, following the curvature of the long muzzle that poked toward him, the pink-and-black nose twitching slightly amid the rusty brown fur.

Grant realized then that the nurse was some kind of animal, a dog. A German shepherd or maybe a timber wolf.

And as he looked up, gazed across the room, the surgeons and the other nurses and personnel in the room all appeared the same. Dogs. He was being operated on by dogs.

BRIGID BAPTISTE'S EYES opened and she looked at the computer screen before her through the small, square-rimmed glasses perched on the bridge of her nose. The glasses were a symbol of office, marking her as a Cobaltville archivist, but were also a medical necessity. Years of computer work had left her slightly shortsighted. Her eyelids felt heavy, and the information on the glowing screen seemed unfamiliar. Her vivid emerald eyes scanned the glowing screen for a few seconds—it showed an archival report on an island in the Pacific that had been used for bomb testing back in the 1900s.

Strange, she thought, glancing surreptitiously around her, seeing the familiar forms of her colleagues as they worked at their own terminals, running through and amending the documents from the old days, the days before skydark. Everything seemed normal, and yet there was something that Brigid felt in the back of her mind, and the feeling had begun when she looked at the document on her screen.

I blinked, she thought, going through her preceding actions, and when I looked at the screen again it was like seeing it for the first time.

Perhaps there was something in the document? Perhaps she had seen something, or noticed something, or perhaps something had changed even as she was looking at it, almost subliminal and yet different.

"Refresh," Brigid ordered into her mike pickup. A wipe panned down her terminal screen at the instruction, refreshing the information as though she was loading the file from scratch.

Nothing. No differences. Brigid's eidetic memory would alert her instantly if something had changed.

"Go back," she instructed into the pickup.

The screen blinked and refreshed as it went back to the previous document, exactly the same as the item that she had been looking at.

"Go back," she said again, her voice soft, eyes flicking around the room for a moment to check that she wasn't drawing any attention.

Before her, the screen blinked and refreshed once more, taking her back to a previous document. It appeared to be a schematic of an underground military facility—a redoubt—and Brigid's brain automatically decoded the cryptic coordinates as she read them from the top right corner of her screen. The Tennessee River Valley, she realized, close to the barony of Beausoleil.

She had seen this before, she told herself, reassured. She had to have looked at the Pacific island stuff and just not taken it in. Mind wandering or maybe just tired. Yes, Brigid realized even as the word came to mind. Tired—that was it.

She sat there for a moment, looking at the schematic on the screen. "Revert," she instructed, and the computer returned to her most recent file, the military report on the Pacific bomb tests. She looked at the report for a moment and a smile crossed her lips. There was a satellite picture of the island under discussion, and from this angle it looked sort of like an animal. Four legs, a body, a head with open mouth. No, not a head. Two heads. She giggled as she thought of the words "two heads are better than one."

Must be tired, she realized. I'm seeing things. She removed her spectacles and glanced around the library room, but no one seemed to have noticed her giggle. Her section leader was across the far side of the room, leaning over Meredith Burrt's desk, running through a file with the short, blond-haired woman.

Placing her glasses on the desk before her, Brigid raised her hand and waited for the section leader to come over and relieve her of her post. She needed to rest; maybe she was even coming down with something. She couldn't recall the last time that she had felt so tired.

KANE OPENED the door to his apartment. It was unlocked, a carryover from the Program of Unification, when the Council of Front Royal had decreed that privacy bred conspiracy and, hence, deviant thinking.

He pushed his way into his compact two-room apartment, taking in its familiar walls and familiar smells. The whole place seemed faceless, with barely any sign of individuality or anything that could really be considered decoration. A single shelf against one wall of the main room included three books, one of them his precious, hidebound copy of *The Law*. Like all Mags, Kane could access all rules, amendments and subsections of the Cobaltville penal code merely by engaging the computer system, but there was something reassuring about having a genuine physical copy of the codes to refer to in his quiet moments. Three tall windows shed light onto the shelf and the wall to which it was attached, and Kane glanced through the panes for a moment, taking in the familiar lights glittering on the Administrative Monolith, which loomed over the ville.

Exhausted, he slumped down on the sagging cushions of his old couch, pondering what to eat. It was strange, he thought, to feel so tired after waking from a dream.

# Chapter 5

Trent, a sallow-faced Cerberus tech with tired eyes and a messy mop of dark hair, checked the diagnostics as the mat-trans unit powered up. They were expecting Kane, Brigid and Grant to emerge momentarily, but the redoubt had received unexpected guests in the past.

Lakesh leaned over Brewster Philboyd's desk as the tall man went back to monitoring communications frequencies for the various Cerberus field teams. "I feel increasingly uncomfortable with this part of the operation," the elderly scientist admitted. "One never quite knows what may jump through the gateway."

Philboyd's lanky six-foot frame seemed to be hunched over the communications terminal as he nodded his agreement. "Hopefully they won't bring back any monsters this time around," Philboyd said. In his midforties, Philboyd wore black-rimmed glasses above his acne-scarred cheeks, with pale blond hair swept back from a receding hairline. He had joined the Cerberus team along with a number of other Moon exiles over a year before, and his dogged determination to find the cause of a problem or uncover the basic workings of a system had proved invaluable. Although he wasn't a fighter, Philboyd was as determined as a dog with a bone when he was faced with a scientific or engineering quandary.

Mist began to fill the armaglass cubicle that housed the mat-trans itself, and the howling noise grew louder as the emitter array powered up. The vanadium-steel bulkhead that sealed the ops center off from the rest of the redoubt slid into place. When the mist cleared and the howling subsided, Kane, Brigid Baptiste and Grant stood revealed, none the worse for wear, and a collective sigh of relief went out from the Cerberus operations team.

"…where someone doesn't start shooting at us?" Grant was asking as he stepped out into the anteroom.

Kane smiled and shook his head. "You don't really want me to answer that, do you?"

Grant glared at his partner. "Not if it's going to depress me," he growled.

Brigid stepped forward, the leather satchel slapping against her thigh as she strode through the anteroom. A moment later, the three-person field team stepped out into the ops room.

"My dears," Lakesh said as he approached them, "how did it go?"

"You mean initially or overall?" Kane asked as he shrugged out of his faded denim jacket and stretched his tense muscles.

"A summary will suffice," Lakesh said hopefully.

Pushing Kane gently aside, Brigid stepped ahead of the others and addressed Lakesh, giving the distinct impression that Kane's response had struck her as juvenile and unnecessary. "It all went fine," she explained, shirking off the leather satchel and placing it to one side. "We'll need to speak with the trader again, but everything's in place."

"Yeah." Grant laughed, slapping Kane on the back. "Thanks to Romeo here."

Lakesh glanced across to Kane, who was looking just a little self-conscious as he busied himself with removing his wrist holster. "Would you care to explain, my friend?"

Kane looked away from Lakesh, glancing around the ops room for a few moments before he replied in a mutter, "Nothing to explain. Just the usual story of bullets, women and, well, mostly bullets."

Lakesh laughed at that, watching as Kane continued to scan the room. It was strange, but just for a moment, Lakesh saw a side of Kane that he had only really noticed on the few occasions when he had accompanied the ex-Mag on a field mission. If he didn't know better he would swear that Kane was checking out the room, searching for enemies with that old "point-man sense," as he called it.

"I'm glad you're all okay," Lakesh concluded, "and that we've made a new friend."

"'Friend' may be overstating the case a little, Lakesh," Kane said, "but it is what it is."

With that, the three warriors marched through the ops room and out into the corridor.

Working at the desks closest to the mat-trans unit, Skylar Hitch tapped Donald Bry lightly on the arm and indicated Kane and his colleagues. "What's eating them?" she asked in a whisper.

Bry shook his head. "I didn't notice," he said.

"They just seemed a little, I dunno, pissy?" Skylar suggested, keeping her voice low.

After a moment's thought, Bry shrugged. "No one likes traveling by the mat-trans," he reminded her.

Skylar sat there for a half minute, lost in thought as she looked at the door on the far side of the room.

"Are you okay, Skylar?" Bry asked when he noticed that she had ceased working at the motherboard before her.

"Hmm?" Skylar said, turning to look at him, her eyes coming back into focus. "It's nothing." She sighed, rolling her dark eyes and returning to the job at hand.

KANE CHECKED his wrist chron as the three of them strode, shoulder to shoulder, down the wide corridor that stretched the length of the Cerberus redoubt. "It's 12:34 local time," Kane told his colleagues, his jacket and holstered Sin Eater slung over one shoulder.

"One, two, three, four," Brigid stated, smiling as she broke down the time into separate numbers. "That's lunchtime."

"Then we should eat," Grant stated practically.

They slowed, purposefully looking around the twenty-foot-wide corridor as they realized that they were its sole occupants. The vast corridor was carved directly into the mountain rock, with curving ribs of metal and girders supporting its high stone roof. The air never really seemed to heat up here, and it often felt more like working in a mine shaft than being inside a high-tech military facility.

Brigid stopped walking, and her eyes rolled back in her head as she brought to mind the floor plan of the redoubt. After a moment, her emerald eyes reappeared and she pointed to a doorway a few paces behind them. "This way," she said. "Stairwell B."

Kane nodded. "Lead the way, Baptiste," he encouraged as the redhead pulled at the door handle.

The door didn't move and Brigid turned and smiled

with embarrassment. Then she pushed the door to open it and the three of them walked through.

THE CANTEEN WAS BUSY when Kane, Brigid and Grant entered the room. The lunchtime rush had begun, and the cooks and serving staff were busy trying to keep the lines moving as almost forty people waited to be served, trays in hand. Several friendly faces turned to acknowledge the three newcomers as they entered the room and Kane nodded back—albeit self-consciously—in return.

At the far side of the room, Domi sat with Shizuka, the lone occupants of a long table. The remnants of a late breakfast remained on the table between them. Domi rested back in her seat, keeping her back to the wall while Shizuka faced her, bemoaning some of the more mundane political aspects of her leadership of the Tigers of Heaven.

"Sometimes," Shizuka was saying, her eyes on the water jug that stood a few seats along from her in the middle of the table, "I wonder that there might be more to life than politics and war. And by more, quite naturally, I truly mean less."

Domi nodded, enjoying the company of the fascinating warrior woman whose background was so unlike her own. The two hadn't always seen eye to eye, but they had a healthy respect for each other. Domi certainly felt more comfortable around Shizuka than she did around many of the big brains who resided at Cerberus on a permanent basis.

As Shizuka took a sip of her green tea, Domi noticed the new arrivals and waved them over. "I think lover boy's returned," she told Shizuka with a meaningful wink as Kane, Grant and Brigid spotted her and approached the table.

Shizuka's eyes flicked delicately to the silvered surface of the water jug that sat just beyond her grip once more, then she smiled indulgently at the albino woman. "You're slowing down, Domi," she said. "I saw them enter almost a minute ago. Everything after that was just distraction."

Domi shook her head, a cardsharp solidly outplayed. Shizuka's eyes went back to the water jug as she watched the three figures approach, and unconsciously her left hand reached beneath the table to where her *katana* rested in its scabbard.

"Hey, guys," Domi said, gesturing to the empty, molded seats of the table. "How did everything go?"

Kane looked at the albino woman for a long moment, blue-gray eyes like steel lingering over her small frame before affixing on the quiver of arrows that she had propped against the wall behind her. "It went fine, Domi," he stated. "Planning a hunt?"

Domi looked confused for a second, before she saw where the ex-Mag was looking and realized what he meant. "Ha, no—just doing a little exploring this morning," she explained. "Haven't had the time to put things back."

Kane nodded, then he glanced back to Brigid and Grant before he sat down. In that moment, it seemed, a significant look passed between the three, and Domi wondered if they were mocking her. "You could join me sometime," she said defensively, though she didn't relish the thought of company on her morning jaunts.

Grant took the seat to the left of Shizuka, and a broad smile played across his face as he watched her sip from the teacup. "Miss me?" he asked as she placed the cup delicately back on its saucer.

"An infinitesimal amount, perhaps," Shizuka allowed, turning to look at him. After a second, a smile broke across her face and her hand reached out to entwine with his beneath the table.

Kane took the seat on the other side of Shizuka. Brigid walked around the table and took the seat opposite Kane, leaning back and surveying the other denizens of the cafeteria.

"Aren't you guys eating?" Domi asked, looking from Kane to Brigid. Neither of them responded, and she snapped her fingers to get their attention. They both looked at her, their expressions inscrutable. "What's up with you? Hey, you're not doing that *anam-chara* thing again, are you?"

Brigid tilted her head indulgently as she looked at the albino woman. *"Anam-chara?"* she asked. Then, after a long blink, she continued, looking significantly at Kane. "The bond of the soul friends. No, Domi. Why do you ask?"

"Because the last time we were all together like this," Domi began, "you were all—" she waved her hands around "—*wooo-ooo!* Soul-friend magic shit."

Kane smiled. "We'll try not to do that," he assured her before pushing back from the table and standing. "I'm going to grab a tray and see what's cooking," he announced.

Excusing herself, Brigid followed him to the rear of the queue.

Shizuka leaned close to Grant and asked in a soft voice, "Are you not going to acquire something to eat, Grant-*san?*"

"In a minute," he told her, still clutching her hand beneath the table.

"Keep your energy up," she whispered, a tantalizing twinkle in her eye.

"Careful, Shizuka," Grant whispered back. "That's a threat I may just hold you to."

BACK IN THE OPERATIONS room, Lakesh was placing Brigid's discarded satchel of gold coins back in a secure cupboard, having removed the hidden stash of flash-bangs and other minor weapons and sent them on to the armory for secure storage.

"You're pleased to have them back on-site, aren't you?" Donald Bry said, calling across from the desk where he worked with Skylar.

Locking the cupboard, Lakesh turned and smiled. "Somehow, Donald, the three of them seem to complete Cerberus. The place always feels a little empty in their absence, present company notwithstanding, of course."

Sitting beside Donald, a soldering iron in her hand, Skylar Hitch tsked.

"Something bothering you, Skylar?" Bry asked.

"Just thinking," she said as she replaced a burned-out chip on the motherboard, "how you can get too attached to people sometimes."

Lakesh joined the two of them, wheeling over a chair. "Now, then, what is that supposed to mean?" he asked, concern in his voice.

Skylar looked up at him for a few seconds before averting her gaze and turning back to her soldering. "Nothing, Dr. Singh," she said quietly.

Lakesh and Donald shared a look; neither of them was quite sure what was going on with the normally quiet Miss Hitch.

IN A DARK CAVE many thousands of miles away, Decimal River was checking the results on his laptop's screen for a fifth time. Finally satisfied, he shifted his body, turning away from the screen so that he could see both Cloud Singer and Broken Ghost where they stood across from each other within the small cave. "Infiltration complete," he told them proudly. "They're inside Cerberus."

Cloud Singer felt a flush of warmth over her body at the thought. "What now?" she asked, looking at Decimal River.

In response, the young man simply inclined his head toward Broken Ghost, waiting for her to answer Cloud Singer's question. "We wait," Broken Ghost told them, "showing great patience always."

"Always," Cloud Singer repeated, despite feeling the intense need for action. She yearned to find Kane and the others and make them hurt for all they had done. But, she wondered, just where are they now?

# Chapter 6

The side lighting of the room was dimmed, and Kane lay snoozing on the sagging couch in his two-room apartment. A plate rested on the low table before him, a half-eaten meal left to stew in its own juices. Beside it, catching the lights from the nearby residential towers through the window, brown drapes pulled back, a half-drained glass of milk, the bone-white liquid clinging to its interior sides as it was slowly dragged back down the glass by gravity.

Kane lay in a peaceful, dreamless sleep, head back, mouth open, and a quiet snoring came with his deep breaths. For the first time in a very, very long time, Kane was at peace.

"The quick brown fox never jumps over the lazy dog."

Brigid Baptiste smiled as her fingers raced across the computer's keys and these words formed on the display before her. The phrase contained every letter of the alphabet, an old typist's mnemonic to ensure that all the keys could be reached and were operational.

"The quick brown fox never jumps over the lazy dog."
*Never.*

The computer and keyboard sat on a little desk that was

hidden in a converted wardrobe within Brigid's tiny apartment. Strictly speaking, she should not own a computer. Despite her high ranking as a Cobaltville archivist, Brigid was not legally allowed ownership of a personal computer of any form—the designated work databases should be enough for her, where her data queries could be monitored and questioned at any time.

Her computer at the Historical Division was newer than this one, using voice-recognition commands in place of this clumsy, old-fashioned keyboard with its "quick brown fox." The keyboard felt old and slow by comparison, unable to keep up with the speed of Brigid's thoughts. Still, it did the job.

She had found the computer, a cast-off DDC model, in the trash close to her one-person apartment. It had seemed to be serendipity, a stroke of luck, but she suspected it had been planted for her to find by her friends in the Preservationists, an underground movement dedicated to retaining the complete records of the world as it was before 2001. Brigid's job, as an archivist, was to smooth the rougher edges of history to ensure that it was palatable with the enlightened baronial world view. Which was to say, hide the truth.

They could ask Brigid to smooth and hide all they liked, but her eidetic memory ensured that a perfect, untouched copy of it remained in her mind's eye. She spent long evenings at the DDC's keyboard, re-creating this information into computer files once more before leaving it at a specified drop-off point for the Preservationists to collect.

Sometimes she wondered if the Preservationists really

existed. Sometimes she woke in a cold sweat, convinced that she had been snared in a web of deceit and the Preservationists were a simple fallacy that the emotionless Magistrates had created to prove her guilt.

She sat at the terminal, her rectangular glasses perched on the bridge of her nose, recalling all the files she had seen that day. There had been little that would be of genuine interest to the Preservationists, she realized. Perhaps the nuclear testing on the Pacific island, evidence of the short path that led those same military minds to ultimate destruction. It was hard to say.

Strange, Brigid thought as she sat there, the screen flickering before her. Such an empty day, I can hardly remember it. Which wasn't like her, not at all.

As she sat there, her thoughts wandering, her eyes focused on some imagined point in the far distance, Brigid heard the wind chimes tinkle as the front door to the apartment was opened from outside. She pushed her chair back and closed the wardrobe doors to hide the keyboard and terminal. Then she stepped from the bedroom and glanced down the corridor to see who had entered, her heart racing.

A familiar figure stood beside the doorway, a girl with messy honey-blond hair that fell past her shoulders, a brown leather satchel slung across her small chest so that it dangled beside her knee. She wore the regulation uniform of a schoolgirl, and its insignia showed she was in class 3, for five-year-olds. Abigail.

"Hello, little darling," Brigid said, waving from the other end of the corridor.

Abigail looked up, her eyes wide with trepidation. She

hadn't expected anyone to be home. "Auntie Brigid!" the girl announced with a bright smile.

Slinging her satchel to one side, Abigail rushed down the corridor and into Brigid's waiting arms. "What are you doing home?" she asked "It's really early."

"I got out of work early today," Brigid told her, scooping the little girl into her arms and spinning her. "Wanted to see my little munchkin."

The girl frowned, her green eyes boring into Brigid's. "I'm not a munchkin," she told Brigid sternly. "I'm almost six."

"Oh, that's still a munchkin," Brigid explained with grave seriousness as she placed the girl back on her feet. "A heavy munchkin, though. You're getting too big for me to lift."

"Maybe I can lift you instead?" the girl suggested, and her arms wrapped around Brigid's waist and heaved.

Brigid stood up on tiptoe, looking down at the girl's mop of blond curls as Abigail strained to lift her from the floor. After a moment, Brigid reached down to ruffle the girl's hair. "Not quite yet," she told her, "but close. I think you'll be strong enough to lift me once you've had some dinner."

Abigail's eyes were wide with excitement as she looked up at Brigid. "Really?"

"Go clean up and change your clothes while I put some noodles on," Brigid told her.

Smiling, the girl skipped off to her little curtained-off area in the lounge, while Brigid went back to her wardrobe and powered down the computer. The files could wait— taking care of her niece would always come first.

WAKING UP WAS LIKE trying to get a campfire to catch light; it seemed to take a long time and for a while Grant couldn't be sure if it was really happening. Achieving consciousness felt like wading through quicksand.

Then suddenly he opened his eyes and let out a growl through gritted teeth. He felt raw, all of his muscles inflamed, and yet the edge of their sensation was muted, as though he had exercised to exhaustion. He had hit that point a few times, both on missions and in the Magistrate gymnasium, and he recognized the feeling.

He looked around and realized he lay on his back in a small room, high up on a bed that smelled of freshly laundered sheets. He was tucked within the sheets, and the room itself had been left in semidarkness. A small light off to his left had been placed close to a windowpane, and its reflection cast a double image against the darkness beyond. Grant peered at the window for a moment, making out the spots of a few lights out there—stars or windows he wasn't sure.

The light gave a little detail to the room, and Grant lay there, assessing his current location. It was a hospital room, somewhere in the medical hub, and there was no doubt in Grant's mind that he was on Cappa Level. He was a Magistrate; of course he would be in a Cappa Level facility.

What happened to me? Grant wondered, casting his mind back. Slowly, seen in painful snatches at first, he recalled the operation, the blood splashing against the blue-eyed surgeon's overall, the nurse rushing over to sedate him, the hounds. It was all so unreal, the memory mixed with something else, something feverish, a hallucination.

Grant focused his eyes on the door at the end of the bed, watching it with intensity. The door itself was propped open, and light spilled through from the corridor beyond. Light and noise, the noises of people walking about, going about their business, an occasional comm alert ringing, a PA system blurting to life.

Definitely the medical hub, he told himself. He had been here before, although generally as a visitor for one colleague or another. His partner, Kane, had ended up in here a few times suffering from cuts, bruises, one time a nasty fall from a hovering Deathbird.

He heard the sound of solid heels, clickety-clack on the tiled floor, getting louder, closer. The long shadow of a figure crossed the light spilling through the doorway and Grant tried to speak, to call out, but all that came was a croak that made his throat burn. Have they done something to me? he wondered.

The figure outside stopped, the heels scuffing at the floor tiles, and then a young woman walked in wearing a white nurse's uniform. She stood in the doorway, peering up the length of the bed. In the semidarkness, Grant stared back.

"Are you awake, Magistrate?" the nurse's voice was soft, tentative, as though frightened that she might disturb her guest.

Yes, Grant thought, struggling to push the word out of his mouth. Finally, it came out as a gurgled "yuh."

The nurse stepped closer, and Grant saw her russet-colored hair, kindly green eyes that seemed to smile as she looked at him. "Just take things slowly," she instructed him, the compassion clear in her soft voice. "There's no need for you to rush."

He stared at her, holding her gaze with his own.

"It's okay," she said, so quietly as to almost be a whisper.

"You're safe now. It's all over." And then she smiled and Grant remembered her from the fever dream in the operating theater. The metamorphosis nurse, the woman who had become a dog.

He looked at her, watching her face, waiting for the change to begin, but nothing happened. "I…" he said, the word cracking in his throat, "I remember you…. You helped me…back there." It was a struggle to form the words. The thoughts were there but the words wouldn't come, and the dry pain in his throat just made it all the worse.

"My name's Elaine," she told him quietly. "I was there when they operated on you, Magistrate. We didn't think you'd remember. We hoped…" She stopped herself, and her gaze left his, glancing down the length of the bed.

Grant's eyes followed hers, looking at the swells in the bedclothes that covered his body.

"What happened to me?" Grant asked, the words coming out strained and husky.

"There was an accident," Elaine told him, her eyes meeting his once more. "I'm afraid that I don't have all the details, Magistrate."

"What…what do you know?" Grant asked.

She looked at him, a sympathetic smile on her lips, and Grant realized then that she was afraid of him, afraid of the Magistrates. "You were on patrol," she began, "in the Tartarus Pits when terrorists attacked. Your partner got you out—"

In his mind's eye, Grant saw the explosion, a burning across the lower half of his body, Kane pulling him to one side. "Magistrate down!" Kane was shouting into his comm as figures rushed all around. "Mag down!" Then gunfire, McKinnon and Kane taking shots at an enraged mob as they rushed toward him. And he had blacked out.

"Kane? McKinnon?" Grant asked, his voice still that hoarse whisper. "Are they...?"

The nurse looked uncomfortable. "You will have to speak to your superior," she said diplomatically.

"Please," Grant begged, "tell me what happened."

She looked at him, her sea-green eyes locked on his, sympathy straining her face. "I believe that you are a very brave man, Magistrate," she said. "The surgeons did the best they could, but sadly they were unable to save either leg. I'm deeply, deeply sorry, Magistrate." Then she went quiet, biting at her lip as she looked at him.

Grant listened for a while longer, hearing her words echo in his head. *The surgeons did the best they could. They were unable to save either leg. Unable to save either leg.*

When he returned to the present he realized that she was still standing before him, looking so sad as she watched his face for a response.

Grant laughed, just a single snort from his nose. "Funny, I always wanted a desk job," he told her and, despite herself, the nurse smiled.

THE COMM UNIT in Kane's apartment rang its alert, but Kane continued to sleep, barely stirring where he lay on the old couch, despite the buzzing noise. After a moment, the comm went to answer-message mode and a woman's face appeared in the view window. She was a striking woman, at an indefinable age between forty and fifty-something, with dark hair that fell about her shoulders in a luxuriant cascade, chocolate-colored eyes full of promise and an honest smile that still held the infectious exuberance of youth.

"Kane, darling," she began. "Are you there? No? I guess you must still be working. I was just calling to see if we could move our lunch date an hour forward tomorrow. Nothing important, just some new shipment coming to the gallery that Jeff wants me to evaluate, so I need to be back for three o'clock." On the tiny screen of the comm, the woman gave a genuine shrug, as though the whole thing was ludicrous in the extreme. "Well, anyway, I'll be at the café at twelve-thirty, okay, honey? I'll see you there, I hope. Let me know if it's a problem, okay?" She paused then, and her hand could be seen reaching toward the screen to disconnect the communication. She stopped and looked back at the screen, her beautiful, rich eyes peering into the camera lens that captured her image. "Don't forget how proud of you I am, okay? I couldn't ask for a better son." With that, the dark-haired woman reached forward once more and finished the communication.

Kane, who had slept through the whole thing, wouldn't see the message until the morning.

BRIGID AND ABIGAIL SAT side by side at the little countertop, eating from plates of noodles. Abi had washed and changed into her home clothes, but her blond curls still looked unkempt to Brigid's eyes. Listen to me, Brigid thought, like some mother hen clucking over my little chick.

"They showed us a vid at school today," Abigail was saying through a mouthful of noodles. "It was all about the Program of Uni-fickeration…"

"Unification," Brigid corrected.

"How the whole world was horrible before then and how the barons fixed it all so we could live better, happier lives." Abigail nodded, winding noodles onto her fork.

"Yes, I remember seeing the same vid when I was your age," Brigid said.

"Was it really as bad as they said, Auntie?" Abigail asked, genuine concern in her voice.

"Oh, munchkin," Brigid said, laughing, "I don't remember. It happened before I was born. A long time before I was born."

Abigail looked thoughtful for a moment before she spoke again. "Would my mommy remember it, do you think?"

The girl's words immediately made Brigid feel sad. It was always like this. Abigail would mention her mother, and it was like pushing a button deep inside Brigid Baptiste. Her sister had died almost two years ago in a transport accident, and Abi's father was already off the scene by then and had no interest in bringing up a kid. Brigid had taken the girl in due to family loyalty, despite not really talking to her sister much in those last few years. People drifted apart sometimes, Brigid knew, and it was only Bronwyn's death that had made her realize just how far they had drifted. Sometimes it felt like Abigail was her sister, reborn, a last chance to redeem herself for the unintentional neglect she had shown her sibling.

"Auntie Brigid?" Abigail said, deep concern in her voice.

Brigid looked at her, returning her thoughts to the present. "Your mommy was only three years older than me, Abi," she explained. "You'd need to go as far back as your—oh—great grandmamma before you found someone who remembered the dark days before unification."

Abigail nodded, biting her lip in deep thought. "Oh," she said, deflated.

"So, what else did you learn today at school?" Brigid asked.

"Adding up things," Abigail said after a moment's thought, "and dividing things."

"Math." Brigid nodded. "How did you find that? Was it okay?"

"I guess," Abigail said, scrunching up her face. She worked her fork around the last vestiges of soy sauce on her plate.

"What about," Brigid said thoughtfully, "if we add up some yummy desserts? Would you like that?"

Abi smiled. "Oh, yeah!"

"Okay," Brigid said as she got up from the counter and took the plates over to the tiny kitchen sink. She leaned across and opened the door to the refrigerator, trying to remember if they had ice cream.

"Oh," Abigail said as Brigid looked for dessert, "I'm going to be in a play."

Brigid looked back, a broad smile on her face. "A play? Wow, that sounds really exciting. Can I come see?"

"I'm not the star," Abigail said glumly.

"I'd still like to see you, if you'll let me," Brigid told her as she dished the ice cream into two bowls.

Abigail smiled at that. "They said it was for mommies and daddies only, but I think it will be okay."

Placing the bowls on the countertop, Brigid laughed. "I'm sure they'll make a special exception," she told Abigail as the girl tucked in to her dessert.

Brigid watched Abigail eat ice cream for a few moments

before she reached across and stroked a hand through the girl's blond curls. "Your hair needs a proper brushing, munchkin," she said as the girl continued scooping ice cream from her bowl.

"Mmm. Dessert first," Abi said, nodding.

Brigid laughed. "Dessert first," she agreed. "Definitely."

A DOCTOR CAME TO SPEAK to Grant, explaining in technical terms everything that his team had done, and how they would do everything that they could to make Grant's life comfortable. There would be physiotherapy to increase his upper-body strength, and the Magistrate Division would provide a wheelchair for him as soon as he felt ready.

"Nobody wants to rush you, Magistrate Grant," the doctor said in his sympathetic tone. "You just take your time. This is a team effort—we're all going to pull together."

Grant had thanked the man, looking down the length of the bed at the abbreviated body he had been left with. It was strange. He had seen hideous injuries before, in his time as a Mag, and this was really no different. He felt divorced from the situation, an observer in a dream, as though it were all happening to someone else. But Grant suspected that was just a reaction to the shock, that the whole thing would hit him like a runaway wag in a few days.

The russet-haired nurse, Elaine, returned, standing beside the bed and checking the notes that the doctor had added to Grant's chart.

"Could I get a drink?" Grant asked her.

She nodded, reaching across for the glass of water that

had been placed beside his bed and putting it in his hands, helping him sit up to drink it.

"Thank you," Grant said as he sipped at the water. "My arms are okay, but I'm having a bit of trouble reaching for stuff. Can't seem to stretch the right way, you know?"

Elaine nodded slowly, a sad expression on her face.

"Hey, don't fret," Grant told her. "It'll get easier, I guess."

"You're very brave, Magistrate," Elaine said earnestly, looking into Grant's eyes.

"Comes with the job," Grant told her, and he shrugged. As he did so he spilled water on the bedclothes. "Shit, I'm sorry…. Didn't mean to…"

Elaine took the glass from him and placed it back atop the bedside table. "It's okay," she assured him as she pulled paper towels from a dispenser on the wall and used them to soak up the spilled water. "You were saying…? About the job?"

"Yeah, I guess I was." Grant smiled, and he began telling Elaine all about his Mag training, his childhood in the academy, assignments he had been on and other things that he could tell her, the things that weren't classified.

"It sounds like a lonely life," Elaine said as she sat in a chair beside his bed.

Grant thought about her words for a moment. "I guess it is," he admitted. "Never really thought about it. I have some good friends in the division, great friends." His words sounded defensive to his ears, as though he needed to justify the Magistrate lifestyle.

"I'm sorry, I didn't mean to offend you, Magistrate," Elaine said, turning away from his gaze.

"You didn't," Grant told her. "And please stop calling

me Magistrate. Figure I'm going to be here awhile, so we may as well be friends. I'm Grant."

Elaine inclined her head. "Pleased to meet you, Magistrate Grant," she said with a smile.

They spoke through the night and beyond, until dawn's first light shimmered through the window beside the bed. And, despite everything he had lost, Grant felt at peace at last.

# Chapter 7

It was early morning in the outback. Leaving Decimal River alone at his keyboard, monitoring the trap for any fluctuations, Broken Ghost had led Cloud Singer far from the village, out into the brush that dotted the harsh landscape of the outback. There was a clump of trees, the best of them barely four feet in height, surrounding a shallow watering hole. The watering hole was no more than ten feet across, and reddish-brown earth swilled within its waters, clouding it as the currents ebbed and flowed.

Broken Ghost turned to Cloud Singer, her voice quiet, as they walked among the clump of low trees. "The kangaroos come here to drink," she explained, "sometimes, in the mornings when they think it is safe."

Cloud Singer nodded. She had seen kangaroos out here, hopping across the land, sometimes passing close to the little settlement of huts that stood beside the caves that the Original Tribe inhabited. Strange creatures, always on the move.

They ducked and watched from the cover of the low trees as six 'roos bounded past, two females and four males, hopping close to the muddy waters. Covered with fur an autumnal reddish-brown, dappled with gray, each animal was almost seven feet tall, with powerful tail and huge, sturdy hind legs that propelled them across the unforgiving landscape. The males looked around, noses twitching as they scented the air, while the females leaned down, tongues lapping at the cloudy waters. After a moment, the males dipped their heads and drank from the pool, too, taking turns to lap at the water with their long, fleshy tongues.

Cupping her hand, Broken Ghost leaned close and whispered in Cloud Singer's ear. "Have you ever faced an angry boomer, Cloud Singer?"

Cloud Singer shook her head. She had seen others in the tribe fight with the kangaroo from time to time, but her own encounters had only ever been from afar. Kangaroos were powerful, ill-tempered beasts, good meat, certainly, but not worth the hassle of close-quarters meetings when they could be felled by boomerang, arrow and yo-yo from a safe distance.

"This is a test," Broken Ghost whispered. "I wish to see the extent of your abilities before we proceed, warrior."

Cloud Singer felt her heart thunder in her chest at the thought. The assassin who moved like a ghost wanted her to do battle, unarmed, with an enraged kangaroo. She would do so, but it would be a conditional agreement. "And I, yours," she stated simply.

Broken Ghost's lips broke into a smile, and she nodded appreciatively as Cloud Singer silently pushed herself up from the ground and stalked closer to the beasts at the watering hole. Foot crossing foot, Cloud Singer edged sideways, keeping out of the kangaroos' line of sight as they nervously drank from the pool. In a few seconds she was close, almost upon the troop. Before her, a male kangaroo's head raised and he sniffed at the air once more, sensing something wrong.

Cloud Singer hollered as she swung her right fist into the creature's side. The creature swayed, its mighty legs shifting as it centered itself, ears twitching. It scrambled around to face her, eyes like dark pools, regally peering down its long snout at this thing that had had the audacity to hit it. Its nostrils flared and it spit a mist of saliva into the air as it reared back, using its tail as a tripod, kicking out at Cloud Singer with both of its large feet.

Cloud Singer skipped out of the reach of the boomer's powerful feet, conscious of the movements all around her as the other creatures scattered across the shallow watering hole, surrounding her in an instant. Broken Ghost had wanted a show, proof of Cloud Singer's prowess, and she would get one.

The alpha male leaped forward, its smaller forepaws— perhaps as big as Cloud Singer's own hands—scratching at the air, reaching for her chest. Cloud Singer hunkered down before kicking out with her feet, leaping high in the air. Toes pointed like a knife, Cloud Singer's right foot snapped out and kicked the animal in its thorax before she came back down to earth in a reverse spin. The male tripped backward, spluttering and spitting, shaking its head back and forth.

Cloud Singer was moving immediately, ducking low and kicking out behind her. Her heel crunched against the nearest kangaroo, slamming it in the belly as the others bounded out of the way. A series of clicks came from the boomer's mouth as it righted itself and kicked ahead with one of its huge, muscular feet. The blow missed Cloud Singer by a fraction of an inch, and she danced on the spot to retain her balance as the creature's mighty foot whipped past.

The kangaroo sprang toward her then, head down in a charge, and she swerved to keep clear of this new attack. The boomer's head missed Cloud Singer, but its sloping shoulder clipped against her side, knocking her so that she struggled to keep her footing.

Frightened, the other kangaroos kept their distance, snarling, hissing and spitting as they watched the battle. But the alpha male, the first one that Cloud Singer had attacked, was moving toward the combatants, stalking forward with head down.

Cloud Singer whipped out a punch, driving her fist into the jaw of the kangaroo who had charged her. It swayed on its feet, swinging its head back and forth as it shook off the effects of the blow. Then the other one was upon her, rising up on its thick tail once more, until it towered almost nine feet in the air so that it could kick out at the troop's assailant with both legs. Cloud Singer watched, timing the movements in her head, kicking forward with her own foot in an apparent mirror of her attacker. The kangaroo's blow fell short, and it sprang back to the ground, ready to try again. Cloud Singer's foot cleaved the air, kicking the beast in its long muzzle. It was like hitting a wall, solid bone offering no give whatsoever. She struggled to keep her balance as her foot carried through the arc and came back to the ground.

The alpha male looked at her, head swaying atop its thick, furry neck, foreclaws ripping at the air. It was dazed, Cloud Singer could tell. She swung her left fist at its face, connecting just above the eye, her right fist following through with a jab to the creature's snout. The kangaroo's oblong head swung back and forth on its neck, little hands clawing through the air.

Cloud Singer took three steps back, her eyes locked on the punch-drunk boomer. Then, with a little run, she leaped into the air once more and kicked at the creature's head with both feet stretched out, her weight and momentum propelling her into the majestic creature. The boomer toppled like a tree, legs giving out, and it fell to the hard-packed, arid soil around the watering hole.

The other male who had tried to charge her was moving again, Cloud Singer realized, and she turned to face it, fists up in a defensive pose. The kangaroo jabbed at her with its paws, and the thick, sharp claws tore down the side of Cloud Singer's arm, ripping a bloody line in the flesh as she struggled to keep clear of this fresh attack. The kangaroo hopped on the spot, sizing up its attacker with dark, glistening eyes.

Behind her, Cloud Singer heard the trees part as Broken Ghost finally joined the fray, backing toward her tribe sister. "Enjoying yourself?" Cloud Singer taunted, annoyed that the assassin had waited so long before revealing herself.

The pale-skinned woman said nothing, holding herself in a fighter's stance as she assessed the remaining kangaroos that approached her. There were four in all, plus the one that Cloud Singer was sparring with. It was all just movement and timing now, and Cloud Singer had shown Broken Ghost what she needed to know—that the warrior girl had spatial awareness, as well as the ability to draw power from her muscles to create a devastating attack. She had feared that Cloud Singer's drive for vengeance had dulled her abilities, but she could see now that the girl was still a supreme fighter.

The kangaroo before Cloud Singer bounded forward suddenly, barreling through the air toward her. She kicked out, using its approaching body for leverage as she threw herself into the air, over its head. Without turning, Broken Ghost reached behind her to where Cloud Singer had been a moment before. Her arm wrapped around the neck of the lunging beast, and she used its own momentum to draw it forward, dipping her body as she tossed it over her shoulder and onto its back. The kangaroo whined as it struggled on the ground, preparing to get back up. But Broken Ghost was already upon it, jumping into the air and crashing down on it with both feet plunging into its windpipe. The creature shook as the pale assassin leaped away, then its head slumped to the ground and it ceased moving.

Broken Ghost was already amid the others, grabbing a female by the snout and pulling it toward her before letting go. The creature toppled forward, hitting the ground hard with the flat of its jaw. By then, Broken Ghost was upon the next, shoulder down as she body slammed it in its side, knocking it from its springing, swaying footing. As it crashed to the ground the assassin placed her feet to either side of its thick neck and, with a swift zigzag movement, snapped it with a loud, gruesome crack that echoed across the empty plain.

The remaining kangaroos were terrified now, and they bounded away, leaping past the clump of trees and away from the watering hole. It was like twin fireworks shooting off after their fuses had burned down—a fully grown kangaroo could reach a speed of over forty miles per hour for a short distance when fleeing. But Broken Ghost wasn't finished with them yet. She leaped forward, her arms pumping, her legs racing across the ground as she sped after the fleeing pair.

Cloud Singer watched, incredulous, as the assassin rushed after her prey. The kangaroos split up, taking different directions, and Broken Ghost stayed with the boomer as it tried to hop away. In that moment, the assassin seemed possessed of an inhuman speed to Cloud Singer's eyes. There was no dreamslicer in action, no tricks to make her skip ahead; the assassin just powered her trim body onward with incredible, unimaginable drive.

In an instant, Broken Ghost reached out and was suddenly upon the boomer's back, using her weight to topple it, driving it into the hard ground. Dust kicked up as the assassin wrestled with the kangaroo, its writhing tail snapping out at her as she smashed its head against the ground. After a moment, the movements stopped and Cloud Singer peered at the fallen bodies, wondering what had happened.

Cloud Singer walked through the shallow waters, past the corpses of the kangaroos, toward where Broken Ghost had brought the male 'roo down. As she stepped across the warming, sunbaked soil, she saw Broken Ghost rise from the tangle of bodies, sweeping her braided hair over her shoulders. There was blood on her body, shining as it caught the early-morning sunlight.

"You're fast," Broken Ghost stated as she approached Cloud Singer, "but you're no hunter. You seek new targets when you ought to finish each sequentially before moving on to the next."

"I'll keep that in mind," Cloud Singer responded, nodding. She gestured to the fallen kangaroos—five carcasses lying around them. "What do we do with these?"

Broken Ghost smiled, her grin a sinister thing within her skull-like face paint. "The tribe shall dine well this month," she said.

A LITTLE LATER, the pale assassin led Cloud Singer along the dark passages of the network of caverns, deeper and deeper into the darkness. Broken Ghost had stripped away her baggy shirt, leaving a white harness that held her breasts strapped tightly to her chest. As Cloud Singer followed, she watched the muscles in play on the assassin's magnificent body as she moved.

They were going lower, getting deeper into the rock formation, and Cloud Singer wondered if they were actually belowground now.

"Where are we going?" Cloud Singer asked, her quiet voice taking on a hollow edge with the echo of the tunnels.

Broken Ghost ignored the question, and Cloud Singer chastised herself, realizing that the answer was obvious. They were going where they were going; she would know when they got there.

There were paintings on the walls down here, scribblings and sketches, abstract shapes beside disturbing representations of faces, and their presence added to the claustrophobia that the dark tunnels induced in Cloud Singer. Ever since the mission in Georgia, when she had been forced to hide in the vent and had awakened to find no easy exit from the underground bunker, Cloud Singer had begun to feel terrified of enclosed spaces. The Georgia ventilation shaft had been blocked using explosives before the Cerberus team left the Chernobog base, and Cloud Singer had been forced to dig her own way out of the hidden bunker, using makeshift tools, parts of the bunk beds and her bo staff and, finally, scrabbling at the clogging soil with her hands, breaking her nails in desperation.

Cloud Singer blinked, sending the instruction to her implants, letting the electrochemical polymer lenses slide into place over her eyes, giving her night vision in the smothering darkness of the tunnels. She could hear the sound of rushing water now, and it seemed nearby but perhaps that was an auditory trick of the enclosed, echoing passageways.

Swiftly, Broken Ghost turned left and ducked beneath the low overhang of the ceiling. Cloud Singer stopped beside the rocky overhang, looking all around, trying to get her bearings. She had never been this far into the caverns before, never in all her sixteen years. It felt like another world, a mystical otherplace that the outside world couldn't touch.

"Come," Broken Ghost encouraged, "I have something to show you, Cloud Singer."

Cloud Singer ducked beneath the low stoop and found herself in a little cave, no more than five feet square. Broken Ghost was kneeling on the ground, using the palms of her hands to brush away the dirt until she uncovered a small pouch of animal hide. "Here," she said, opening the drawstring mouth of the pouch.

"What is it?" Cloud Singer asked, bending close to see.

The assassin held the pouch open and let the contents drop into the palm of her empty hand. Cloud Singer stared, the image filtering through the night-vision lenses into a stark green and black tapestry across the windows of her eyes. There, resting atop Broken Ghost's palm, was a bull roarer. Its length of cord snaked around her hand, overflowing and trailing down into the mussed dirt from which

Broken Ghost had retrieved it. At one end of the strong cord, Cloud Singer saw a cup, the noisemaker for the device. At the other end, the woven leather handle with an extra tie to ensure a failsafe grip.

"Is that…?" Cloud Singer began, almost too overwhelmed to speak.

Broken Ghost nodded. "A dreamslicer."

"But I thought that we'd lost them when…" Cloud Singer stopped, unable to conclude the sentence, the memory still too vivid, too painful. She had been one part of the six-strong field team that traveled to Russia to acquire a weapon of incalculable power called the Death Cry. Once there, the Original Tribe strike team had found themselves at odds with an American-based field team from a group called Cerberus. The Cerberus people relied on technology, and yet they demonstrated no real insights into the true nature of their mat-trans unit, how it granted access to the Dreaming World. They saw it merely as a tool, a conveyance, a method to move their people from one arena to another, with no real acknowledgment of the in-between. Trained warriors all, Cloud Singer's team had the upper hand from the moment they clashed with the Cerberus people, but somehow the Cerberus crew had tricked them into detonating the Death Cry weapon inside the Dreaming, destroying their dreamslicer and blocking their access to the Dreaming World in the process. Five men, five brave warriors, had died that day, leaving Cloud Singer the lone survivor.

Her access to the Dreaming denied, Cloud Singer had been forced to travel home via more conventional means, crossing the lands on foot, hitching or stealing rides, navigating the seas in a succession of flimsy boats. Her innate homing sense, hardwired into her skull for use in navigating the Dreaming, had helped guide her to the outback and the waiting members of her tribe.

Broken Ghost's low voice brought Cloud Singer back to the present. "Not here," she was saying. "Down the passage, there is a large cavern where there is more room."

Cloud Singer nodded, backing out of the low entrance to the cave and waiting in the rock-walled passageway for the older woman to join her. Broken Ghost wrapped the strong cord of the bull roarer around her hands and stretched it between them, leading the way ever deeper into the multitudinous caverns.

Eventually, they came to a steep slope that led into an open area. Through her night lenses, Cloud Singer saw a large pool of water dominated this cave, ripples fluttering across its surface with the breeze, and she saw the flitting shadows as a family of bats flew around the high ceiling, disturbed by these newcomers, these humans.

"In here," Broken Ghost said, walking along the narrow path beside the underground pool. After a moment, she slowed her pace and held her hand up, instructing Cloud Singer to wait. Then she turned to face the warrior girl, slipping the ties of the bull roarer over the back of her hand as she adjusted its handle in her grip. "Are you ready?" she asked. "You remember how?"

Cloud Singer gave a single firm nod. "Of course."

Broken Ghost held the bull roarer at her side, letting the cup drop to the rocky ground. Then, with a whirring of her wrist, she set the instrument in motion, raising it above her head as it spun in her grip, unleashing that familiar droning song as the cup cleaved the air of the cave. The bats flew about them, panicked by the sudden currents of air and the howling noise of the bull roarer in motion, its reverberations echoing off the rock walls.

Cloud Singer closed her eyes, feeling for the tingling sensation at the top of her spine where the bull roarer engaged with her implant. After a moment, she felt it, like carbonated bubbles popping against her neck, and she channeled her will into the implant, stepping out of the Realworld and into the Dreaming. When she opened her eyes, Broken Ghost still stood before her, swooping the long cord of the bull roarer over her head.

But everything else had changed.

Her night lenses forgotten, Cloud Singer looked all about her, marveling at her return to the Dreaming World. It was so much more than she had remembered, vivid and full, more than the mind could hold. The familiar caves of the outback swept before them, but they were prettier, with green shrubs and trees dotting their sides. Above, the sun was a deep red ball, a staring eye watching over everything, visible through a skylight that went on and on until it reached the open sky. The whole place smelled fresh, open, newborn.

Cloud Singer could feel the smile tug at her lips. She had thought, over the past few months, that she would never return here, never see the Dreaming again. She turned to Broken Ghost, who was spinning the bull roarer over her head, and the broad smile dominated her face. "You brought us back," she said in wonder, "back to the Dreaming."

Broken Ghost nodded. "Yes," she said, "there was

another dreamslicer, given to me by Bad Father. I have been called upon to use it from time to time, in my journeys." She politely called them "journeys" but Cloud Singer knew what she truly referred to, for an assassin only had one purpose in any journey.

"Do the tribal elders know that you have this?" Cloud Singer asked.

"They suspect," Broken Ghost admitted, "perhaps. It was no secret that Bad Father chose me, paid me more attention than the other members of the tribe. But it need not concern them."

Cloud Singer looked all around her, still astounded at the beauty of the Dreaming. "But they know of my mission, my quest of righteous vengeance upon the Cerberus killers. The elders should—"

"They have other means of entering the Dreaming," the assassin said, hushing Cloud Singer's complaints, "and they are not warriors as we are. Now, come—there are things I must show you."

With that, Broken Ghost turned, shifting her body just subtly, and she was gone. Cloud Singer stood there, looking all over, eyes peering to the distant horizon, trying to see where her companion had disappeared to. Each member of the tribe had his or her own way of traveling through the Dreaming. Cloud Singer's method involved her song, pulling her through the air, drawing her along the lines of music that threaded across the globe. But she had never seen Broken Ghost within the Dreaming, never realized how swiftly the woman moved here.

There was a shimmer, a blur, like heat rising from tarmac, and Broken Ghost reappeared, the impressions of her footprints still on the waters of the underground lake. She inclined her head toward Cloud Singer, the glass and rocks glinting within the braids of her hair, the query clear on her furrowed brow. "Are you coming?"

Cloud Singer was apologetic. "I don't know that I can follow, you move so fast."

With the bull roarer spinning over her head, Broken Ghost reached out and grasped Cloud Singer above the wrist. "Take my hand," she said, "and hold tight."

Cloud Singer did as she was instructed, and in a moment they were rushing together, hand in hand, through the vibrant landscape of the Dreaming, its strange sights and sounds hurtling by like autumn leaves in the fall winds.

"Where are you taking me?" Cloud Singer asked as she felt the wind pour through her hair. Below her she saw land rush by, then ocean, then land once again. Somehow, she realized, Broken Ghost was folding space upon itself so that she could travel immense distances in a few seconds. Cloud Singer was certain that here was a feat that took exceptional concentration.

Suddenly, Broken Ghost took a firm step on the landmass to halt them and the rush ceased as quickly as it had begun.

Cloud Singer stood there swaying, feeling dizzy, the whirl of the ride so fast. She took a breath, centering herself once more. "Where…?" she asked.

Silently, the ash-skinned assassin flicked a pointing finger into the distance, and Cloud Singer saw a burning wave that moved slowly across the land, a rainbow of oscillating color rippling across its oily surface.

"What is it?" Cloud Singer asked as she watched the

wave overwhelm the land beneath it, washing back to leave only black emptiness where once there had been life.

"The Death Cry," Broken Ghost said darkly. "It is progressing across the Dreaming World, destroying it slowly and emphatically."

"But what happens then?" Cloud Singer wanted to know. "When the Dreaming is gone?"

"Who knows?" Broken Ghost replied. "Perhaps something will take its place. Something new or something the same. Perhaps this is a natural part of the cycle."

"A new version." Cloud Singer nodded. "A reboot." That made sense to her, that the Dreaming would re-create itself, better and stronger. She realized that this was the legacy of her battle with Cerberus, the destruction of everything that the Original Tribe held dear. "When will you know?"

Broken Ghost's dark-rimmed eyes stared at her companion, unable to answer the question. "Come, there are other things you must see." She took that firm grip on Cloud Singer's wrist once more and sidestepped into the whirling ride.

From land to ocean to land once more, they skimmed the surface of the globe in a few seconds, the wind of movement rushing by. As they moved, Cloud Singer looked behind her and watched the massive wave front until it disappeared over the planet's curve. Then they stopped again, and Broken Ghost instructed Cloud Singer to look ahead.

Cloud Singer peered but saw nothing, just a mountain beneath her feet, clouds rushing by overhead. "What? I don't see."

Broken Ghost pointed to the ground, her mouth taking care to form her next words. "Look closely."

Cloud Singer peered at the ground, looking at it and then, by relaxing her eyes, looking through it, feeling its substance peel away. There, tucked beneath the earth, a rectangular doorway glowed a deep orange. "A door," she said. "I see a door."

"This is Cerberus," Broken Ghost told her as the bull roarer spun above her head. "We are in Montana, an area known as the Bitterroot Mountains. Their tribe is located here, in these mountains."

Cloud Singer felt the anger rising within her, even at the merest mention of the enemy who had killed her teammates. "Could we step out? Could we attack them now?" Cloud Singer asked.

"To what end?" Broken Ghost replied. "To attack a mountain? What would that prove? How would that benefit us?"

Cloud Singer looked at the glowing orange rectangle in the earth. "The door," she said. "We can use the door."

Broken Ghost nodded. "The door is inside their lair," she explained. "This is their mat-trans. Decimal River spent time working this interface between the Dreaming and their access point, but he cannot open it."

Suddenly, things were clear to Cloud Singer, she began to see the whole of Broken Ghost's ambitious plan. "But *they* will open it for us," she said in realization, "our people."

Broken Ghost nodded once. "When the time is right. Then we shall destroy the Cerberus operation for what they did to us."

"What about Kane and the others in the strike team?" Cloud Singer asked. "Are they dead?"

"No." Broken Ghost laughed. "You do not kill an enemy by cutting off its limbs, Cloud Singer, you do so by lopping off its head. We kill Lakesh, but his people remain, imprisoned in the trap, never able to escape." She counted them off on her fingers. "Kane, Baptiste, Grant—they're gone, they won't bother us now. Trapped in a little cage in Hell."

Cloud Singer looked at the glowing doorway beneath them, remembering the time when she and Rabbit in the Moon had faced Kane in the room of bones beneath the Caucasus Mountains. "I saw vampires in Russia," she said, "out in the daylight, feeding off one another. I fought with them and I stole their sailboat."

"Not vampires," Broken Ghost corrected her. "Cannibals. Just hungry people with nothing left to eat."

"How does the trap work?" Cloud Singer asked then, changing subject in a breath.

"It takes their memories," Broken Ghost explained, "the way a dream takes your memories. And then it gives them more, things to make them stay, to hold them in place. It takes their true hearts, their desires, and it feeds on them like a parasite. A funnel-web spider within their bellies, weaving inside them, locking them in place forever."

"Their desires?" Cloud Singer queried.

"Desires are parasites, Cloud Singer," the assassin explained. "We all have them, deep inside us, even if we think that we do not. We all wish for a place within the world that is our own place, where we can be ourselves."

Cloud Singer nodded in understanding, looking back into the earth where the glowing orange door waited.

"Their time with Cerberus will be nothing but the

vaguest memory," Broken Ghost explained, "like a story they read as children."

"Could we go there, into their new world, I mean?" Cloud Singer asked.

"To what purpose?" Broken Ghost queried reasonably.

Cloud Singer looked at the assassin, then away again, off to the horizon. "How long before the wave, the fallout of the Death Cry, reaches this part of the Dream?"

"Not long," Broken Ghost replied. "A month, maybe six weeks. After that we won't be able to get here, to access the interface."

"Will it take any longer than six weeks?" Cloud Singer asked.

"No," Broken Ghost assured her. "In twenty-four hours Mohandas Lakesh Singh will be dead."

# Chapter 8

Shizuka sat on the edge of the bed in Grant's personal quarters in the Cerberus redoubt, admiring her lover's muscular body as he changed out of his shadow suit and into casual wear. She blushed a little and averted her eyes when she realized that he was looking at her.

"I'd better pop to the armory," Grant explained, unclipping the Sin Eater and its bulky wrist holster from his arm, "put this bad boy into storage. After that, we're good to go."

Shizuka nodded. "I'll meet you at the main door," she told him, still aware of the heat on her cheeks.

Grant reached down, taking Shizuka's *katana* from the bed where it lay in its scabbard. "I'll take this with me, too," he said, "make sure it's safe."

Shizuka reached up, stilling Grant's arm. "No, that's okay," she assured him. "It will be fine here. I'll leave it under the bed, out of the way."

Grant frowned. "Well, if that's what you think is for the best…" he began.

Shizuka smiled. "Swords aren't like guns, Grant," she reminded him. "They don't just go off when the wrong person touches them. Besides, a true samurai would never trust their blade to another—you know that."

Grant looked offended for a moment, but he took it in good humor. "You know you can trust me, right?"

Shizuka's petite hand reached up to stroke Grant's cheek as she looked him in the eye. "With my life, Grant-*san*," she assured him. "With everything that I am and all that I will ever be."

"Okay," Grant grumbled, "but don't blame me if you shish kebab your foot when you go to the bathroom in the middle of the night."

Shizuka pulled the sword close to her side. "I'm touched by your concern," she told him.

Grant shrugged, muttering amiably about trying to help as he left the room and made his way to the armory to store his blaster.

Alone in the two-room quarters, Shizuka shifted on the bed and looked around. Grant seemed to have so little personality on display. The walls were blank gray, the shelves almost empty. She had known Grant to open out the small table that slotted into the wall, decorate it with candles and a vase of flowers, just for a private meal with her, but he still had that Magistrate sensibility at the core of his being, that need for order, for neatness with no frills, no fuss.

Standing, Shizuka took the *katana* from the bed and broke the seal between scabbard and sword for just a moment, looking at her reflection in the inch and a half of gleaming steel that emerged before she pushed the hilt back to meet with the sheath. Crouching, she placed the scabbard gently on the floor and carefully pushed it away until it was tucked far beneath the double bed. It would be safe here, she knew.

Then she stepped across to the tiny wardrobe and

pulled back its door. Grant's Kevlar-weave long coat was on the foremost hanger, slightly askew. She smiled as she straightened it—a poor performance for the regimented manner of the ex-Magistrate. Then she reached for her travel bag and took out her comm device, checking it for messages. Nothing had come through, no urgent Tigers of Heaven business. She had told her second in command not to bother her with anything less than critical priority, and for once it seemed that he had obeyed. Perhaps she would actually get to spend the whole day with Grant after all.

Replacing the comm unit in the bag, Shizuka pulled the wardrobe door closed and left the room, making her way to the main door of the redoubt.

THREE FIGURES PACED slowly through the shadows of the vast, machinery-filled room that controlled the ventilation system for the Cerberus redoubt. They walked in semi-darkness, their discussion held in low whispers despite the churning sounds of the ventilation system that operated beside them.

"This is the main router for the system," Brigid Baptiste told the others, pointing to a large silver unit that took up almost one-third of the room. "It pulls all the air into the Cerberus facility, purifies it and distributes it via the pipes you can see here and here."

Grant nodded, carefully noting in his mind where the red-haired woman had pointed. He wore a white undershirt with loose combat pants and boots now. "And where then?"

"The pipes filter into the air shafts that run all over the building. These connect to vents that can be altered for some rooms while, in other areas such as the main thoroughfares, they're fixed and will always remain open."

Still wearing his shadow suit, Kane looked at the vast, churning machinery as it continued to feed air to the Cerberus complex. The unit itself was old and had a thick layer of dust across its surface. The dust was deep enough that when he ran a fingernail through it he left a shiny silver streak there. "Is there a backup system?" he asked Brigid.

Brigid shook her head. "The redoubt's self-contained," she explained. "In a normal day they could, in theory, open the main door and let the air flow through. Hence, essentially, this is the backup system."

"But it's in use all the time," Grant pointed out, confused.

"As a convenience rather than a necessity," Brigid told her colleagues. "This facility was designed to hold perhaps two hundred personnel at any given time. Without this air-conditioning system, it would become very warm very quickly. Not unbearable, mind you, but certainly unpleasant."

"Sweaty, too." Kane smiled, adding two more strokes beside the line he had drawn in the dust, then dotting them with the tip of his finger so that they looked like three letter *i*'s.

"Death by body odor." Grant chuckled quietly. "An ignominious way to go."

Kane looked up from his sketching on the dusty surface. "We can do better than that, partner."

Brigid agreed. "I'm sure there are plenty of interesting and useful items in the Cerberus armory," she proposed, a catlike smile playing on her lips. "Phosgene would be ideal."

Grant glanced from Kane to Brigid. "You're going to

have to do it alone," he told them. "Shizuka's got a whole afternoon of fun planned for her favorite ex-Mag."

At Kane's nod, Grant took his cue to leave, trotting across the vast room, ducking under the low-hanging pipes and making his way to the maintenance door.

Once Grant had gone, Brigid's eyes flicked to Kane. "He okay?" she asked, raising her eyebrows meaningfully.

"Who, Grant?" Kane asked, looking at the closed door where his partner had just exited. "Grant's solid. Rock solid. Always will be." He turned back to face Brigid then, taking in the whole, vast machine room as he did so. "I can handle all this. What about the other thing?" he asked, his voice still low. "The gateway?"

"You want me to take care of it?" Brigid asked.

"It's more your field than mine, Baptiste," Kane acknowledged.

"Could be tricky, though," she told him.

Humorlessly, Kane smiled. "You like tricky."

She held his gaze. "I like good food and good wine. Tricky I merely endure," she told him.

"When all this is done," Kane assured her, "we'll have us a champagne breakfast on their fucking graves. You, me, Grant and dead Lakesh."

"I'll keep you to that, Kane," Brigid told him before weaving her way through the low-hanging pipes and making her way out the northernmost access door to the room.

Standing alone, Kane let out a low whistle as he looked around the vast room at the groaning, whirring machinery. "This is going to get a whole lot more fun," he muttered before ducking beneath an air pipe and leaving via the room's south exit.

SHIZUKA WAITED beside the large accordion-style door at the main entrance to the Cerberus redoubt, her eyes closed, letting the breeze from the open door play through her hair and fill her nostrils. She heard the footsteps, recognized the tread and, without turning, acknowledged Grant. "I thought you were going to be one minute, Grant-*san*," she said, but there was no irritation or judgment in her tone.

"Weapons all safely back in the armory," Grant told her. "Had a little business to take care of, as well."

Shizuka opened her eyes and looked at Grant. "Sometimes it's like you never stop working," she said.

Grant ran a hand through his cropped hair, looking a little embarrassed. "I'm sorry, I'll try harder."

"No, you won't," Shizuka assured him. "It's what I love about you."

Grant stepped close to her, and Shizuka glanced over his shoulder, ensuring that they were alone before she pecked him on the cheek.

"So where do you want to go?" Grant asked close to Shizuka's ear, his voice low.

Shizuka looked through the open door, watching the long shadows as the afternoon sun began to sink lower in the sky to the west. "It's such a glorious day, let's just walk," she decided.

Grant took a step forward, holding his hand out for Shizuka. The warrior woman looked at him and began to laugh playfully.

"What's up?" Grant asked, raising an eyebrow as he looked at Shizuka.

"I was just thinking," Shizuka replied, "how funny this is. We have a mat-trans on the base and the interphaser, too. We could literally go just about anywhere for the afternoon."

Grant held her gaze firmly, and his expression darkened. "Walking is just fine," he said firmly, tugging Shizuka's hand just a little as he strolled across the plateau.

Shizuka laughed. "I think so, too," she told him as they trekked away from the redoubt.

THE OPS ROOM WAS QUIET when Brigid Baptiste entered, that lazy midafternoon feeling washing over everyone who worked there. Lakesh was sitting at his desk near the door, leaning back in his chair as he read a printed report. The operational staff worked at their designated tasks, checking the feeds from the satellite links and monitoring the steady flow of information. Donald Bry and Skylar Hitch were still working at the deconstructed computers on the far side of the room, and beside them sallow-faced Trent was blowing on a hot beverage between tired yawns.

As Brigid made her way down the aisles of computers, heading for her usual desk beside Brewster Philboyd's communications-monitoring station, Lakesh glanced up and smiled, offering her the briefest of nods before getting back to his reading. Brigid smiled back before sitting down at her desk.

Smile all you want, you old goat, she thought. Pretty soon the whole operation's coming down around your ears.

KANE ACKNOWLEDGED the sentry at the doors to the armory with a curt nod as he entered. The guard greeted Kane pleasantly, recognizing him from around the redoubt, even though they had never shared more than a few words. Her name was Johnson, five foot five with blond hair cut into a severe bob that ended in line with her earlobes. Mentally, Kane dismissed her immediately—she was clearly more inventory clerk than guard. Which made sense while the Cerberus complex wasn't under attack or in any immediate danger.

Kane paced the aisles of the vast room, spying Dragon missile launchers, propellant tanks, handguns, shotguns, automatics, semiautomatics, rifles, scoped rifles, scoped rifles with silencers and numerous other weapons, all stored and cataloged by shelf number.

"Are you looking for something particular?" Johnson spoke up, her voice nasal with a slight drawl.

Kane glanced over his shoulder as the shorter woman approached. "I'm not quite sure…Johnson, isn't it?" he said, offering his most disarming smile.

A blush rose across Johnson's neck and up into her cheeks. "My friends call me Henny," she said. Responding to Kane's confused look, she added, "Henrietta."

"Hi, Henny," Kane said, offering her his hand. "I'm Kane."

Henny Johnson shook Kane's hand as she spoke. "So, what are you looking for, Kane? Something I can help you with?"

"The techs are running some tests upstairs," Kane lied. "Asked me to pick up something called, um, phosgene. You know what they're talking about?"

"Sure, sure," Johnson said, pulling a tiny two-by-three-inch notebook from her pocket and flipping through the handwritten pages. "Phosgene, phosgene…" she muttered as she flipped past numerous notes. Kane glanced around the room as she did so, noting where his Sin Eater pistol had been stored beside Grant's.

"Aha," Johnson said, tapping a triumphant finger against the open page of her tiny pad. "Phosgene, toxicant, aisle 8, shelf C." She continued reading from her pad as she led Kane through the aisles to the appropriate shelf. "This thing is a pulmonary agent, Kane, so you're going to want to be shit careful with it. I mean, if this stuff gets loose it would clog up your lungs in a few hours."

"Is that so?" Kane asked emotionlessly.

Johnson nodded, warming to her subject. "Oh, yeah, this stuff was produced prenukecaust, and it is lethal. Colorless under normal conditions, this gas is heavier than air, which means it sinks and remains at a low level, filling a room or building until the occupants breathe it in."

"What then?" Kane asked.

"Inhalation results in massive pulmonary edema, which reach—"

Kane held up a hand to stop Johnson in midflow. "Pulmonary edema? Translation?"

Johnson looked at him and blushed once more before she explained. "Sorry, it's the lungs filling with fluid, like when you have a chest cold. I've been on my own down here for too long," she added with a shrug.

Kane nodded. "And then what?"

"After exposure, the symptoms max out in about twelve hours," Johnson said. She looked up at Kane and added conspiratorially, despite them being the only people in the room, "That's some fast-acting shit."

"Sounds pretty hard-core," Kane agreed. "Do you have anything else written down there?"

Henny Johnson checked the numbers on the shelves before locating a series of large, bucketlike canisters that stood on the floor like tins of paint. The canisters showed a series of military stickers regarding their toxic nature, with the ominous warning Danger Of Death written on their sides. "Within twenty-four to forty-eight hours after exposure, this stuff will kill you," she told Kane.

Kane smiled. "Wouldn't do to drop it on my foot then, huh?"

Johnson laughed at that. "I'd say that's a definite negative, soldier," she told him between guffaws.

Kane reached down and picked up two of the canisters by their carrying handles, hefting them off the floor with a tensing of powerful arm muscles.

"Will you be okay with that?" Johnson asked. "I can lend you a flatbed, then you can wheel them out if you want."

Kane shook his head. "I'll be fine," he assured her. "Not far to go."

Johnson fell into step beside Kane as he made his way toward the exit. "You need me to sign for these, Henny?" he asked.

"Protocol says yes," she told him, "but you've got your hands full and I don't want to keep you. Are they leaving the Cerberus base?"

Kane shook his head and smiled. "Definitely not," he said.

"Then I'll sign for them, no problem," Johnson assured him, walking back to her reception desk, which overlooked the main doors to the room.

"Thanks, Henny," Kane said, "I owe you one."

Johnson watched the ex-Mag as he shuffled through the doors with his heavy burden. "Hey, Kane," she said, "what about, I don't know, maybe dinner sometime?"

"Definitely," he replied before letting the armory door close behind him. *If there's still breath in your lungs, Cerberus scum,* he added to himself.

# Chapter 9

The glass double doors swished back automatically as Kane approached them to enter the medical center on Cappa Level. He was dressed in his Mag street clothes—dark T-shirt and pants, Kevlar coat and dark glasses—and he felt the eyes of the people in the facility turn to him warily as he walked straight up to the main reception desk past the waiting patients.

"C-can I help you, M-magistrate?" the desk clerk stuttered, afraid to meet Kane's hidden gaze. The clerk was a young man, barely out of his teens, with a few spots of acne dotting his rosy cheeks.

"I'm here to see a friend of mine," Kane told the clerk. "A Magistrate by the name of Grant."

"I'll just look…" the clerk began, knocking papers from his desk in his haste to reach the computer indexing system that sat across from his desk. He spoke several commands into the computer mike, was forced to repeat one because his voice was trembling so, until he retrieved the information. He grabbed a sheet of notepaper and scribbled down the information from his screen before turning back to Kane. "He's in room 7D17. That's on the seventh floor," the clerk explained, handing the scrap of paper to Kane. "I wrote it down for you."

Kane took the paper and glanced at it as he made his way across the buffed floor to the bank of elevators. The note was written so poorly as to be almost illegible, the clerk's hand had been shaking so much. Maybe Kane should come back sometime soon and find out what it was this young punk was so afraid of, what it was he was hiding.

Kane tossed the note into the trash can as he waited for the elevator. A moment later, the elevator doors opened silently and he stepped inside, his finger jabbing at the button for the seventh level. The doors closed and, with a shunt, the elevator began to rise.

A moment later the elevator halted and the doors trundled open upon a bland corridor, its walls painted a light tan color. Kane stepped out into the corridor and found a sign pointing him toward D wing. As he strode down the corridor he heard a familiar booming voice and, looking up, saw a man in his late thirties approaching from the other end of the corridor. The man had gray hair, trimmed so close to his scalp as to be almost bald, and his intense dark eyes held the arrogance of authority before he slipped his dark glasses over them, hiding them from sight. This was Salvo, Magistrate watch commander and Kane and Grant's direct boss.

"Kane," Salvo boomed as he approached. "I wondered how long it would take for you to come see your little friend." There was some veiled suggestion in the man's statement, Kane knew. Salvo disapproved of any Magistrates striking up friendships; the job should be enough and any ties would, according to Mag doctrine, only hold an individual back.

"Good to see you, too, sir," Kane said, saluting his superior officer automatically. "How is Grant?"

"Alive," Salvo assured him, "thanks to your quick

thinking. That was some good work you did in the field there, Magistrate." The compliment seemed to irritate Salvo, and he said it through gritted teeth.

"Thank you, sir," Kane responded emotionlessly. "My only regret is that I couldn't save McKinnon, as well."

"Rookies go on PPP for a reason," Salvo lamented. "Some of them don't survive, and that's all there is to say about it."

Kane inclined his head once in acknowledgment. "Sir."

They stood in silence for a moment, Salvo looking intensely at Kane's shades and the hidden eyes behind them. "You're back on duty tomorrow," Salvo said, finally, "when I'll be assigning your new partner."

"Yes, sir," Kane replied, saluting once again before Salvo strode away toward the bank of elevators.

Kane made his way to room 17 and rapped his knuckles lightly against the open door. He heard muttered cursing come from inside before Grant's voice invited him in.

"Hey, tough guy," Kane said as he entered the room. Grant lay before him, his large body filling the top half of the high bed. Kane's eyes took the whole scene in in less than a second, realizing that Grant's body stopped just beneath the torso. "What's all the cussing about?"

"I thought you were someone else," Grant admitted. "I'm sorry, buddy."

"Yeah." Kane smiled. "I just saw our esteemed commander in the corridor. I guess you're popular."

"That's popularity I could do without," Grant admitted. "So, how are you? Things were pretty nasty yesterday, man. No broken bones?"

"Not even a scratch," Kane told his partner apologetically, propping his dark glasses up in his hairline. "I'm sorry you didn't come out of it quite so well, Grant. Really."

"Yeah," Grant responded. "Well, that's the job."

Kane looked at Grant lying there, and his eyes flicked once more to the place where Grant's legs should be.

"You can look," Grant told him, "it's okay. I know they're gone."

Kane shook his head and cursed under his breath. "I wish I could have done something," he told Grant.

"You did do something, Kane," Grant assured him. "That's why I'm here. We're partners, and you did what you had to to get me out of there alive."

"Yeah." Kane nodded. "Partners."

Grant held his gaze, considering his words carefully. "You know you're a good guy, Kane," he finally said, "and I appreciate what you did."

"But…" Kane began.

"No *buts*," Grant cautioned him. "Salvo's promised me a job behind a desk somewhere in command and, well, you know, I've been longing to get off the beat for a while now. It's a good thing, man, it really is."

Kane shook his head, looking at Grant. "What am I going to do without my partner?" he asked, yet he felt selfish for even saying it.

"There are other partners," Grant told him. "Good people, good Mags. You'll do okay."

"You and me?" Kane began. "We were more than a team. We knew each other, knew how to react to situations. We were like one of those mythical beasts, one creature with two heads."

Grant laughed at that. "Yeah, like—what was it?—

Cerberus, the dog at the gates of Hell," he said. "Yeah, that's us, all right."

"The hound of Hades." Kane chuckled, then he felt the hairs rising on the back of his neck as he remembered his discussion with the psychiatrist the day before. He shook his head, dismissing the coincidence. "Weird," he grunted.

"You know," Grant said after a moment, "this is a good thing. Really. I wasn't kidding about the desk job. It's so stupid to think, but I kind of feel like this is a good move for me. The very thing I wanted. I kept applying for it and, well, now I've got it."

"And all it took was a terrorist with a molly," Kane growled. "Careful what you wish for, and all that."

"Well," Grant conceded, "there were probably easier ways to get a transfer. But it's done now."

Kane smiled bitterly as he looked out the window. "Yeah, I guess it is. Can only live the life you're given, right?"

BRIGID BAPTISTE WORKED at her terminal in the hushed Historical Division of Cobaltville. She sat before her computer in the little cubicle facing the stone wall, her red tresses tied back in a severe bun, wearing a tight blue bodysuit, her rectangular-framed eyeglasses perched on her nose. This day she was altering the details of a document concerning the clinical trials of a certain medicine. A derivative of the medicine in question was in general use among the lower levels, and it wouldn't do to trigger a panic with such out-of-date information.

"Delete paras two, three, seven," Brigid spoke into her mike pickup. The computer highlighted the paragraphs and eliminated them in a blink. "Insert new para two as follows," Brigid continued, still seeing the original paragraph in her mind's eye. "Test dates as previous. Subjects tested—150. Period of trial…"

Just then, the comm unit that was attached to her computer buzzed and Brigid issued the instruction to halt the rewriting program before she answered. The operator for the Historical Division appeared in a window on Brigid's computer display.

"Miss Baptiste," the operator explained, "there is a call for you from the educational facility. A Miss Hargreaves, J clearance level confirmed."

"Accept," Brigid said, and the teacher's face appeared on the comm screen window of her terminal. Hargreaves was a young woman, younger than Brigid, with dark blond hair that brushed across her shoulders, and a pair of circular, wire-framed spectacles on the bridge of her nose, her own symbol of office.

"Miss Hargreaves, how may I be of assistance?" Brigid invited.

"It's your daughter," Hargreaves began before correcting herself, "I'm sorry, I mean your niece."

"That's okay." Brigid laughed. "It's a mistake I even find myself making sometimes."

"We were rehearsing Abi's part in the play and she had a slight fall, nothing major, I assure you. She seems quite upset and has become disruptive, so I think it would probably be better if she were to be taken home."

"I'll come right over," Brigid replied, glancing to her side to see where her elderly supervisor was.

"Honestly, Brigid," Miss Hargreaves continued, "it's

absolutely nothing to worry about. I think she just needs a little love and attention, someone to make a fuss over her."

Brigid assured the woman that she would be there as soon as she could.

"It's absolutely nothing to worry about," the teacher repeated before disconnecting.

Worried, Brigid waited for her supervisor to relieve her.

GRANT SAT in a wheelchair as Elaine pushed him around the bland corridors of the Cappa Level medical hub.

"It must be nice to get out of that little room," Elaine said, smiling down at him.

"Yeah," Grant agreed, "it's a party."

Elaine stopped pushing his wheelchair then, bringing him to a halt. "Magistrate Grant," she said sternly, "we're going to be positive, aren't we?"

Grant looked at the nurse, her russet hair shining beneath the strip lights of the corridor. "*We'll* try," he said, nodding.

"I believe you are a very brave man, Magistrate," Elaine told him, pushing the chair along as a doctor rushed past them toward the theater, "and I would like to ask a favor of you."

That was unexpected, Grant thought, but he nodded encouragingly. "Ask away," he told her.

"I appreciate that it may be difficult at first, even for a very brave man, to manage by himself, after all you've been through," Elaine said earnestly. "I live alone, but my apartment is large and it's on the first floor, so there's no elevator, no stairs. I wonder if perhaps you might come live with me. Is that allowed? For a Magistrate, I mean?"

Stunned, Grant looked at her. She was a beautiful woman, healthy and probably fifteen years his junior. He saw then what she had meant when she called him a brave man so many times in their conversations. She had really meant, "I'm falling in love with you, Magistrate," and he hadn't noticed it at all. She had spent so much time with him, it never dawned on him that she had other patients, that she was with him because of something other than her responsibilities.

"Elaine," he asked, "can you do something for me?"

She leaned down, her wonderful smile showing beside his face. "What would you like me to do, Grant?"

"It's hard for me to see you at this angle," he told her. "I'd like you to stand there, in front of me, just for a moment." He pointed at the corridor ahead of his wheelchair.

Elaine stepped from behind the chair and walked ahead, her head bowed a little and her feet dragging slightly with self-consciousness. Grant watched her walk with her back to him, peering over her shoulder through the curtain of her hair, dressed in the pressed white linen garment of her post. She was tall, long of limb and thin, with just enough flesh on her bones to add womanly curves where she needed them.

After six paces, Elaine turned and stood there, facing Grant in his chair, giggling just a little and blushing as he admired her. The curved hips, the swell of her breasts, accentuated where the white linen clung to it. Her hair, that wonderful reddish-brown that reminded him of fall days when it was still warm, when the summer had yet to really make way for winter. The top button of her dress was open, the collar of the uniform spreading like petals, accentuating her long, pale-skinned neck. The smooth, rounded chin, that wonderful, elfin smile, a little stub of nose and her hazel eyes, so full of promise and mischief.

She was a dream.

CLOUD SINGER WAS BACK in Realworld along with Broken Ghost, who had gone to speak with the elders, requesting spiritual support before the final push against the devils of Cerberus. Cloud Singer was left alone in the cave with Digital River as he monitored the three Cerberus warriors who were held in stasis within the trap.

"How are they?" Cloud Singer asked, her sudden question surprising Decimal River.

The young man turned to her, his fingers never leaving the keyboard. "Everything's as expected, Cloud Singer," he assured her. "They're not getting out anytime soon."

"Could they get out?" she asked thoughtfully.

Decimal River shrugged. "With enough willpower coupled with a dreamslicer or something similar, it's theoretically possible," he mused. "But it wouldn't happen. Everything they want is there. There's no reason for them to wish to leave."

"What about their physical bodies?" Cloud Singer suggested.

"The body's just an extension of the mind," Decimal River told her. "A physical manifestation. If the mind tells us it's there, then it's there, whether we are connected to it or not."

Cloud Singer nodded once, conceding his philosophical point. "And the world? What of the world?"

"It's their world," Decimal River said. "It's where they

grew up, with just a few alterations to make it more attractive."

"They didn't grow up in the Cerberus facility?" Cloud Singer asked.

"No," the computer expert replied. "I hacked into the personnel files that Cerberus has on them. All three were born in a settlement called Cobaltville, a utopian city in Colorado."

"Then why did they leave?" Cloud Singer wondered.

"Who knows?" Decimal River replied. "They're back home now, with no knowledge of any other life. I've attached a piece of coding to their digital files that we now hold in stasis, a tail code that affects their thinking. Like endorphins, pumping into their brains, making them happy."

"I don't want them to be happy," Cloud Singer spit angrily. "They killed Neverwalk. They killed Rock Streaming and Rabbit in the Moon and Good Father and Bad—"

"Enough!" Broken Ghost's sharp voice came from behind Cloud Singer, and the pale assassin stood in the doorway to the cave, a frown on her painted face. "Are you a warrior or a child, Cloud Singer?"

"They killed them," Cloud Singer yelled. "We should bathe in their blood for what they did—" Cloud Singer stopped, suddenly aware that both Broken Ghost and Decimal River were looking at her with disappointment. Cloud Singer took a long, deep breath, tamping down her fury. "I don't want them to be happy," she said finally, her voice low.

"Do you remember what I told you in the Dreaming?" Broken Ghost said calmly. "How desire was a parasite?"

Cloud Singer nodded.

"Desire and happiness are intertwined," Broken Ghost

continued. "We lose ourselves in our lover's embrace, Cloud Singer. We lose ourselves in happiness." And then Broken Ghost posed a question. "And if we are too happy…?"

"We lose ourselves," Cloud Singer reasoned, "until we cease to be."

The assassin nodded in silent response.

IT WAS HER SMILE, Kane thought. That's what really did it.

He sat at a patio table outside the café, his long black coat hanging from the back of the chair, his regulation shades still covering his eyes as he tucked in to the light salad before him. Sitting across from him was a beautiful dark-haired woman with chocolate-colored eyes, explaining the fundamental differences between the current, prevailing art schools of Snakefishville, Mandeville and Cobaltville. She smiled as she spoke, warming to her subject despite Kane's ignorance. Her smile was wide, and it reached up to touch the tiny creases at the edges of her dark eyes.

"Right now the Snakefishville school are doing some interesting experimentation with color, very bold strokes, really expressive," the woman—Kane's mother—continued, that beautiful, infectious smile touching everyone who looked at her, "but it's a retread of things we've seen in the history books."

"Is that a bad thing?" Kane asked, taking a mouthful of salad.

"Like life, art should always move forward, Kane," his mother explained. "Haven't I drummed that much into you by now?"

Kane looked a little embarrassed. "I have trouble

keeping all the different pieces straight in my head," he confessed, looking down at his plate. When he looked up and saw his mother's disappointed look, he shrugged and added, "If I'm honest."

Kane's mother laughed. "Yes, your father did a very good job of ensuring you knew all about the laws and the reasons for unification, but he didn't have much time for the other things in life. The…" She stopped herself.

"What?" Kane inquired. "What is it?"

"I was about to say 'the nobler things,'" his mother said, pushing a lettuce leaf around her plate, "but, of course, what you do is very noble indeed."

Kane put his fork down. "Well, it's a job."

His mother reached forward, touching Kane gently on his tanned arm and smiling with sincerity. "Kane, being a Magistrate isn't a job—it's a calling. I couldn't be more proud of you, and I would never expect you to do anything else."

Kane nodded. "That means a lot," he said. It felt strange to say that, as though he had never said such a thing to his mother before. It felt right somehow, having her here, a part of the puzzle that had been missing all his life. "Did you go away?" he asked suddenly, wondering why he felt that way.

"Me?" his mother asked, taken aback. "Oh, no, Kane, I never went away. Why do you ask?"

"I don't know," Kane said, shaking his head as though that might loosen the nagging feeling that was there.

When he looked up again, there was a young man, perhaps fifteen or sixteen, running past the café tables that lined the promenade. Incredulous, Kane watched as the boy's hand reached out and plucked a patron's bag from the next table to theirs before he ran on. The bag's owner, a chubby, olive-skinned woman in the clothes of a lab tech, stood and pointed, dumbstruck. "That boy..." she uttered, watching the young thief run off into the crowd.

Kane was on his feet immediately, automatically grabbing his coat from the back of the chair as he rushed onto the sidewalk. He uttered a single word of explanation—"Duty"—to his mother as he dashed into the surging crowd after the disappearing thief. Proudly, his mother watched him work.

PROPPED AGAINST A STACK of pillows, Grant sat up in bed and gazed out of the medical room's window at the familiar buildings of Cobaltville. It was a beautiful place, the result of a hundred years of desperation and a hundred more of struggle to perfect peace. He could conceive of nothing right then that might ever drag him willingly away from this place, this idyllic ville.

"*Drag* would be right," Grant muttered, glancing down at the stumps of legs he now had.

There was something else, though, something at the back of his mind that kept trying to emerge, like an image seen beneath a flicking overhead lamp. He closed his eyes and took a deep, steadying breath as he focused on whatever was nagging at him.

Kane, his partner.

A man whom Grant trusted more than anyone else in Cobaltville, anyone else on the planet. Kane was always in sync with him, always able to cover for him and second-guess his moves.

What was it they had said? Like a mythical beast. Like Cerberus, the hound of Hades.

The image appeared then, fully formed, a vivid, garish painting of the three-headed dog, its powerful legs and snapping jaws, the reflection of the fires of the underworld in its eyes. It wasn't alive; he knew that. It was something else, a picture, a vid, a dream.

Grant opened his eyes. "Cerberus," he mumbled, feeling the play of the syllables on his mouth. "Cerberus, the hound of Hades."

KANE'S EYES WERE locked on the retreating figure of the thief as the boy weaved through the crowd. People were already stepping aside, recognizing Kane as an off-duty Magistrate because of his clothes and the dark lenses over his eyes. Those who didn't step out of his way were shoved aside by Kane as he chased after the boy. His automatic instinct was to call the Sin Eater to hand with a tensing of his wrist tendons, but off duty he wasn't armed—the weapon was held in a secure locker in his small apartment.

BRIGID CARRIED Abigail's satchel as she walked her niece to the school gates. She could see that Abigail was fidgeting; she kept pulling at the sleeve of her top.

"Leave it alone, Abi," Brigid warned her.

Abi looked up at her, her emerald eyes wide. "But it hurts!" she whined.

"I know it hurts, munchkin, but it will only hurt more if you pick at it," Brigid warned her.

Abi set her face in an annoyed sneer and stormed along beside Brigid. "It's all Lakesh's fault," she huffed.

Brigid stopped in her tracks and just stared at the girl. "What?" she asked after a moment. "What did you just say?"

"I said it was all Lauren's fault," Abigail whined. "She pushed me and I fell off the stage. She did it deliberately."

Brigid stood stock-still, her hand reaching out and holding on to the open gate to the school for a moment as she held a breath. "Lauren," she finally muttered.

"I'm going to punch her on the nose," Abi insisted, "and pull all her hair out."

Brigid looked at her niece, who was just a bundle of fury right then. "Don't do that, little darling," Brigid said calmly. "It was just an accident."

The sleeve of Abi's top was ruffled and torn, and there was a nasty scab running along her arm, with dried blood in blotches on the sleeve itself. However, the fall from the stage hadn't done any permanent damage. It had just shaken Abigail up a bit and left her feeling resentful toward her classmate, reason enough to remove her for the day, according to Miss Hargreaves. Looking at her furious niece right now, Brigid was inclined to agree.

Brigid crouched on her haunches, bringing her head level with Abi's. "Don't be like that, munchkin," she told her gently. "It's fun skipping school sometimes, and it's even more fun when you're a grown-up."

"Auntie Brigid, you don't even go to school," Abigail reasoned.

"That's true." Brigid smiled, her hand reaching up to untie her red hair from its tight bun. "I get to cut work instead, which is way, way better," she explained, shaking her hair out so that it fell halfway down her back. "And I get to eat ice cream."

Abi's eyes lit up. "You do?"

"If we stop and buy some," Brigid admitted. "Which means we're going to have to walk. Is that okay, munchkin?"

Abi stuck out her bottom lip as though in deep concentration. "Ice cream monster says yes," she decided.

Brigid stood up, taking Abi's hand as they walked along the sunny promenade toward the market area. "What's an ice cream monster?" she asked.

"I am," Abi said reasonably. "I got taken over by an ice cream monster and now I can only eat ice cream."

Brigid looked at Abi as they wandered along, feeling a sudden shiver run down her spine. Possessed by an ice cream monster? she thought. Did that happen to Abi once? Did it happen to me? She shook herself, realizing how foolish it sounded. Get a grip on yourself, Baptiste, she thought. Ice cream monsters aren't real.

AHEAD OF KANE, the thief was making good progress, his thin, wiry form slipping through the crowd like liquid, instinctively drawn toward the path of least resistance. Kane called out to the boy, instructing him to halt immediately, using the Magistrate voice of command.

The crowd parted around Kane as he rushed on, head down, breath coming faster now as he pumped his arms and legs to increase his pace. "I told you to stop," Kane instructed as the boy leapfrogged a concrete bollard and dashed into the busy market square.

Kane hurdled the bollard and rushed into the market,

as well. The teen thief looked over his shoulder, fear in his eyes as he saw the Mag bearing down on him. The woman's bag was still in his hand and he tipped it upside down, shaking the contents loose as he rushed through the main thoroughfare between the market stalls.

Kane powered ahead, ignoring the strewed contents of the bag in favor of catching the perp. He'd sling this little idiot in a cell, get him off the streets, let the system bury him. No one ran from a Magistrate.

The running thief leaped sideways, narrowly avoiding a collision with a woman pushing a baby carriage along the paved area, then he ducked between two stalls and out of sight. Kane followed, vaulting over the carriage and shoving his way along the thoroughfare, keeping pace with the retreating thief running behind the stalls. The thief continued to run, but his pace was slowing now, and Kane knew that he had him. The Mag fitness regime demanded exceptional endurance from personnel. Kane could easily outrun one teenage thief; the only things working to the boy's advantage up until now had been his head start and his smaller size.

Suddenly the boy stopped, finding himself trapped at the end of an aisle of stalls. Kane waited at the other side of the stall, peering beneath and seeing the thief's feet as he seemed to dance on the spot, looking for another escape route. Suddenly, the boy pushed straight ahead, and the stall before Kane trembled and began to topple, its collection of trinkets and old books slipping from their displays. Kane held out his arm, catching the top of the stall and rocking it backward with a powerful shove, trinkets falling all around him, clattering to the sidewalk.

"Give it up, boy," Kane instructed. "There's nowhere left to run."

But the thief wasn't done yet. He began running back the way he had come, and with a curse, Kane followed. In a moment, Kane zipped between two stalls and found himself in the area behind them, the thief's wiry figure ten paces ahead. The space behind the stalls was a narrow alleyway, with a high brick wall towering to Kane's right, green moss attacking the mortar between the red bricks.

Kane ran on, conscious of the boy's sagging shoulders. Adrenaline was keeping the thief moving now, but he was running out of energy. With a spurt of speed, Kane picked up his pace once more and reached forward. With a swift movement, Kane had grabbed the boy by the collar of his shirt, dragging him backward as his feet kicked ahead. As Kane came to a sudden, decisive halt, the boy tumbled to the floor, hitting the cobbled paving stones back-first with a solid thump. The thief cried out as he hit, pain painted across his face.

"What the fuck! You almost killed me," the boy panted as he lay on his back on the hard ground.

"You'd deserve it, too," Kane snarled, looming over the fallen figure. "Never disobey the command of a Magistrate."

The boy struggled to a crouching position, then pulled himself up by leaning against the solid wall beside him. Kane stood over him, glaring at the thief through his dark lenses.

"You got the bag, didn't you?" the boy snarled. "That's what you wanted, right?"

Kane looked emotionless as he replied. "I got the perp. That's what I wanted."

Kane marched the boy out from behind the market stalls, and the crowd of shoppers parted. Something caught Kane's eye as he walked behind the thief. He glanced around, spotting a beautiful girl, perhaps five or six years old, with honey-blond hair falling halfway down her back. The girl stood at a stall specializing in frozen foods, and for a moment her eyes rested on Kane.

The girl's eyes were a vibrant emerald, familiar and yet he couldn't place it.

As Kane walked past with the perp, a tall woman stepped out from the cover of the stall, folding the top over on the brown paper bag she held. The woman was slender, with pale skin and a curvaceous body wrapped in the blue bodysuit of the Historical Division. Her hair was a vibrant red-gold, flowing in a cascade over her shoulders and down her back, falling level with the underside of her breasts. The woman inclined her head to speak to the girl, the afternoon sun catching the rectangular lenses of her spectacles, and her smile seemed warm and honest. Behind her glasses, her eyes were that distinctive, familiar emerald color.

Even as he walked past her, Kane knew he had to see this woman again.

# Chapter 10

It was night, and the Original Tribe was mostly sleeping. Decimal River dozed before the glowing screen of his laptop, a blanket over his legs.

Cloud Singer entered the cave silently, her dark skin and bloodred clothing making her just another part of the shadows, only the whites of her eyes giving away her presence. On bare feet, she walked across the cave and stood over the laptop, staring at its screen. The screen had been set to energy-save mode and was much duller than normal, but she could still read the details there.

Subject: Kane. Status: Active.

Subject: Grant. Status: Active.

Subject: Baptiste. Status: Active.

Their minds were trapped; that was the essence of the situation. Their minds were trapped, never to free themselves, never to reenter Realworld, digital files held in stasis forever, or until someone pulled the switch, wiped the program. And what would happen then? Cloud Singer wondered. Would they dissipate into nothingness, would their souls float free without bodies or would they somehow re-form or even acquire new shapes, like a chrysalis becoming a butterfly?

Beside her, Decimal River stirred, rolling his muscles

as he woke up. "Cloud Singer," he gasped, his tongue thick with sleep.

"I need to go inside," Cloud Singer told him, her voice firm, "into the trap."

Decimal River was still for a moment, trying to make sense of her words as he came to full awareness. "Broken Ghost said not to," he reminded her.

"Broken Ghost wasn't there when our friends died," Cloud Singer told him, "and I was. Neverwalk was fifteen, and they killed him. It was his first field mission—he didn't even get the chance to fight. They didn't just kill him—they ripped his throat out. His death was slow agony, Decimal River."

Decimal River nodded, absorbing this information.

"Broken Ghost didn't see him," Cloud Singer continued after a moment, "and I did. And now I want to go inside the trap to make sure, to see for myself, that they are truly stuck, that they will be lost forever."

Decimal River nodded wearily. "I understand," he told Cloud Singer, "but I don't think that you should."

"Can it be done?" Cloud Singer urged, ignoring his concerns. "Can you put me inside the trap?"

Decimal River nodded again. "I included a back-door coding into the program. It will allow one of us to enter, to become a character within their new world," he said.

Cloud Singer stood, arms outstretched, head back. "Send me, then," she said.

"And what do I tell Broken Ghost?" Decimal River asked.

"Broken Ghost is asleep," Cloud Singer said. "I checked before I came here. She need never know."

"Better that she doesn't," Decimal River agreed, rifling through a box of attachments until he brought out a reel of cable with a USB jack at one end and a headset at the other.

"What's that?" Cloud Singer asked, looking at the cable with its headset.

"I cannibalized a mike headset," Decimal River said, proud of his own ingenuity. "It will pick up your brain-waves and let you operate inside the trap while your body remains here."

Cloud Singer nodded, taking the headset from Decimal River and placing it over her head as she sat before the laptop. "I see," she said.

Decimal River attached the USB spike to a port in the side of the laptop, and began running a series of codes through the mainframe. "Where do you want to go?" he asked. "Which one of them do you want to see?"

Cloud Singer thought back, remembering the savage battle in the bunk room beneath the Caucasus Mountains, the skeletons of Russian soldiers all around them as she and Rock Streaming fought with the tall, muscular American with eyes of steel and the build of an alpha male dingo. "Kane," she said. "Take me to Kane."

SHE FELT AS THOUGH she was caught in a sudden downpour, the sort that soaks the dry plains of the outback with much-needed water, that comes with sheet lightning and deafening thunder, the type that's all energy and exhilaration. And then, whatever the barrier was, the change of thinking, the rewiring of the brain, she was through, inside another world that seemed every bit as real as the cave in Australia where her body resided, its sounds and smells and the taste of the very air itself a definable quality.

Cloud Singer looked about her, saw the huge tower that dominated the center of the walled man-made settlement. This was Cobaltville, she understood, or a Cobaltville simulation, at least.

Figures moved about her, indistinct, unreal, like phantoms, forming from polygons and blocks into human shapes as they walked away from her. Concerned, Cloud Singer looked at her hands, down at her body. She was intact, the bloodred strips of her battle clothes perfectly reproduced in this new world. As Broken Ghost and Decimal River had explained, whatever a prisoner took to the trap would be remade here, their wants twisted.

Cloud Singer was standing in an alleyway between two buildings.

She stepped warily out into the street beyond. Directly opposite the alleyway where she had arrived was a towering structure that dominated the entire ville. Cloud Singer read the words beneath: Administrative Monolith.

As she watched, the phantoms around her became people, solid and fully realized, each now an individual with character and distinct mannerisms. Cloud Singer turned to her left and saw two new figures approaching. One was a boy, still going through puberty by the looks of him, about the age that Neverwalk had been when he had been killed. The boy walked with his head bowed as though afraid. Behind the teenager, a large figure walked purposefully forward, a commanding presence, shoving the boy between his shoulder blades whenever he tried to slow down. She recognized the man instantly, despite the dark lenses that he wore to mask his face: Kane.

Cloud Singer began moving, picking up her pace as

she headed directly toward Kane and his charge. She wanted to run, to attack the man, kill him for what he had done in that underground bunker in Russia. She saw his head turn slightly, some intuitive sense realizing that he was being approached, and in that instant, she realized her folly. She turned, blending into the crowd, hiding herself from his view.

KANE GRABBED THE PERP by the collar and yanked him to a halt just before the wide concrete steps that led up to the Administrative Monolith. Someone was watching him. He knew it instantly, some sixth sense, his point-man instinct kicking into high gear and automatically scanning the faces in the crowd.

The people seemed normal, ordinary Cobaltville residents going about their business, no two faces alike. He watched the pedestrians walking past, always busy, always with places to go, living their carefully ordered lives. A rickshaw passed by, pulled by a dark-haired man with an olive complexion, probably of outlander stock.

"What are you doing, man?" the teenager's whiny voice came to Kane. "I thought you were going to turn me in."

"Hush," Kane told the perp as he clung tight to the youth's collar, not bothering to look at him. He continued scanning the crowd, examining the faces with practiced speed, moving through them like the pages of a flick book.

A little way back, across the far side of the street, a figure was retreating, trying to lose itself in the crowd. A woman, not very tall, her form svelte but muscular. Her skin was dark and, as gaps appeared in the crowd about her, Kane saw that she was covered with tattooed designs, lines and swirls that looked like circuitry. Her clothing was strange, too, strips of cloth of a very dark red, so dark as to be almost black.

The woman was facing away from Kane, her head down, but she seemed nervous, her movements anxious. That wasn't so unusual; people got that way around Mags sometimes. And yet there was something odd about the woman, and not just in her clothes or her strange, almost tribal tattoos.

Kane couldn't put his finger on it. He filed the information away for later and shoved his prisoner up the steps and through the main doors of the tower.

TURNING AWAY, Cloud Singer watched Kane's reflection in the glass windows of the buildings she walked past. She saw the Magistrate enter the Administrative Monolith with his charge at last. As the doors closed behind the two figures, the crowd around her faded, becoming ghostlike blocks, then just strips of code as she watched them. Suddenly, she was in the street alone.

The street, too, was an artificial construct, she realized as the people-codes evaporated. The map had to be finalized, however, a complete construction that was available at all times while the people only appeared as needed. As soon as Kane, or one of the others—Grant or Baptiste— appeared, the details of the world would form around them, a radial pattern of activity that surrounded them no matter where they were. The perfect illusion of a living, breathing world; they would never know any difference.

How many people do we truly interact with in our world? Cloud Singer wondered. How much of it could be artifice, sleight of hand, a confidence trick feeding our perception of what a world should be?

She stood there, looking at the tower, wondering what activity was occurring inside, convincing Kane that this play-world was real.

KANE MARCHED THROUGH the double doors into the high-ceilinged lobby of the Hall of Cappa Level, watching the slouched shoulders of the perp who stomped ahead of him.

A tall statue loomed over the wide room, a robed woman holding scales and wearing a blindfold—justice. The statue towered to almost three full stories, bearing down on proceedings within the large, open area. Kane walked the perp past it to the main reception desk, recognizing the Magistrate on duty there.

"One for the cells, O'Brien," Kane announced, pushing the teenager against the desk and pinning his arms in a swift, practiced movement to ensure that he could not move. The teen grunted in discomfort.

The desk Mag glanced contemptuously at the pimple-faced teen before looking up and acknowledging Kane with a warm smile. "Kane, I thought you were off duty today."

Kane nodded sourly. "I am. This sewer rat happened to bust in on my free time."

O'Brien tsked and shook his head, his gaze returning to the teenager. "What did you do, son?"

"Nothing," the teen replied far too quickly.

"Bag snatch out on Market Square," Kane elaborated when O'Brien threw him a questioning look. "Toss him in a cell until I come on shift tomorrow. Run him through the system, let me know if he's got any priors, okay?"

"Sure thing, Kane," O'Brien agreed, pulling a pair of plastic riot cuffs from his desk.

Muttering under his breath, the boy turned and let the desk Mag cuff him as Kane made his way past the statue of justice and through the Cappa Level lobby. As he stood by the doors, a Mag in riot gear came striding through, his black visor splintered where it had taken a hit. Kane acknowledged the Mag with a curt nod, holding the door open for the man.

CLOUD SINGER HAD FOUND a drop-down fire ladder running up the side of one of the buildings opposite the Administrative Monolith, which she clambered in a matter of seconds. The ladder led to some iron stairs, and these in turn brought Cloud Singer to the roof of the building where she could look out over the ville. Birds flew through the air up here, pigeons and white gulls, cawing and chirping as they swooped through the high canyons between the interconnected towers of the Residential Enclaves.

There was a caste system in operation here, Cloud Singer understood, yet another vision of utopia built upon the structured limitation and suffering of others, and the system expressed itself through proximity to the sky. The closer one's apartment and workplace to the apex of the towering Administrative Monolith, the higher one's social standing.

Not that any of it mattered, Cloud Singer knew. The whole thing was just an artifice, a construct to imprison the Cerberus warriors. A mirror that lied, a cruel trick.

She looked out across the ville and spotted a pocket of activity across from her.

The boulevard that ran along an apartment block across to the south showed people walking up and down. As they got farther from the building's windows they disappeared, ceasing to exist, their roles all played out. One of the Cerberus people had to be entering that building, or perhaps was already inside, gazing out of the windows at the seemingly normal street scene beyond the glass, utterly unaware of the brief lives that the people he or she saw were living.

Hearing street sounds waft up toward her, Cloud Singer turned back and saw people on the street once more, becoming substantial as the main doors to the building opened and a dark-clad figure stepped out. It had to be Kane, of course.

Cloud Singer stood at the roof's ledge, peering down, watching the broad-shouldered man make his way along the busy street. He was utterly unaware that the people around him ceased to exist as he turned a corner, with new ones forming wherever he went.

She could kill him right now, she realized, kill him in this world.

Kill him in his own world.

She began to walk along the rooftop, mirroring Kane's movements, several stories above where he walked. He continued moving, heading south, the bubble of activity massing around him all the while, like moths around a lamp.

Cloud Singer had reached the end of the roof, and she peered down, watching Kane's retreating figure surrounded by the buzz of activity.

Cloud Singer stood at the very edge of the roof, her bare feet on the ledge, toes curled around it, watching the violent man walk freely through this strange playground. It didn't seem right to her that he had all of this after killing her colleagues. This was a trap, true, but she wanted him to suffer, to feel the pain that her friends had felt, that Neverwalk had felt.

Kane's figure became smaller as Cloud Singer watched, then the man turned into a cross street and disappeared from view. She stood atop the roof, and her hands clenched into tight fists, remembering Neverwalk with the missing piece of his neck, the bloody pool that his body lay in. Kane reappeared, striding across the gap between buildings, other people passing him.

Cloud Singer stepped back from the ledge, looking over her shoulder. Then she backed up, walking backward until she was midway across the roof. She leaned down, coiling her muscles, settling her breathing as she adopted a runner's crouch. And then she sprang into action, legs racing, arms pumping, running as fast as she could at the far ledge of the rooftop. A moment later she was at the edge, kicking off from it, leaping high into the air between the buildings.

Slam! She hit the far rooftop with curled toes and the balls of her feet, and her legs bent to cushion the impact. She didn't stop, not even for an instant. Her body was already moving ahead, arms cleaving the air in rhythm at her sides, feet pounding against the grit-covered rooftop beneath her.

Ahead, in the gaps between buildings, she saw Kane reappear once more, still making his way south. Cloud Singer ran onward, vaulting a boxy air vent slick with condensation, then veering to her left to follow Kane.

Again the edge of a roof appeared, but Cloud Singer didn't slow, just held her head low to her body, arms and legs pumping as she leaped out into free space, cutting the air with her body until her feet met with the next rooftop and her body navigated over one obstacle, around the next.

Cloud Singer reached the edge of the building in a few seconds, muscles powering her onward, kicking out into the air above the street, letting her body land where it may. The building facing her was constructed in a series of glass tiers, shaped like an Inca pyramid, and she landed on one of the steps, rolling her body to diffuse the momentum of the leap. She looked about her—the building continued up, reaching ten stories into the air, higher than the structures around it.

Looking down at the streets below, she spied Kane once more, easy to spot by simply looking for the crowds. He was just a block away; she could reach him in twenty seconds.

The buildings around her were low, four- and five-story structures, pristine clean, glimmering in the afternoon sun. Two window cleaners worked on a mobile scaffold along one side of one of the buildings, going about their business in silence. As she looked more carefully, Cloud Singer realized that they weren't cleaning the windows; they were burning off the grime from the brickwork using some kind of acetylene blowtorch. The rulers of Cobaltville believed in utter cleanliness, complete, near fanatical order.

She ran along the step tier of the building before leaping from it, arms outstretched, flinging her body like a dart at the next building. Her hand slapped at the building's edge and she pushed herself forward, driving her body over the lip and onto the rooftop, running across it in a few seconds. The service alleyway was just ahead of her, and she flung herself into the air feetfirst. Her bare feet slapped against the wall before her, and she seemed to almost run down it for the first two stories, using gravity and momentum to her advantage before kicking off and tracking from one wall to the other, back and forth to shed her speed before she reached the ground.

Kane turned at the last moment, realizing that something untoward was happening in the alleyway beside him, but he was too late. Nine feet above him, Cloud Singer kicked off from the wall and dived through the air at the darkly clad Magistrate, raising her other leg into a sweeping kick that connected fully with Kane's chest.

The Mag dropped, arms windmilling as he fell backward. Kane swiftly pushed himself up and looked around. He saw the dark-skinned woman coming up from her crouch, her fierce eyes fixed on his. It was the same woman whom he had spied on the street, the woman with the eerie tattoos and the red-black rags of clothing.

Automatically, Kane tensed his wrist tendons, calling the Sin Eater to hand, his finger crooked to begin shooting immediately. Nothing happened, and—damn!—he remembered that he was not wearing his weapon.

Before him, the girl spun on one foot while her other kicked out in a high circle, clipping the side of Kane's head so that he saw bright flashes for a second. He blinked back the disorientation and pain, positioning his left arm before him to block the girl's follow-up kick. Her foot slammed into his elbow with solid finality, and Kane staggered sideways, struggling to retain his balance.

The girl was fast; he'd give her that. Fast and powerful, and she clearly had no intention of holding back. She looked so young, probably not even in her twenties, Kane realized. Her hair was braided, thick, clotted twists arrayed all about her head. Her skin was dark, but lighter than Grant's, and she was naked other than the straps of material along her arms, legs, chest and groin, her bare skin glistening with sweat, her feet bare also. Her body was covered in tattoos, lines etched along her arms and across her chest. The tattoos were strange swirls mixed with fiercely straight lines, the latter so much like circuitry.

Kane realized then that he knew the girl, but he didn't know from where or how. He recognized her as someone he had seen in the past. Not in a book or a Mag video, but in the flesh, in combat.

The girl rushed at him, sweeping her hand along the ground and tossing gravel at his eyes before she swung a punch at Kane's chin. He blinked away the gravel rapidly, fending off the punch at the same time and feeling its tremendous impact jar along his blocking arm.

"Die," the woman spat, angling her right foot behind his and sweeping it toward her, dropping Kane to the ground like a sack of grain.

Kane swept her punches away as he struggled on the hard surface of the street. Then his right fist powered forward, knocking into the girl's face as she tried to attack him once more, and she sank back, her legs giving out from under her.

Kane took a moment to catch his breath, watching the tattooed warrior and wondering why she seemed so familiar. There was a room, he remembered, with no windows. The room was full of bones. Skulls and ribs, arms and legs, dead people all about them. And she had come at him in a series of blinks, as though she weren't really there at all, or as though she moved so fast as to be beyond his comprehension.

There had been another one, too, a man in his twenties, tattooed like her and wearing loose clothing that left his firmly defined muscles on show. He had attacked Kane in the room of bones with a knife. No, not a knife, it was larger than that. A cleaver? A sword?

The girl stood and gave him an up-from-under look, her thick braids dropping over her face, her teeth set in a grimace. Kane couldn't place her, couldn't place the fight in the room of bones, but he was sure that it had happened. It felt so real.

Then the girl moved, leaping high in the air, her right foot snapping out at Kane's face. He arched his back, pulling himself just clear of the arc of her attacking kick. The tattooed woman landed, her body sinking into itself to absorb the impact. And then, still in motion, she spun and ran off.

INCREDIBLE AS IT SEEMED, Cloud Singer had forgotten how fast Kane could be. The man was as powerful as a stallion and yet he used that brute strength with subtlety. He was a true warrior, able to weigh and outthink an opponent, learning from every move of their developing conflict. That was how he had trapped and presumably killed Rock Streaming, pinning the man down in the room of bones, preventing her blood brother from dreamslicing to escape.

He was following her, she knew. She felt his presence behind her, his long-legged, powerful strides eating up the distance between them, relentlessly driving himself after her.

Cloud Singer ran, remembering the cleaners working at the outside of the building. Kane was stronger than her, yes, and more powerful, that was also true. But she knew something that he didn't—none of this was real.

She drove herself onward, heading for the cleaners in their rig over the street. They were at the building just ahead of her, using the acetylene torch to peel layers of residue from the third-story window frames. Cloud Singer looked about her, her eyes narrowing as she spied the drainpipe running down the side of the building, the trash can affixed at the edge of the sidewalk. She leaped, her speed never slowing, kicking against the trash can so hard that the metal popped with a loud gong, a dent appearing in its side. From the trash can, her body was already in motion, twisting as she hurtled up in the air toward the building. Her left foot slapped into the side of the building, followed by her right an instant later. Then her left hand was swiping at the drainpipe, grasping it and driving herself upward as she continued to sprint up the wall.

KANE COULD ONLY watch in amazement as the tattooed female warrior clambered up the wall like a cat, her movements seeming to defy gravity in an astounding display of *parkour.*

In a few seconds she was at the cleaning rig, three stories above the street. Kane tracked the girl's movements, cursing that he didn't have his Sin Eater to hand. Atop the scaffold, she kicked out, hitting one of the cleaners full in the face so that his teeth burst from his jaw in a spray of splintered shards. The man crashed against the base of the cleaning rig, making it wobble to and fro on its support wires. The girl spun, and her hands grasped the collars of the other man on the rig, yanking him off his feet and tossing him over her shoulder. The man cried in pain as he landed heavily on the blowtorch he held, and he began screaming as his clothes caught fire, becoming a human torch as Kane watched helplessly from the street below.

All around Kane, people stopped and stared, muttering in amazement at the bizarre turn of events. The residents of Cobaltville lived in a perfectly ordered society. They had never imagined such a situation was possible outside the Tartarus Pits. Kane looked about him, wondering if there was another way up to the cleaning rig. The rig used a pulley system that was attached to the roof of the five-story structure and its controls were on the rig itself. There was no way to operate it from down here. If Kane was to enter the building, either to work the controls from the roof or to try to ambush the girl at the rig itself, he would have to lose sight of her and, in that time, she could seize the opportunity to escape, to disappear once more into the crowd.

"Damned if you do and damned if you don't," Kane grumbled to himself as he watched helplessly.

And then he saw the woman warrior do something extraordinary. She took the acetylene torch in one hand and, holding her free arm extended, she set the torch on her arm, playing its thin blue flame up and down her skin until it caught fire. The flesh popped and burned beneath the fierce power of the torch, the strips of material fizzing into flame, and all the while the girl simply gritted her teeth, watching the flames dance higher and higher along her arm.

CLOUD SINGER TOSSED aside the torch and placed her hands together, almost like praying, bringing her elbows forward until they touched. The flames flicked from her left arm to her right, dancing to and fro in the breeze as she watched. The sensation was unearthly, a pain of such intensity that it threatened to overwhelm her.

She stood on the swaying rig above the street and spread her burning arms out to her sides, hands outstretched, palms facing the skies above. A flock of white gulls flew by her, cawing and squawking their endless chatter, and Cloud Singer reached out and snatched one from the air, holding its body in her burning hand. Its pure white feathers caught light in a second, turning gray as an oily smoke poured from its squawking body.

Whatever the pain is, she reminded herself, none of it is real. It's all just a part of the illusion, the trap, the mirror that lies.

With that confirmation running through her mind, she tossed aside the burning carcass of the gull and leaped into the air, plummeting toward the ground below where Kane waited, watching her.

KANE BRACED HIMSELF as the warrior woman came at him through the air, her arms bright as the fires played along her flesh. She had to be high on something, whacked out on some illegal hallucinogen that was being produced in the Tartarus Pits or imported from the Outlands. No one would voluntarily set fire to themselves during battle, would they?

Kane jumped aside as the girl landed on the sidewalk, crouching there as she watched him with fierce eyes, the flames licking up and down her arms.

"I don't know what your problem is," Kane told her, "but you need to turn yourself in right now if I'm to help you."

The tattooed woman ignored him, leaping up and swinging her burning fists at him, left then right then left again, closer and closer, the flames whooshing dangerously close to Kane's face and chest. He took a step back, then another, cursing again that he didn't have his Sin Eater pistol with him so that he could deal with this rapidly moving nut job at a safe distance.

As her right fist swung again, Kane saw an opening and he kicked out, his booted foot knocking the girl's forearm and staggering her. She spun, recovering instantly as Kane stamped out the flames that now licked at the toe of his boot.

The woman looked at him, her eyes narrowed in contempt as the flames reached her shoulders and began to play across her chest and torso. She uttered one word before driving at him again: "Die."

Kane slapped her blows aside, feeling the heat of the flames on his bare skin as the crowd around them kept their wary distance. The girl was a whirlwind of movement, moving faster and faster, increasingly frantic as she attacked him.

It hadn't been a sword, Kane remembered suddenly, thinking back to the battle in the room of bones, it had been a boomerang made of steel or titanium.

The girl kicked at his solar plexus and followed up with a right cross of such power that it felt like it would remove Kane's head from his shoulders. He avoided the kick but took the punch to the side of his face, feeling the heat of the flames beside his ear.

Grunting, Kane lashed out blindly, sensing rather than seeing where the tattooed girl was. His fist connected with something solid, and he opened his eyes in time to see the girl stagger and trip, her burning hands reaching for her chest.

As the tattooed woman fell, Kane lunged forward, his foot outstretched, ready to pin her to the ground where the flames could do the least damage to him. His foot raced toward her chest and slammed down hard...*against solid ground.*

The girl was gone. Disappeared.

Openmouthed, Kane looked at the paving slabs beneath his foot, then up and down the street. The cleaning crew was back at work on the building, seemingly as though nothing had happened. The pedestrians and gawkers who had been watching the battle just moments before were all wandering off, heads down, going about their business as though nothing had happened.

Kane grabbed a passerby, pulling the bewildered man by his shirt and pointing at the ground where his foot rested. "You saw her, right?" Kane demanded.

The man shook his head.

"A woman," Kane continued, "about five foot five, body covered in tattoos, arms on fire."

The man looked at Kane as though he were insane, and Kane shook him angrily.

"Do I need to remind you that lying to a Magistrate, even an off-duty one, is an offense?" Kane snarled.

The man answered in a timid voice, his eyes wide. "I didn't see anything," he admitted. "I'd never lie to a Mag. Really I wouldn't. Please let me go. I didn't do anything wrong."

Kane looked at the man, detecting his fear and trying to press for untruths, but he felt nothing. The man's body language, his tone and stance, they all pointed to one thing: he believed every word he said.

Annoyed, Kane let the man go. He watched him make his way along the street, glancing over his shoulder once to see if the "crazy Magistrate" was still watching him.

Kane stepped back, pacing to the spot where the woman had lain. There was no evidence of her, no scorch marks or charring where the flames would have burned, nothing. People walked to and fro along the sidewalk, ignoring the confused Mag standing there, eyeing the scene.

It was odd. Like…like something that hadn't really been happening at all, Kane realized. Like a training simulation after you pressed Reset.

"What the hell is going on here?" Kane muttered under his breath as he stared at the empty paving slabs.


THE FIRST THING that Cloud Singer became aware of was Decimal River, staring into her eyes. "She's coming out of it now," he said, his voice betraying no emotion.

Cloud Singer reached up, momentarily surprised to find that her hands were no longer on fire, and touched at her skull. "What…?" she began, struggling to comprehend what had just happened. Hadn't she been fighting with the Cerberus man on a sunlit sidewalk in some majestic, towering ville so beautifully integrated that it looked for all the world like an artist's sculpture?

"What did I tell you?" The woman's voice came in a harsh whisper from Cloud Singer's right and she looked there to see Broken Ghost's skeletal face bearing down on her. "What did I say about desire, Cloud Singer?"

"That it is a parasite," Cloud Singer replied automatically, "that ensnares the individual."

"So why did you go into the trap, Cloud Singer, tell me that?" Broken Ghost snapped angrily.

"Because I wanted to see how the trap worked," Cloud Singer replied, feeling embarrassed and humble now before the fierce warrior. "I wanted to ensure that it was working as you had promised."

"You 'wanted'?" Broken Ghost mimicked.

"Well," Cloud Singer said, "what if there had been a flaw, what if you hadn't realized it until it was too late?"

"Desire is a parasite that traps the individual," Broken Ghost said, her voice low and ominous. "You went inside the trap because you wanted to, Cloud Singer, no other reason than that. And so your desire almost trapped you there, too."

Cloud Singer was about to respond when she stopped herself, considering the assassin's words. "Desire is a parasite," she said, "within me, too."

Broken Ghost nodded. "Very good, Cloud Singer. You've learned a lesson."

# Chapter 11

"I took the data held by the mat-trans," Decimal River told Cloud Singer as she humbly stared at his laptop screen, "and added a transgenic alternator to their DNA sequences."

Cloud Singer looked at him blankly.

"Essentially, I made them obey us," Decimal River expanded. "Doubles of the Cerberus warriors that follow our commands."

"What are they doing now?" Cloud Singer asked.

Decimal River enlarged a window on his glowing screen, upon which data flows raced by. "The three of them are active," he assured her, "pursuing their primary objective."

GRANT SAT ON THE GROUND with his arm around Shizuka, watching the sun set behind Trapper Peak. The beautiful warrior woman looked up at him, admiring the firm set of his jaw, the intensity that burned in his eyes. "It has been nice," she said quietly, "just spending a day like this, with no dangers."

Grant looked down at her and smiled. "No dangers," he repeated. "Long may it last."

Her arms wrapped around him, Shizuka pushed herself closer to Grant's warm body.

## The Gold Eagle Reader Service — Here's how it works:

Accepting your 2 free books and free gift (gift valued at approximately $5.00) places you under no obligation to buy anything. You may keep the books and gift and return the shipping statement marked "cancel." If you do not cancel, about a month later we'll send you 6 additional books and bill you just $31.94* — that's a savings of 15% off the cover price of all 6 books! And there's no extra charge for shipping! You may cancel at any time, but if you choose to continue, every other month we'll send you 6 more books, which you may either purchase at the discount price or return to us and cancel your subscription.

*Terms and prices subject to change without notice. Prices do not include applicable taxes. Sales tax applicable in N.Y. Canadian residents will be charged applicable provincial taxes and GST. Offer not valid in Quebec. Credit or debit balances in a customer's account(s) may be offset by any other outstanding balance owed by or to the customer. Offer available while quantities last.

NO POSTAGE
NECESSARY
IF MAILED
IN THE
UNITED STATES

## BUSINESS REPLY MAIL

FIRST-CLASS MAIL    PERMIT NO. 717    BUFFALO, NY

POSTAGE WILL BE PAID BY ADDRESSEE

GOLD EAGLE READER SERVICE
3010 WALDEN AVE
PO BOX 1867
BUFFALO NY 14240-9952

If offer card is missing write to: Gold Eagle Reader Service, 3010 Walden Ave., P.O. Box 1867, Buffalo NY 14240-1867

# Get FREE BOOKS and a FREE GIFT when you play the...

# LAS VEGAS

## GAME

*Just scratch off the gold box with a coin. Then check below to see the gifts you get!*

**YES!** I have scratched off the gold box. Please send me my **2 FREE BOOKS** and **FREE GIFT** for which I qualify. I understand that I am under no obligation to purchase any books as explained on the back of this card.

▲ DETACH AND MAIL CARD TODAY! ▲

© 2008 WORLDWIDE LIBRARY ® and ™ are trademarks owned and used by the trademark owner and/or its licensee.

**366 ADL EVMJ**

**166 ADL EVMU**
(GE-LV-09)

FIRST NAME

LAST NAME

ADDRESS

APT.#

CITY

STATE/PROV.

ZIP/POSTAL CODE

| | | |
|---|---|---|
| **7** | **7** | **7** |

Worth TWO FREE BOOKS plus a FREE Gift!

Worth TWO FREE BOOKS!

TRY AGAIN!

Offer limited to one per household and not valid to current subscribers of Gold Eagle® books. All orders subject to approval. Please allow 4 to 6 weeks for delivery.

IN THE SHADOWS of the machine room, amid the thrumming and whirring of the various units, Kane was using a heavy wrench to loosen bolts on the main air-conditioning processor. The two bucketlike canisters of phosgene were resting on the floor, close to his feet, and both of them were still sealed tightly. He groaned as he tried to loosen another of the tremendous bolts that held the front panel onto the blocky unit. The bolt wouldn't move, no matter how hard he strained—it may well have been stuck in the same position for two hundred years, he knew, and it wasn't going to budge for all the sweat he expended.

"Damn it," Kane grunted, tossing the wrench aside with a loud clank. He took a step back and stared angrily at the processing unit, hands on hips. "Well," he decided, "there's more than one way to crack a nut."

Kane took up the wrench once more and ran his free hand across the front panel of the processor. It was thick with a black, powdery dust, though whether this was an accumulation of weeks or months or years he couldn't tell. Beneath the dust, the cold metal of the unit thrummed against his touch. Kane pushed against it, driving the heel of his hand into the panel and feeling it give just a little. It wouldn't buckle to his touch, but it was thin enough that he might bust through it with a few good swipes of the heavy wrench.

Kane took a half step back, holding the wrench in a two-handed grip and raising it behind his shoulder, like a baseball player in the batter's box. With a loud cry, Kane swung the metal wrench into the front panel of the boxy unit. The wrench hit with the loud clash of metal on metal before rebounding back along its arc, dragging Kane with it.

He looked and saw a jagged, silvery scar had appeared in the black dust where the wrench had hit. The metal panel had dented just a little, a tiny, silver kiss against its flat surface.

Pulling the wrench over his shoulder once more, Kane swung another heavy blow to the machine.

He worked like this for more than fifteen minutes until the panel finally came loose, a large rent across its surface, one corner torn from its housings. By the time he had created the hole, Kane was wet with sweat, his hair damp, his shirt clinging to his back.

"There we go." He smiled, placing the wrench atop the huge unit and pulling at the rent with his hands, enlarging the separation. After separating the sharp edges of the broken panel, Kane eyed the bucketlike canisters on the floor beside him. He wanted to open both canisters of phosgene while they were inside the unit, both to ensure that they did the maximum damage and also to hide the evidence of his sabotage from a casual viewing. He yanked at the panel but it wouldn't bend far enough, and he realized he needed a lever to properly open it. Picking up the wrench once more, Kane got to work, bashing and levering the torn panel to widen the gap he had created.

As he worked, cursing and hammering, Kane was unaware that a man called Ben Michaels had entered the vast processing room and was watching him, his brows raised in a mixture of surprise and confusion. Michaels, like so many of the staff at Cerberus, was a Manitius Moon Base exile. In his late forties with tanned skin and a balding pate, Michaels was an engineer and he had adopted the role of maintenance man for the redoubt along with a number of other people best suited to the task.

"Hey, hey!" he called as he saw Kane take another swing at the front panel of the main processor with the wrench. "I don't think you should be doing that."

Kane looked up at the man, his eyes narrowed. "What's it to you?" he snarled.

"Wait," Michaels said, "I know you. Kane, isn't it?"

Kane just glared at him, an unspoken challenge in his erect stance.

After a moment, Michaels continued, his tone wary now as he spoke to the larger man. "I don't know what's going on, Kane, but this wasn't okayed by me, and that's no way to handle a wrench, friend," he explained. "I don't want to rain on your parade or whatever, but whatever your orders were, no one told me you'd be doing this. That is to say, I mean, whatever it is you're doing."

Kane continued to glare at the engineer from the darkness, feeling the heavy weight of the wrench in his hand. "I'm sure we can straighten it out," he said, and all emotion drained from his voice. "Here, let me show you my orders."

Kane swung then, cracking Michaels across the side of the head with the heavy wrench. The engineer fell, crashing into the tall processing unit, yelping in pain. Kane pulled the wrench back and swung again, smashing with full fury at the man's head once more.

Blood was smeared across Michaels's face. His nose had caved in and his left eye was turning red as he staggered to keep his balance, his breath coming in ragged gasps. With one hand resting against the processor,

Michaels leaned forward and spat. A great gob of blood, saliva and two shattered teeth landed at Kane's feet. "What the devil are you doing?" he muttered, the words coming out strained through his swelling lips.

"Showing you how to handle a fucking wrench," Kane told him, lunging forward and swinging the tool again.

Michaels's screams of pain were masked amid the churning sounds of the air-conditioning units as they processed fresh air for the Cerberus personnel.

"DAMN IT!"

In the Cerberus operations center, Skylar Hitch flung down her miniature screwdriver in annoyance. Donald Bry looked up at her from his monitoring post beside Lakesh on the other side of the room.

"Something wrong, Skylar?" Bry asked.

Hitch looked at him, her frustration turning to embarrassment as she realized that everyone in the room had turned to watch her when she had let out that cry of annoyance. "Just… I can't get this stupid capacitor to… Argh!" The normally timid computer tech looked as though she was going to punch the desk in front of her, where the circuit boards that she was working on resided.

Next to Donald Bry, Lakesh checked his desktop chron and spoke to Skylar in a soothing tone. "It's almost 9:00 p.m.," he began, "and I rather suspect you were working at this problem before I came in this morning, Skylar. Why don't you go to your quarters and get some sleep."

Skylar looked about to argue until Lakesh added reasonably, "Our old, worn-out computers will still be there in the morning."

"Thank you, Dr. Singh," Skylar acquiesced after a moment's thought. She ran a hand through her hair, pushing at her dark bangs where strands had escaped the ponytail she wore, before standing up. She reached for the screwdriver and placed it carefully beside the motherboard at a perfect ninety-degree angle to the edge of the desk. "I'm sorry," she said apologetically as she passed Lakesh's desk on her way to the main door.

"Think nothing of it," Lakesh told her, his smile warm and sincere. "See you tomorrow, Skylar."

When the tech had left, Lakesh turned back to the report that he had been assessing with Donald Bry before pausing, a thoughtful, faraway look in his eye.

"Shall we get back to this report, Doctor?" Bry asked after a moment.

Lakesh glanced at him and smiled. "You know, it is getting late for all of us," he decided in a loud voice. "Why don't we conclude this tomorrow, when fresher heads will prevail, I'm sure." With that, he dismissed the bulk of the monitoring team, leaving only a two-man crew to watch things. With no one out in the field, the Cerberus operations center could function with a skeleton staff quite easily; most of the monitoring systems functioned automatically and rarely needed input from a human being.

The remaining crew were Brewster Philboyd, who stayed at the communications desk to monitor any incoming calls, and Trent, the sallow-faced operator whose primary responsibility this day was for the mat-trans, but who would double as general systems checker and button pusher until the next shift came on at 1:00 a.m.

Brigid Baptiste remained behind, too, despite Lakesh's suggestion that she call it a day. "You were out in the field this morning, and you're still working on your reports," he chastised her.

"It's a field report," she explained, peering up from her desk over the rectangular frames of her eyeglasses. "I like to get these finalized while all the information is still fresh in my mind."

Lakesh snorted with laughter. Brigid's notorious eidetic memory made her statement a fallacy, he knew, but he didn't bother to argue. Some things you just wanted to get out of the way rather than putting them off for another day. He had known Brigid a long time, since way back when he had been her section supervisor in the Historical Division at Cobaltville, and he had always admired her dedication to a given task, her utter attention to detail. "Make sure you get a proper night's sleep, though, Brigid," he instructed her as he made his way through the operations room door.

"Oh, don't worry," Brigid assured him, "when I'm finished here I'll sleep like a baby."

IN THE HIDDEN CAVE in the outback, Cloud Singer turned to Broken Ghost, a frown creasing her brow. "So, they're clones?" she asked.

Broken Ghost smiled indulgently. "Not really," she said patiently. "Their technology, the mat-trans, works by generating and replicating digital files, downloading and uploading the matter that makes up human beings, their belongings, their essence. Like a computer, it's essentially the transfer of a file containing information, nothing more than that."

Decimal River broke into the conversation then, proud of his handiwork. "The files are held by the mat-trans units, but they are instantly wiped when the person rematerializes from quantum space. If they weren't, there would be the risk of two, three or—" he shrugged "—a hundred of the same person running about. It's a basic failsafe. I broke the failsafe, adding a strip of code to the transferring files. A virus worm that makes the reborn Kane, Grant and Baptiste pursue our needs over their own."

"Is that possible?" Cloud Singer asked, astonished.

"There are limitations," Decimal River admitted. "Their memories are flawed, so they will paint in the details of their pasts as required, like characters in a story."

"With more time," Broken Ghost added, "without the pressure of the Death Cry wave front, we would have made them perfect."

Cloud Singer nodded, finally understanding the full scope of Broken Ghost's audacious plan. "You promised me the head of Cerberus," she said. "That was our agreement."

"His greatest warriors are imprisoned beyond reach," the assassin assured her, "and Cerberus itself will fall next. Then I will move in and kill Lakesh, completing our contract."

Cloud Singer bowed her head in acknowledgment, cursing her own impatience.

KANE HAD WRAPPED Michaels's body in a black trash bag he had found among a stash of materials in a corner of the vast machine room. He had placed Michaels's body on the floor of the room, wedged beneath a series of wide pipes that distributed the air flow around the whole redoubt. Then he had gone back to working at the front panel of the huge processing unit, pulling at it, using the blood-spattered wrench as a lever to pull the rent wide.

Once Kane had the front section fully open, he crouched beside it and took a cloth from his pocket, tying it over his nose and mouth. Then he placed the first canister of phosgene inside the main junction of the processing unit, where three large pipes met, and pulled at the seals until the canister opened and began leaking its deadly, near odorless, colorless payload into the air. Pulling at the seals of the second, he placed it across from the first, wedging it where two wide pipes met, cooled by rushing water before they fed the Cerberus base with fresh air.

Once he was finished, Kane put hand and shoulder to the misshapen front panel and shoved until it bent back in an approximation of its former setting. The repair wouldn't stand up to scrutiny, but in the darkness of the room it would suffice. It only needed to remain undetected for twelve hours; by then the lethal toxins would be in every air shaft, feeding the Cerberus personnel with the deadly phosgene gas.

Kane stood back, admiring his handiwork, and beneath the kerchief he had placed over his mouth he smiled, a broad and terrifying grin.

Kane tossed the bloodstained wrench beneath the piping before he made his way to the service door and departed the air-processing room.

IT WAS AFTER MIDNIGHT, and the lighting in the Cerberus operations room had been dimmed, giving the large area a cozy feel. Brigid Baptiste sat at her desk running through the details of her report on the screen. At one of the desks beside her, Brewster Philboyd looked about ready to drop off to sleep, his large frame slumped in his chair at the communications desk.

Brigid leaned across to him, speaking quietly. "Brewster?" she said tentatively. "Why don't you go catch some sleep. You look beat."

Brewster removed his spectacles and rubbed at his eyes before he turned to look at her. "I'd love to," he admitted, "but my shift's over in an hour. Not long now."

Brigid shrugged. "I can monitor communications if you like," she told him. "I'm only doing a final run-through on my report here. I don't mind pulling double duty."

Philboyd smiled, glancing around the large room. It was only himself, Brigid and Trent left now, since the mass exodus over three hours before. "Well," he said, "I don't really want to leave you alone."

Brigid pointed to Trent. The sallow-featured man was scratching at his neck and looked thoroughly bored. "Trent will keep me company," she assured him. "Go. We'll be fine."

Brewster thanked her and made his way to the door, offering a weary "good night" to Trent as he exited.

Trent looked up, stifling a yawn. "I'm dropping off myself," he told Brigid as he stood up and stretched his limbs. He paced across the room to the small coffee percolator that sat behind Lakesh's desk. "You want some java?" he asked Brigid as he picked up the pot.

She nodded. "That would be great," she told him as she watched him peer at the pot. It contained just a tiny dribble of the rich, brown liquid and nothing more. "Think we'll need more coffee, though."

Trent laughed. "Heh, yeah. Y'know, I'll just go up to

the canteen and grab us a couple of cups," he decided. "This pot's not been cleaned in a week, I swear to you."

Brigid offered an innocent expression. "I thought that all added to the flavor."

"Sure, Ms. Baptiste," Trent told her, nodding very seriously. "Someone who didn't like washing up told you that, I reckon."

Brigid shooed him away, assuring him she could handle the ops room for ten minutes on her own. As soon as Trent had left, Brigid stood up from her desk and walked swiftly across to Trent's terminal. She sat down, brought up a live data stream regarding the mat-trans system and began working through her task. She estimated that Trent would return in twelve minutes. She would be finished in four.

SKYLAR HITCH STOOD before the mirror of her tiny bathroom, looking for spots on her skin as she cleaned her teeth. It had been a long day, and dark circles were definitely appearing under her eyes. She had begun work on the computers in the ops room at just after 6:00 a.m. and she had still been working at the motherboards at 9:00 p.m. when Lakesh had dismissed her.

She leaned forward over the compact sink, spitting toothpaste foam into the basin as she ran water from the faucet. As she did so, something occurred to her. It wasn't a big revelation, just a little idea of how to repair the aging computers without going through the laborious process of cleaning and resoldering the components on the motherboards. Swishing her mouth out with water, Skylar grabbed her dressing gown and rushed out of her quarters, her furry-faced bunny slippers slapping against the tiles as she headed back to the main operations room.

When she reached the Cerberus ops room, Skylar found the lighting had been dimmed, and she was surprised to find only one other person working there. Brigid Baptiste sat at the main mat-trans terminal, punching in code at an incredible speed.

As ever, Brigid looked fantastic, her tall, agile body wrapped in one of the tight-fitting jumpsuits of the Cerberus operation, her red-gold hair radiant, cascading over her shoulders in a luxurious wave. By contrast, Skylar was five foot nothing, wearing an old dressing gown over the long T-shirt she habitually wore to bed, and the slippers that were shaped to look like cartoon bunny rabbits on her feet.

"Hi, Miss Baptiste," Skylar said self-consciously as she scrambled across the room to the three desks that contained bits and pieces from the deconstructed computer units she had been working with that day.

Brigid looked up at her, a fierce look in her narrowed eyes. "Hello" was all she said before getting back to her work at the keyboard.

Skylar sat down at one of the three desks and looked at one of the circuit boards. It showed a dark line where smoke had damaged it, and Skylar sighed as she tilted it to the light. She couldn't quite see what strength the capacitor ran to, and she leaned across and flicked on the desk lamp. Brigid glared at her as the light came on.

"Sorry," Skylar said quietly, as though she had been caught making noise in a library. "I just had this idea.... Won't disturb you."

Brigid went back to her work at the mat-trans-linked

computer, ignoring Skylar as the IT expert went back to her own work.

Skylar realized that she needed something to pry the capacitor loose, and she reached across the desk for the little screwdriver that she had left beside the ancient circuit diagrams that she had printed out earlier that day. As she stretched across the desk, she happened to glance at Brigid's terminal screen and, without really thinking, asked what she was up to.

Brigid's head remained focused on the screen for a moment, but her typing fingers stopped their furious movement. "What am I up to?" she asked darkly. Slowly, Brigid's head turned, and then she was facing Skylar, a dark, angry look on her features. "Do you recall what happened to the curious cat, Skylar?"

"Um, excuse me?" Skylar asked, wondering what on earth Brigid was so mad about.

Brigid stood up and stalked across the room, her hands forming into fists as she walked the five paces to bring her before Skylar's desk.

"I'm sorry, Miss Baptiste," Skylar said, "I didn't mean to disturb you. I can come back later, it's fine." Skylar stood up then, looking across to the large door that led into the room.

Brigid took a step to the left, blocking Skylar's path. "I never liked you," she said ominously.

Skylar couldn't believe what she had just heard. Where had that come from? "I'm…I'm sorry?" she stuttered. "I'll go. I'm going. Sorry."

The IT expert took a single step, but Brigid's right arm shot out, her fist punching at the smaller woman's face. Skylar maneuvered out of its path just in time, and Brigid's fist smacked against her collarbone instead, forcing her to stumble backward.

"Please," Skylar began, "I don't…"

Brigid didn't let her finish the sentence. Her booted foot kicked high, thumping Skylar hard in the chest, knocking her backward once more until she slammed into the side of the desk. "The curious cat was killed, Skylar," she said.

"What's gotten into you?" Skylar wailed fearfully, struggling to keep her balance as she was forced against the desks.

"I never liked you," Brigid said again, leaping forward, her hands closing around Skylar's throat. "Nosy and arrogant because you know how to operate computers. That's not a talent, Skylar, that's barely even an ability."

"P-please," Skylar croaked as Brigid's grip tightened around her neck, "Miss Baptiste. I think something is very wrong with you.… Please try to—" She could tell that Brigid wasn't listening, and she struggled vainly to loosen the grip of the taller woman. There was a dark, determined look in Brigid's narrowed eyes, a horrible joy in the set of her smiling jaw. Skylar thought that she knew what it was—bloodlust.

Skylar's throat was aching now and it was getting harder to breathe. She couldn't shake the other woman's grip. Brigid was a trained fighter, powerful, her body a tool, a weapon. And Skylar Hitch? Skylar Hitch was just an IT consultant; all she ever did was sit at a desk working on a computer problem. She had never even visited the Cerberus gymnasium. Her hand scrambled across the desk, grabbing for something she was sure had to be there.

The screwdriver.

Her hand brushed against it and Skylar saw it in her

mind's eye. Her fingers clutched at it, grabbing the handle of the little four-inch tool. Her vision seemed darker now, but with the dim lighting it was hard to really be sure. Brigid pushed down, hands clamped around Skylar's tiny throat, pushing inward, ever inward, wringing her neck.

Suddenly, Skylar's arm swung, jabbing the screwdriver's blade into Brigid's side, just below the taller woman's rib cage. Brigid howled in pain, and her grip loosened on Skylar's throat. Skylar pushed her away and stood there, leaning against the table, retching and coughing.

Although she did not look up, Skylar heard Brigid wrench the blade from her body and toss it aside. The plastic handle of the screwdriver tinkled as it hit the tiles of the floor.

"You fucking bitch," Brigid growled behind her, and Skylar turned to see the red-haired woman stomp up to her and reach for her face with outstretched hands. There was a tear in Brigid's jumpsuit along the left-hand seam, and a small circle of red was forming on the white material there. Brigid's hands played across Skylar's head for a moment, securing their position before she began twisting. Skylar Hitch felt the enormous, screaming pain as something in her neck gave, and then she blacked out.

SKYLAR'S TINY BODY fell to the floor in a heap as Brigid let go and stepped away. The IT expert's neck was broken, and Brigid knew she was either dead or dying. It was a move that Kane had shown her once, years before, one that Brigid had committed to memory, like everything else she saw.

She leaned down and dragged the smaller woman's limp body across the room by her hair. Opening the arma-glass door to the mat-trans, Brigid tossed Skylar's body inside. She closed the door behind her and walked back to the terminal that she had been working at. After a half-dozen keystrokes, the emitter array began to whine and mist began to fill the mat-trans unit before the body of Skylar Hitch was digitized and spirited away.

Brigid glanced at her wrist chron. Seven minutes. Trent would be back in five more and it wouldn't do for him to see her working at the mat-trans terminal.

STANDING IN A SILK dressing gown so short that it left her legs almost entirely bare, Shizuka watched from the doorway as Grant admired himself in the bathroom mirror. He had removed his shirt and shoes, and he stood there in his pants, examining his face as though wondering whether he needed to shave.

Silently, Shizuka watched him, intrigued by the strange ritual he was going through before coming to bed. Suddenly, Grant turned and looked at her, a smile on his lips. "Ha, caught me," he said, the trace of embarrassment in his tone.

"Doing what?" Shizuka asked in her soft, musical voice.

"Looking at old scars," Grant admitted. "Thinking about things that happened. Just remembering, really."

Shizuka stared at him for a few seconds before turning and walking across the little bedroom that formed the main part of Grant's private quarters. "Don't take too long," she told him, "or I'll be called back to New Edo."

Undoing the silk ties on her short dressing gown, Shizuka sat on the bed. She removed the dressing gown as she watched through the open door while Grant stood at the basin. It was a little unsettling the way he seemed to be watching himself so intensely, examining his eyes, his teeth, as though he didn't quite recognize who he was supposed to be. But a moment later, the feeling left Shizuka as Grant switched off the bathroom light and paced across the room to join her in bed. He removed his pants and underwear, tossing them to the floor and joining Shizuka under the covers.

Shizuka felt desire rise in her as she smelled his skin so close, felt his lips push against hers. She kissed him back, pulling him closer, her hands running down the curved muscles of his familiar, scarred body. Grant was strong, and Shizuka felt that strength as he pushed at her, his body over hers, his kisses so passionate that they drove her back against the pillow. His mouth pushed into hers, his body pressed against hers, and Shizuka wanted him so much in that instant.

And then he bit her, his teeth catching her lip in his passion, and it jerked her back to reality, out of the forming fires of her passion, and she yelped. "Careful, lover," she admonished, pulling her face away from his.

Grant ignored her, his face looming closer in the semi-darkness of the room, kissing her once more with heat and passion. And violence—above all else, violence.

Shizuka pushed him away. "Slow down. You hurt me," she said quietly.

Yet still he ignored her, pushing against her naked body, positioning her beneath him so that he could enter her, have her. As Grant thrust against her, Shizuka rolled, flipping his weight off her.

"I said slow down," she said, louder this time, a slight edge to her voice now.

Grant lifted his torso above her, his smile showing bright in the dimly lit room. And then he said one single word, and it both scared and repulsed Shizuka as she lay in the bed before her trusted lover: "No."

He was upon her again, holding her wrists, forcing her down against the mattress as she squirmed beneath him. "Let me go," she demanded. "Let go of me. This is not funny, Grant-*san*."

Grant yanked her wrists above her head, and Shizuka stretched her body taut, gasping in pain. Grant brought her wrists together, holding them down with a single, large hand, leaving his other hand free to probe her body, working its way down her torso as she squirmed.

Shizuka didn't want him. She didn't even want to be in the same room as him now. Grant had never done this before, never been violent with her. He was a strong man, used to war, driven by rage sometimes, but with her he had always been gentle.

Suddenly Shizuka knew. As Grant forced his body against hers, pawing at her breasts, smiling sadistically as he listened to and ignored her pleas, Shizuka suddenly knew. *It wasn't Grant.*

Whatever it looked like, whomever it appeared to be, this man—this monster—wasn't Grant.

She shifted her weight, sinking into the mattress before kicking out with her legs like a beached fish. It was difficult to get any leverage while Grant held her like this, but she kicked hard enough to dislodge him, make him rear back.

Grant still held her wrists tight against the mattress, and Shizuka rolled, kicking backward before kneeing him hard in his side, pulling her leg back to kick again and again.

Grant—or whoever he really was—howled in rage, and his grip on her faltered.

Finding her hands free, Shizuka moved with lightning swiftness, scampering up the length of the bed toward the wall behind it, her legs kicking out as she scrambled away from the huge ex-Mag. The monster with Grant's face reached out, grabbing her by her ankle and yanking her down onto the mattress and back toward him. She let him pull her, going limp as he hoisted her toward him, lunging at her with his body. Then her free leg snap-kicked into his face, the ball of her foot catching him in the side of his nose so that a spray of blood shot across the room and spattered the wall.

The Grant thing roared in pain, letting go of Shizuka's ankle as his hands went to his bloodied nose. A few spots of blood dripped from it, and Grant tossed his head to shake them away, taking his eyes from her for a moment.

Shizuka was off the bed then, diving to the floor. She landed beside Grant's pants where they lay in a heap there. Something in Shizuka's mind set off an alarm then. Grant was once a Magistrate; he was extremely disciplined. She had never known him to discard his clothes in such a casual, messy manner, never in all the time they had been together. And then she recalled the coat hanging in his wardrobe, slightly wonky on its hanger. The devil was in the details, she realized.

Grant placed one foot on the floor, hard, and he leaned down to grab Shizuka by her flowing hair. At the same moment, Shizuka was reaching underneath the bed without looking, feeling the scabbard that she had placed beneath it for safekeeping while they had enjoyed the surrounding countryside of the Bitterroot Mountains.

Shizuka yelped as Grant pulled her up to her knees by her hair, and his hand drew back, preparing to slap her, a savage grin on his face. "Don't tell me this isn't fun," he said, laughing at her.

Shizuka pulled the *katana*—still in its scabbard—from under the bed and jammed it against her lover's ribs. The blunt edge of the scabbard wasn't enough to do any real damage, but the shock made Grant tip from the bed, letting go of Shizuka's hair, a few strands tearing away in his hands as he dropped backward. It was all the time she needed.

Her left hand clutched the uppermost part of the scabbard, pulling it down and toward her as her right held firmly to the sword's grip. Twenty-five inches of tempered steel appeared from the scabbard, glinting as the blade caught the dim bedside lights of the room, singing a quiet, pure note as its length emerged.

"Whoever you are," Shizuka warned him, "you have just made one very big mistake."

The thing that looked and moved like Grant stared at her from the bed, and a cruel smile crossed his face once more. "You've got me all wrong, Shizuka, my love," he cooed, "my dearest heart."

"Fuck you," Shizuka screamed, swinging the blade at Grant.

The Grant thing moved fast, powering himself from the bed and out of reach of Shizuka's swinging blade. She jumped forward, balancing atop the bed in a fighting stance, the blade poised over her head as she watched her cruel target scamper across the small room until he reached the wall.

"What did you do with him?" Shizuka demanded. "What did you do with Grant-*san?*"

"You crazy slut," Grant snapped back. "I didn't do anything with him. Come now, put the sword down. You're fucking delusional."

Shizuka's eyes fixed on Grant's, on this thing that pretended to be Grant, and she shook her head ever so slightly. "No, I'm not," she assured him. "Slow on the uptake, maybe, that I'll accept. But you're not Grant. You're nothing like him."

The huge ex-Mag smiled confidently, deciding to change tack. "Not what you thought this afternoon," he said, goading her. "You were all over me like a bitch in heat back there in the woods. Surely you haven't forgotten—"

"Shut up," Shizuka snarled.

"I certainly haven't forgotten," he continued. "I can't wait to tell Kane all about it...."

"Shut up," Shizuka said again, more insistent this time. But she realized something even as this vile creature spoke—Kane was in on this, too. The pair of them were different, no longer themselves. And it stood to reason that Brigid Baptiste was one of "them," too, whatever they were. The three of them traveled together, a single unit, and what affected one of them had likely affected them all.

"Come on, girl," Grant cooed, his arms stretched wide, "let's get back to bed. Kiss and make up. What do you say?"

Shizuka's eyes tracked across Grant's naked form, the familiar muscles, the scars and moles. "Never!" she told him, leaping from the bed and across the room, her *katana* thrusting forward in a lethal strike.

The blade hummed as it rushed through the air, and

Grant attempted to spin below it in a swift, frantic movement. Something clipped the side of his head and he felt hot liquid pump down the side of his face. He looked up and saw, lying stuck to the gray wall of the little room, his left ear, a splatter of blood shining all around it.

"You crazy bitch," Grant cursed, driving himself toward Shizuka with his left arm outstretched, ready to grab her thin, swanlike neck.

Hating the close quarters of the small room, Shizuka swung the blade again and its razor-sharp edge smacked into and through the wrist of Grant's outstretched arm, spraying blood across the room in a pumping geyser.

Grant skipped backward, looking at his twisted hand in incredulity. The hand was intact but it hung at an odd angle now, a whole chunk of his wrist severed down to the bone, leaking blood over the floor. "I'll make you eat that knife before I'm done with you," he assured Shizuka as she shifted to a two-handed grip on the blade.

Shizuka wasn't listening. Her feet pounded against the floor and she ran at Grant, two, three, four paces across the tiny room, the *katana* poised before her. As Grant tried to dodge he found himself right up against another wall, nowhere left to run. And then the blade drove through him, tip first, cutting a path through the center of his rib cage, just below the breastbone. The blade tilted upward, piercing Grant's body at a thirty-degree angle, cutting through muscle and organ as Shizuka drove a path through her "lover's" body. There was a violent thump, and the blade ceased moving—it had hit the back wall behind Grant.

Grant's eyes were wide open, the whites showing all around the pupils as he stared at Shizuka; his body gradually slid down her blade under its own weight. "Shizuka, my darling," he breathed. "How could you?" Then his knees buckled, and Shizuka extracted the blade as the thing that looked like Grant sank to the floor, surrounded by a pool of its own blood.

She stood there, her breathing heavy, her heart racing, looking at the familiar body that lay before her. "What on earth have I stumbled onto?" she asked in a low, frightened whisper.

Whatever it was she would have to tell Lakesh, and he in turn would need to alert the whole Cerberus crew as to just what was going on. Killers with the faces of friends in their midst. And more. A killer with the face of her trusted lover, and he had almost fooled her, had fooled her entirely for a time. It almost didn't bear thinking about.

Shizuka grabbed her silk dressing gown from where it lay across the cushions of a chair, put it on and left the quarters, the bloody sword still clutched in her hand. She had to find Lakesh right away.

# Chapter 12

"I was attacked just off Market Square," Kane was explaining to Grant as he watched the red orb of the sun sink over the Cobaltville skyline through the window of the hospital room. "She targeted me, Grant. I'm sure of it."

Grant looked at his long-term partner from his position on the hard-mattressed, high bed. "You okay?"

"Yeah." Kane nodded, bitterness in his voice. "The woman packed a hell of a punch, but I came out of it pretty much unscathed, just a couple of bruises."

"And what happened to her?" Grant urged.

"I lost her," Kane admitted. "She disappeared. And I don't mean that she ran off or anything like that—I mean she disappeared."

Grant thought for a moment. "Like what? I don't get it."

"Like this," Kane said and he snapped his fingers. "Poof, gone. Just evaporated as I looked at her."

"You were close to Market Square, right?" Grant clarified. "Did anyone else see this?"

"Well, that's the strange part," Kane explained. "Once she disappeared, it was like no one even remembered her, like I was the only one."

Grant looked at his partner, concern furrowing his brow. "When we were attacked in the Pits," he said gently, "there was a lot of stuff flying about. Homemade grenades and things. Maybe there was something—I don't know—to make you hallucinate in among all that junk? Is it possible you imagined this woman who attacked you?"

Kane leaned against the windowpane and watched the people below as they made their way to and fro, busy at their designated tasks. "Other people saw her," he said firmly, "got out of her way. I know they did."

"Which could all be a part of the hallucination, pal," Grant suggested.

Kane turned to the bed, looking at his trusted partner. "She was like nothing I've ever seen, Grant. Tattoos on her arms and body, and her clothing was crazy. She wasn't from Cobaltville. She wasn't from any ville at all. And yet I knew her. Or at least I think I did. I just can't tell you from where."

"Outlander maybe?" Grant said. "They go in for some weird stuff out there. How long ago was this?" he added.

"A few hours, just after 3:00 p.m.," Kane said. "I've been thinking about it for a long time before I came here to talk to you. And there's something else."

Grant watched his friend standing beside the bed, encouraging him to continue after a moment.

"I saw a woman in the market, too," Kane said. "A different woman, a redhead. This was much earlier. And I think maybe I knew her, too. I got the same feeling off her, déjà vu."

"We've chased down a lot of criminals," Grant said. "It's possible you arrested her, arrested both of them at some point."

Unconsciously, Kane's hand moved to his jaw and his fingers rubbed against the rough stubble that was forming there. "I don't think it's that," he said hesitantly. "This is like something ethereal. I can't lock down the memory, but I know it's there. You know?"

"All points to the hallucination theory," Grant said. "That would fit with what you're saying. Did you receive a medical when we came out of the Tartarus Pits?"

Kane nodded. "Usual checkup."

Grant shrugged. "Maybe they missed something," he said.

"Or maybe we missed something," Kane said. "Something so fundamental we can't see it. You ever think that, Grant?"

"How do you mean?" Grant asked, intrigued.

"We are Magistrates," Kane said slowly. "But what if we got caught? What if we were trapped in a prison cell, a cell so subtle that we cannot see its edges, its walls?"

"Don't talk to me about cells. I'm already stuck in one room," Grant reminded him, "and I ain't going nowhere for a while."

Kane shook his head, realization dawning. "Yes, you are," he told his longtime partner. "You're going to your ideal job. A cozy desk job with no need to ever be in the firing line again."

"But that's a good thing," Grant said. "That's not a cell. That's not punishment."

"What if it is," Kane asked his partner, "and you just don't see it?"

Grant looked at him, turning the idea over in his mind. "So what are you saying? That we're inside a prison and we don't realize it? Is that what you think? Kane?"

Kane was silent, lost in his own thoughts, and Grant considered what he had just suggested.

"What is Cerberus?" Kane blurted, the question coming from nowhere.

Grant looked up at his partner, distracted. "What?" he said. "A dog. A mythological dog, right? Three heads."

"Yeah." Kane nodded. "That's what I think, too, but it's not what I feel. I feel it's something else. Something just out of sight, like this thing I've been saying about the two women, about the 'prison.'" Kane was silent, groping for a train of thought he found more and more difficult to grasp, almost as though his very thought process had been blocked from proceeding along this line. "I think…I think I need to talk to the redhead," he said finally.

"You think she has something to do with this?" Grant asked.

"I don't know," Kane admitted, his hands forming into fists, white lines appearing across his skin as he clenched them tighter and tighter. "I can't see it, Grant," he said, "but it's there. Whatever it is, it's there." With that, he turned and headed toward the exit of the room.

Grant rested back on his pillows, gazing at the ceiling, turning the thoughts over in his mind. What was Kane alluding to when he asked about Cerberus? And why had Grant seen the nurse, the doctors with dog faces? Could Kane be right? Could a prison truly exist that couldn't be detected by its inmates? What purpose would it serve? And, if such a thing did exist, who were the jailers?

KANE STOPPED at an info port in the lobby of the medical hub, standing before the screen and punching in his security clearance code with impatience.

"Welcome, Magistrate Kane," the screen read. "How may I be of service?"

Tapping into the Cobaltville mainframe, Kane brought up a full list of his arrests over the past two years, requesting details and photographs of each perpetrator. The photos appeared on-screen and he scrolled through them rapidly. After a few minutes he was certain that the redhead wasn't among them, a fact that didn't surprise him in the slightest.

Kane stood beside the column that supported the data screen, glancing around at the waiting patients in the lobby of the medical hub, wondering what else to try. The redhead was familiar to him somehow. Perhaps he had seen her before, a perp or a witness for some case he had not been personally involved with. He could search all of the records, but that would take hours, perhaps days. Kane tsked and rolled his eyes, wondering how to approach such an immense problem. Then he remembered the nervous clerk at the reception desk. He tapped the three-digit code that would erase any record of his use of the info port and prevent anyone assuming his security clearance. Then he turned and made his way to the reception desk.

The nervous, spotty youth was still sitting behind his desk, slightly slouched as he flicked through a yellowing book of single-frame cartoons. Kane stood before the desk, casting his shadow across the clerk's book. The man looked up and almost toppled from his chair as he attempted to tidy himself. He sat more erect, casting the book to one side.

"M-magistrate," the clerk stuttered, and it looked to Kane as though he was about to salute him, thought better of it and ran the hand through his greasy mop of hair. "Can I… How can I… That is, may I help you?"

Kane's expression was emotionless and stern, his eyes hidden behind the dark lenses of his standard Mag glasses. "I need you to run a check for me," he said. "I'm looking for someone. I don't have a name but I can give you a description." Everyone in Cobaltville had to take booster shots at least twice a year, which meant that the woman with the red-gold hair, like everyone else, would have a medical file.

The clerk nervously swallowed as he pushed himself across to his DDC computer unit and attached the mike pickup to his ear. "I'll do what I can, Magistrate," he promised. "There are a lot of records, of course," he added as the number of available files appeared on his screen.

"You have pictures, right?" Kane said, leaning against the high desk so that he could see the man's computer screen. "Once I see her I'll know."

"Okay." The clerk nodded. "I'll need height, weight, age, distinguishing characteristics?"

"I'm looking for a woman," Kane began.

"Patient is female," the clerk said into his microphone, and Kane watched the number of applicable files halve in an instant.

Kane thought back to the woman he had seen in the Market Square purchasing frozen goods with the girl, presumably her daughter. "Height—five-six, maybe five-seven. Weight, about 125."

The clerk fed the information into the computer via his mike pickup, watching as the number of applicable files continued to drop.

"Late twenties," Kane decided, "with red hair and green eyes."

The clerk turned to Kane, waiting to see if he wanted

to add anything else. "Any distinguishing characteristics, Magistrate?"

Kane thought back. "Pretty," he said. "No, not pretty—beautiful."

"We, um, we don't have a field for that," the clerk admitted, "um, sir."

"It doesn't matter," Kane told him, still envisioning the woman in his mind's eye. She was beautiful, stunning, like no one else he had ever seen. An angel. "What do you have?"

The clerk spoke into his mike once more, and a series of medical case notes appeared on-screen, running to several dozen individuals. "Thirty-eight files," he said. "You were lucky. If she'd been a brunette that figure would have run to several hundred."

Kane nodded. "I don't know if I'd call it lucky," he muttered. Not if this angel is trying to kill me, he added to himself. He would need to arm himself before he investigated further.

BACK AT HIS APARTMENT, Kane knelt beside the small equipment locker that was hidden behind the sagging couch, and worked the combination lock. He swung the door open and reached inside for the Sin Eater handgun that was stored there beside its holster. With a heavy heart, he strapped the holster to his wrist and placed the compact pistol within.

Kane didn't like this. The gun would give him an edge over any attacker, especially if the redhead turned out to be as much of a whirling dervish as the tattooed warrior he had met in the street, but somehow he felt like he was making his way to an execution. Furthermore, he had a nasty feeling that it may just turn out to be his own, especially if the redhead was, as he was beginning to suspect, one of his jailers.

Warily, he made his way from his apartment and headed to the address of the suspect.

ABI SAT ON THE OLD couch in the main room, scraping the bowl balanced in her lap with a spoon. From her bedroom, Brigid leaned out of the wardrobe cubbyhole to check that her niece was all right.

"Are you okay, ice cream monster?" she asked.

Abi looked up, seeing Brigid's face peering through the open door, and nodded as she licked the last specks of ice cream from her spoon. One advantage to living in a one-person apartment was it meant that Brigid could pretty much see everything that Abigail got up to. The downside, of course, was that Abi slept in the lounge, and the place could feel awfully cramped. And then there were the Magistrates—if they ever learned that Brigid Baptiste had an unregistered "lodger" here she'd be fined a heavy penalty, and Abi would probably be taken away from her. She couldn't imagine how that would feel, couldn't imagine ever letting go now. That was the single reason that Brigid had never tried to register herself as Abigail's legal guardian, her fear that such status may not be conferred upon her.

Brigid turned back to the computer screen, her voice loud as she called to Abi again. "Would you like anything else, munchkin?"

"No, thank you," Abi said in her pleasant singsong voice. "Can I play with the fume, Auntie?"

"Well, okay," Brigid decided, "but put your bowl in the sink first and don't play for too long, okay?"

Abi uh-huh'd back and Brigid began tapping at the computer's keyboard once more, bringing to mind all the documents she had seen in her half day at the Historical Division. The words on the screen glowed back at her as she read them through the rectangular frames of her eyeglasses.

"The quick brown fox never jumps over the lazy dog."

Had she just typed that? It seemed a strange thing to type, the old mnemonic, but she had to have. No one else was operating the computer but her, the device wasn't networked, no one could obtain remote access.

"The quick brown fox never jumps over the lazy dog."

*"Never."*

She knew the phrase by heart, and yet it nagged at her for a moment, as though there was some hidden meaning waiting to be revealed.

"The quick brown fox."

*"Never."*

She shook her head and her finger hovered over the delete key, about to get rid of the silly, pointless phrase.

Just then she heard a noise at her door, and Abi's footfalls as her niece rushed to see who was coming in. Brigid's apartment, like every other in Cobaltville, had no lock; it was a foundation stone of individual responsibility that ensured that all citizens of the ville were safe.

Brigid stood up and shoved her chair across the room as she closed the wardrobe doors, hiding the illegal computer from sight. She stepped out from her bedroom, into the lounge that ran past the kitchen nook and straight to the front door, and saw the black-garbed Magistrate standing there. He was huge, towering over Abi's tiny frame as she peered up at him. The man was dressed in street clothes but wearing his Sin Eater sidearm in a holster attached to his wrist.

Oh, sweet baron, Brigid thought, they've come for Abi.

"Abigail," Brigid said warily, "come over here."

Abi looked over her shoulder, confusion on her face. "But I want to see…"

"Abi, munchkin," Brigid insisted, "come here, come stand with me."

Through his dark lenses, the Magistrate watched the little girl rush across the room to stand behind her aunt.

Once Abi was with her, Brigid took a tentative step forward and smiled as best she could. "Can I help you, Magistrate?"

"Are you Baptist?" The Magistrate barked the question like a command, his voice rough.

Some of the terror dimmed from Brigid's eyes then, and her playful humor emerged. "Are you asking my name or my religion?" she teased, her voice melodically husky.

The Mag stood there, blocking the doorway, his face an emotionless mask. Something was blocking his thoughts, something making it hard to concentrate. "What?" he finally asked.

"The way things are," Brigid continued, feeling her confidence grow, "I presume you're asking my name. It's pronounced Bap-teest. Brigid Baptiste. Why didn't you knock?"

"I'm Magistrate Kane," the Mag began.

"And Magistrate Kane doesn't have to knock?" Brigid pressed, determined to keep the intruder off balance.

The Mag stood there, a huge presence in her tiny apartment, his body tense with a bubbling fury. "That's right,

Baptiste," he growled. "Magistrate Kane doesn't have to knock."

Brigid looked him up and down, peering over the rims of her glasses, wondering what to say. He seemed confused, and he hadn't mentioned Abigail yet. "So, what can I do for you, Magistrate-Kane-who-doesn't-have-to-knock?"

Kane knew that he wasn't controlling the situation as well as he should. Almost casually, he raised his right arm and the Sin Eater shot from its holster into his hand, the barrel pointed across the room at Brigid Baptiste. "Why don't you start by telling me just what the hell you think you're up to, Baptiste?"

Brigid moved then, moved so quickly that she would look back and wonder that she had actually done so. She turned, shoving Abi through the doorway and into her bedroom, instructing her to hide and not come out until all of this was over.

"What th—" Kane began, but Brigid was already darting across the small lounge, leaning down and scooping the little fume unit—no bigger than a baseball—from the floor.

"Don't come any closer," she warned him.

"Or what?" Kane snarled. "Are you going to throw your kid's toy at me?"

Brigid looked at the fume, realizing that the Magistrate was right. It was not much bigger than her palm, made of plastic and weighed next to nothing. All the unit did was project images to the retina, giving Abi a huge playground to stir her imagination. Her own thoughts were in turmoil, emotions swinging back and forth, almost as if something had broken inside her. "I just want you to go," Brigid said, "to leave us alone. Abigail's a good girl, she doesn't have anyone but me. You have to understand that."

"I don't understand a word of it," Kane admitted, thoroughly confused by the woman's actions.

"Won't listen, you mean," Brigid accused, glancing this way and that as though searching for another exit where Kane stood blocking the first.

"You need to calm down, Baptiste," Kane instructed, still pointing the gun in her direction. "Sit down, where I can see you."

"Where you can see me?" Brigid spat back. "Is that your idea of a joke? It's a one-person apartment—I know that. But don't take Abi from me, please. I'm all she has."

The woman was babbling about the girl, Kane realized, the cute little tyke he had seen at the Market Square, the one who had come to meet him at the door before this Baptiste woman had called her away.

"I don't care about the child," he stated.

"Of course you don't," Brigid said, her voice becoming strained with a mixture of fury and fear. "It's just the rules, right? That's why you have to take her away."

"No," Kane said, "you misunderstand." But as he began to explain, the leggy redhead ran at him, three steps across the lounge, swinging her clenched fist, fume and all, at his head.

Kane sidestepped, bringing up a protective arm to shield his face, but Brigid was ready for him. Her foot had caught behind his leg, and as he stepped she shifted her weight, dropping him to the floor. Kane slammed against the floor, grunting as the air rushed from his lungs. Above, Brigid hurdled over his prone form and into the bedroom.

"Abigail," Brigid shouted, "come on, munchkin, we're leaving. Right this instant."

Sitting on the bed picking at the bandage that ran along her arm, Abi peered at her aunt with wide, innocent eyes. "Now? Where are we going?" she asked.

"Doesn't matter," Brigid said, and she scooped Abi from the bed and pushed her to the open doorway. "Outside, into the corridor, quick, quick."

Magistrate Kane stirred, shifting his body, pushing himself up into a crouch. "Halt!" he shouted.

The girl with the honey-blond hair ran past him, slowing for just a second until Brigid urged her on with an urgent "Go, go!"

Kane brought up the Sin Eater, taking aim at the retreating form of the little girl. Brigid's heeled boot came crashing at his wrist, throwing his aim.

"Don't you dare!" she screamed. "Don't you dare do that!"

Kane charged then, driving himself up off the floor and slamming into the woman's stomach with his hard head. She staggered backward, her windmilling arms knocking a vase of flowers and a paperweight from the bookshelves before she slammed against the wall.

Brigid's left hand swung out, smacking into Kane's neck with the flat edge of her palm. It was a nasty, painful blow, light but well placed into the little cluster of nerves there. He grunted and shook off the blow, bringing up his free hand to block her next attack. With his right hand he raised the Sin Eater pistol once more, bringing the gun up toward Brigid's chest.

"You know, you shape up pretty good for a bookworm," Kane told her, a slight trace of admiration in his voice.

In response, Brigid kicked out at him, the sharp toes of her boots digging into his shins, and he leaped backward.

Brigid looked away from her opponent then, saw that Abigail was still standing in the doorway to the little apartment, watching the whole fight with worry drawn on her face. Her hand was on the bandage again, pulling at it nervously, her nails ripping at the scar beneath. Brigid saw the scar rupture then, a trickle of blood running along her niece's arm. "No," she cried. "Abi, don't."

The Mag was on her again then, his hand snapping forward and slapping against Brigid's breastbone, shoving her into the wall. His other hand, the one holding the gun, moved and Brigid's breath burst out of her as he shoved the muzzle into her gut—hard.

"Now, you quit wriggling," Kane growled, "and together we'll figure out if there's any reason I should let you live."

# Chapter 13

Shizuka's bare feet slapped against the hard surface of the main corridor as she sprinted toward the Cerberus ops room. It was past midnight, and the redoubt was down to a skeleton staff as the facility powered down for the night. As such, Shizuka found the main corridors empty, and she had taken the stairs two at a time to reach the wide ground-level corridor that led to the operations center itself. Sword in hand, she pulled at the large door and rushed into the operations room.

"Where's Lakesh?" she demanded breathlessly, looking around the large room with its twin aisles of computer terminals.

The room was quiet, its lighting set to a pleasing dimness to suggest nighttime, and Shizuka saw only one figure in the room, sitting over by the mat-trans terminal. "Quickly," the warrior woman demanded, "it is imperative that I speak with…" She stopped, the words turning sour on her tongue as the other figure in the room looked up at her.

"Hello, Shizuka." It was Brigid Baptiste, her vibrant red-gold hair framing her head like a halo in the subtle lighting, a thin smile on her lips. She looked, for all the world, like the cat who had got the cream. "What are you doing?"

Shizuka watched warily as Brigid stood and took an unhurried step toward her, that self-satisfied smile never leaving her face. Shizuka calmed her breathing, her eyes on Brigid's approaching form, using her other senses to check the room. They were alone—she was sure of it, just the two of them in the operations room.

"Where is everyone, Brigid?" Shizuka asked. The woman looked like Brigid, that much was true, but Shizuka could feel the tension in the air, sense something askew, not quite right in the familiar movements of the other woman. The movements were right but the body language seemed aggressive, domineering. She tightened her grip around the hilt of her *katana,* preparing to defend herself once more.

"They all went to bed, alas," Brigid said, taking another slow pace toward Shizuka. "Boss's orders."

"And Lakesh left with them? Left you alone?" Shizuka asked, shifting her right foot behind her to better secure her balance should she be called upon to fight this woman who looked like her friend. She couldn't quite be sure, she told herself. It may be Brigid. It may just be her, and her battle with Grant, with the thing that wore Grant's face, had scared her, made her overly suspicious, paranoid.

Brigid's smile widened. "Trent's around somewhere," she said, "and you just missed Skylar. What's with the sword?"

"I had a little run-in with trouble," Shizuka said guardedly. "I think it would be best if I were to speak with Lakesh."

"No," Brigid snapped, moving into swift action. Her foot whipped out and she clambered atop the desks as she made her way toward Shizuka at a dead run.

Shizuka brought her left arm up, reaching out toward

Brigid in perfect balance for the sword held behind her head in her right hand. She saw the rip on the left side of Brigid's tunic then, the trickle of blood running across her porcelain skin, the scarlet mixing with the white material of the jumpsuit along its seam.

Suddenly, the sword was swinging through the air, the steel blade whistling a musical note as it arced toward the woman who looked like Brigid Baptiste. At the last instant, Brigid was in the air, leaping high over the blade, her right leg snapping out and kicking Shizuka in the jaw.

Shizuka was silent as the blow hit her in the face, and she staggered back just a single step as Brigid landed across from her. Shizuka watched the redhead spin toward her, readying her next attack. "Brigid," she said, "if you're in there somewhere I am truly sorry for what I am about to do."

Brigid looked imperiously at the shorter woman, and that contemptuous smirk crossed her lips once more. "I reckon you'd be pretty tough," she said, sneering, "if you came full size." As the words left her mouth, Brigid was already moving, a whirlwind of punching arms and kicking legs, driving Shizuka back, forcing her to give ground in the crammed walkways of the operations center.

Shizuka cursed herself as she deftly avoided the rain of blows, cursed herself for not being ready to attack. She was a warrior, a samurai born and bred, and yet she couldn't bring herself to attack Brigid. In her mind she knew that this thing, this familiar face, was her enemy now, but in her heart she wasn't ready to accept it.

"What are you?" Shizuka cried, swinging her sword toward Brigid, forcing the other woman to back away.

Brigid just smiled, dismissing the question. Her hand

touched Lakesh's desk and came up with a sheaf of loose papers as Shizuka stood a few feet across from her. Instantly, Brigid flung the papers at Shizuka's face, doing no harm but obscuring the samurai's vision for just a moment. In that moment, Brigid stepped inside the reach of Shizuka's *katana,* rendering the weapon clumsy and near useless, and her fist jabbed out at her opponent's face, catching the higher ridge of bone above the woman's left eye socket. Shizuka groaned, head snapping back with the impact.

"Brigid, please," Shizuka pleaded. "If you're in there, try to stop this."

"If I'm in there?" Brigid mocked. "I'm all there is, you simpering piece of samurai filth!" She swung her fists again, smacking Shizuka in the face with her left, then her right, then the left again, pounding her senseless.

Shizuka struggled away, pushing out with her free hand, not so much knocking Brigid away as shoving herself back. She concentrated on her breathing, shook her head, clearing it in a fraction of a second. It had been easier with Grant, she realized. The way he had treated her, tried to violate her, and the things he had said, things a lover should never say. But fighting Brigid was different. She didn't know this woman the way she knew Grant, couldn't shut off the fear that just maybe this really was her friend— broken, perhaps, but her friend nonetheless. Whatever the answer was, whatever the truth, Shizuka wouldn't find it if she was dead. Grimly, she steadied her nerve and prepared to battle with Brigid once more.

"I have to warn you," Shizuka said, "I killed your friend and I'm not afraid to kill again."

Pacing between the desks, Brigid circled Shizuka, darting

as though to pounce and then stopping, edging back, laughing as Shizuka flinched. "On the contrary," she mocked, "I think you're very afraid. I think you're wetting your little kimono wondering what's about to happen to you."

Shizuka's eyes narrowed as she watched the red-haired woman stalk around the room, waiting for her opportunity. Just then, the door opened and, from the corner of her eye, Shizuka saw the broad figure of Grant step into the ops room. Impossible—she had killed him.

"Grant?" Shizuka asked, her eyes still on Brigid. "Is that you?"

"You know it is, babe." Grant's voice, with its deep richness, was so familiar to her.

Shizuka turned then, hoping, willing, praying that it was Grant, the real Grant, come at last to assist her, to protect her whether she asked it of him or not.

Then she saw the man standing before the closed door. Grant had put on a pair of undershorts to preserve his modesty, before following her to the ops center. The dark skin of his bare chest glistened with sweat mixed with red runnels of blood, and besides the shorts, he wore a white bandage taped to his chest, just below his rib cage. The bandage puffed out, stanching the flow of blood from where Shizuka had driven the sword through his torso. As he moved, she saw that his left hand hung limply, twisted in on itself with a white stub showing where the ulna bone now poked through the flesh. He smiled, causing thick liquid to ooze from the hole where his ear had been, but his eyes blazed with a barely contained fury as he held Shizuka's gaze. "Now, my darling Shizuka, why don't you come back to bed?" he asked, a red wash of blood showing between his teeth as he spoke.

"Get away from me," Shizuka spat. "Get away from me, you abomination."

Brigid shoved one of the chairs at Shizuka then. It raced across the floor on its casters, and the samurai woman deftly avoided it. But the chair's movement had distracted her for just one precious second, and when she looked up once more both Grant and Brigid Baptiste were upon her.

Brigid high kicked, driving the toe of her boot into Shizuka's stomach before following through with a brutal left hook to her face as her head sank forward. At the same time Grant grabbed Shizuka's right hand—the one clutching the *katana*—in his. He didn't bother trying to break her grip. Instead, he simply crushed, tighter and tighter, preventing Shizuka from moving the sword, the force of his strength making the bones in her hand crack as they tightened together.

Shizuka cried out, flailing at Brigid with her free hand only to have it slapped aside by the fierce redhead as she renewed her attack. It wasn't really a fight anymore; now it was just a beating.

It took two minutes before the samurai finally collapsed on the floor, ultimately drifting from delirium into unconsciousness.

"Do you think she'll wake up?" Brigid asked Grant as she stood over their fallen foe.

"Not for a long time," Grant responded, assessing the bruised and bloodied face of the woman at his feet, "and by then it'll be too late."

"Any idea how we should dispose of her?" Brigid asked. "We could use the mat-trans, but Trent is liable to walk in at any second."

As if on cue, the ops room door opened once again and Trent strolled in, holding two steaming cups of coffee and smiling amiably. He stopped suddenly, taking in the scene of carnage before him, the scattered files, the askew chairs and desks, the blood and the body.

"What…happened here?" he asked, looking from Brigid to Grant to the bloody form of Shizuka lying on the floor between them.

"Things got a little rowdy while you were gone," Brigid said, leaning down and reaching for the bloodstained belt of Shizuka's silk dressing gown.

"Why don't you come on in and join the party, son," Grant growled, and he darted forward to fix his hand on the technician's tunic, yanking the young man toward them.

"What the…?" Trent babbled. "I don't understand. Isn't that Shiz—"

Grant viciously backhanded the man, dropping Trent to his knees, silencing his questions in an instant. Then Brigid was behind him, the belt from Shizuka's robe wrapped tightly in her hands, coiling around Trent's throat and squeezing tighter and tighter until the technician could no longer draw breath.

Trent blacked out, kicking wildly for a moment before he finally keeled over, his body still at last. Grant looked at the young technician's unconscious body.

"I was going to suggest we take Shizuka down to recycling, let her get mushed up into compost," he told Brigid. "Figure she'll have a friend there now, if she ever wakes up."

Brigid nodded. "One for sorrow, two for joy," she said.

Grant began to laugh in agreement, then he grimaced, sucking in his breath through clenched teeth.

"You okay?" Brigid probed.

Grant closed his eyes, letting the wave of pain pass through him. "She got me real good with that pig-sticker of hers," he growled, his hand pushing firmly against the bandage he had applied to his abdomen. "I actually followed her here by the trail of blood her sword was dripping. That's my blood, Brigid. Can you imagine that?"

Brigid leaned closer to Grant, removing the bandage with delicate hands. "This needs proper medical attention, Grant," she said after a moment. "You're losing a lot of blood."

"What's it going to matter?" he asked her, reaching down and patting the bandage back into place over the bloody wound. "If Kane's done his job, we'll all be dead in a day or so anyway, right?"

Standing before Grant, Brigid held his gaze with her beautifully clear emerald eyes. "I don't want to lose you, Grant," she told him, putting her arms around him and pulling herself close. "We've been through too much over the years, leaving Cobaltville and facing the barons and the Annunaki."

Grant thought back as Brigid held him, old memories slipping into place, masking the flaws in his rudimentary programming. He wondered for just a moment why they had to kill Lakesh. Was the man evil? Was he part of the Annunaki conspiracy to enslave humankind? He had to be; that had to be why. Grant stroked a hand through Brigid's long hair and she looked up at him and smiled, tears in her red-rimmed eyes. Then she stepped away.

"Almost over now," he assured her, and she nodded, turning away to hide the tears that began washing down her cheeks.

Slowly, forcing himself to keep moving, Grant hefted

the bodies of Shizuka and Trent onto a cart that he pulled from the corner of the ops room. "Someone's going to notice they're gone soon enough," he told Brigid as she sat at her desk, quietly weeping.

"I know," she said, wiping tears from her eyes as she turned to him. "But like you said, it's almost over now. Pretty soon it won't matter what they know—they'll all be dead."

Grant nodded silent agreement and began to push the cart and its grim burden toward the exit door. As he bumped the front of the cart against the door to open it, Brigid stood and pointed to the shining sword that rested on the floor where they had beaten Shizuka senseless.

"Take the sword, too," she said, "and dispose of it. No point tipping our hand if we don't have to."

Grant took the *katana* and tossed it atop the bodies, then he wheeled them out of the room and into the high-ceilinged corridor.

As soon as Grant had left the room, Brigid wrapped her arms around herself and sighed. "Oh, Grant," she whispered. She was no expert, but Brigid Baptiste's medical knowledge was sufficient to tell her, just with one look, that the sword wound in Grant's torso had pierced right through, doing immeasurable and—without swift medical attention—fatal damage. But she knew he was right. The mission was almost over now. Wounds wouldn't matter after today.

She walked across the room, gathering up the detritus of the battle and replacing it where it had come from, using a screen-wipe cloth to wipe away a few spots of blood from the desks and floor. Her white jumpsuit was stained with red, too, most of it rubbed off from Grant's body when she had hugged him. She grabbed the suede jacket that hung over the back of her chair, draping it over her shoulders to disguise the bloody jumpsuit, before she got back to work on her report. It was more than a standard field report, however. The text contained a rootkit—a hidden, very pervasive bug that even now was attacking the Cerberus data stream. Pretty soon, Mohandas Lakesh Singh's pet project would be blind, its air polluted, its staff trapped. And then the endgame could begin.

GRANT PUSHED the cart along the tunnel-like central corridor to the service elevator, and from there he descended with his grim cargo to the recycling plant in the basement of the Cerberus redoubt. When Cerberus was constructed, it had been foreseen that there may come a time where food and water were scarce, where the unit had to be utterly self-sufficient, and so a vast recycling facility had been built in one of the basement areas of the compound. Like any other self-contained military compound, Cerberus had been designed to recycle and reuse as much of its own waste as possible, and to safely dispose of the remainder.

The elevator doors pulled back and Grant pushed the cart along the empty corridor, through the twin doors into the recycling plant room. As soon as Grant walked into the plant room, the stench assailed him. Food and chemical waste were piled upon a slow-moving conveyor belt that gradually trudged to a deep pit where metal teeth would sort it, crush it and dispose of it. The system was automated, requiring only occasional supervision by a human operator. The machinery rumbled and groaned, hissing steam and grumbling out a mechanized symphony as the conveyor trudged twelve feet and the metal teeth began grinding the next mass of trash, mashing it into smaller, more manageable blocks and spewing these out before finally beginning the long process of sorting it and extracting needed nutrients and other components of interest. Despite the masses of rotting food, there were no insects in the room that Grant could see—this deep down in the concrete Cerberus compound, deep into the mountain itself, it had been almost entirely overlooked by everyone. There were no gaps or doors to the outside world, no way for a fly to find its way this far into the secure military base.

Grant looked down at the worn, stained conveyor belt that led to the grinding teeth. It was a drop of ten feet from the level he stood at, and he saw the remains of today's dinner and lunch and breakfast piled there, along with similar remains from the day before. With a grunt of effort, he wheeled the cart to the end of the walkway, as close as he could to the grinders, and rocked it on its wheels until it finally tipped over, dislodging the two bodies and the bloody blade of the sword over the side.

"This man's work is never done," he muttered as he watched the bodies drop over the side of the walkway and plummet for a moment until they slapped against the mush of trash that was spread over the surface of the now-static conveyor belt.

"Goodbye, Shizuka," he snarled, shoving the cart over the side, too, before he turned away from the walkway's edge and pushed through the exit doors.

As Grant left the room, he heard the whir of machinery hum as the conveyor belt trundled another few feet forward, dropping the next lot of waste over its side and into the waiting jaws of the grinder, ripping the cart to pieces in a matter of seconds.

IT WAS A LITTLE LATER, almost 1:00 a.m., when Grant found Kane standing alone on the plateau outside the entrance to the redoubt, puffing on a cigar as he examined the clear night sky overhead.

"Hey," Grant said, "what are you up to?"

Kane turned to him, offering a smile to his longtime partner as he pulled the cigar from between his teeth. "Nothing much, just counting the stars." He reached into his jacket pocket and produced a cigar for Grant, passing a little silver lighter along with it.

Grant clipped the end and sheltered the flame from the wind as he lit the cigar, taking a few swift drags to get the cigar going. "What do you think it'll be like up there," he asked, "when we get to Heaven?"

Kane shrugged, peering at the stars once more. "Like here, I guess, only with better cigars. Do you remember those ones we used to get back in Cobaltville, back when we did Pedestrian Pit Patrol? Man, I really miss those."

Grant nodded, even though Kane had turned away, thinking about their times together, feeling the memories fade into place. "I don't think it will be long," he said, his voice low.

"What's that?" Kane asked, turning once more to look at his friend. He seemed to notice the bandage across his friend's ribs for the first time. "Hey, Grant, what happened to you?" he asked, concerned.

"Me and Shizuka had a fight," Grant explained. "She stabbed me, did some other damage, too." He held up his left arm, showing Kane the ruined wrist joint. "I don't think I'm going to last to the end. I'm sorry."

Kane looked at Grant, seeing the scabs, the wounds, the broken wrist. "You've been a good soldier, and before that a good Magistrate and always, *always* a good friend," he said. "Heaven's going to be everything they promised us. Baptiste and I will be with you before you know it."

Grant took another long drag on the cigar, feeling the heavy smoke fill his throat and lungs. "Did you get everything you wanted done, Kane?" he asked as the blue-gray smoke coiled around him.

Kane nodded. "In forty-eight hours everyone here will be dead, friend."

Grant coughed then, hacked as he tried to draw another drag from the cigar. As he did so, he felt the pain pulling again at the spot just above his belly, where the point of Shizuka's *katana* had pierced his body. He walked a few paces in a circle before sinking down and sitting on the packed soil beneath him.

"You want me to do anything?" Kane asked, realizing that his old friend was in pain. "Get anyone?"

"We'll all be dead soon enough," Grant replied, looking up at the stars. "Then we can finally enter the Dreaming for all eternity."

Silent, Kane stood watching as the cigar held by his oldest friend burned slowly down to a stump in his curled fingers, and the white material of the bandage turned a deeper and deeper shade of red.

Once Grant's cigar had burned itself out, Kane turned and walked back inside the redoubt, closing the door behind him. Accessing the emergency controls, he sealed them. Not even a nuclear attack would open them now.

DECIMAL RIVER LOOKED UP from his screen in the outback cavern. "We've lost one," he said, "but our door is now open."

Silently, Broken Ghost nodded acknowledgment, and Cloud Singer followed suit. Soon they would travel through the Dreaming World and enter Cerberus via the mat-trans gateway. And then they would finally execute Lakesh for his crimes against the Original Tribe.

# Chapter 14

"I'm sorry," Brigid was babbling as the black-garbed Magistrate pushed the muzzle of his Sin Eater painfully into her midriff. "I just tried to take care of her. She's my niece. Please…"

Magistrate Kane's expression, his eyes hidden behind the dark lenses of his glasses, didn't change, but there was a note of confusion in his furious voice. "What? What the hell are you talking about?"

"I should have registered, I know," Brigid continued, her words rushing out, "but I was so scared, so scared I would lose her, that the Mags would come and take her away. I'm good for her. I'm a good mother to her. Please don't. Please don't take her."

"Lady," Kane growled, "I do not have one clue about what you are talking about." His head seemed muzzy, his thoughts unclear, almost as though they were being blocked by an exterior power. Hadn't he known whom she was talking about just moments before?

"Abigail," Brigid said. "You came for Abigail."

"Who the heck is Abigail?" Kane asked, easing the pressure of the Sin Eater from the archivist's belly.

"My niece," Brigid told him, the tension clear in her

muscles as she stood pushed against the wall with the intimidating Magistrate right before her.

Kane turned then, peering at the doorway to the little apartment and seeing the girl pulling at the bandage on her arm, tearing the scabs away with her nails. "The girl," he muttered, as if to himself. Then he turned to Brigid and spoke firmly, holding the Sin Eater where she could see it. "You stay right there, Baptiste. Don't even blink unless I tell you otherwise. Understand?"

Brigid nodded, defeat clear in her stance now.

As Kane walked across the small lounge and into the little corridor that led to the doorway where the child stood, he heard Brigid sobbing, "Please don't hurt her." He ignored her. He wasn't here to hurt a child, but he could see the blood on the girl's arm, the pained satisfaction in her grimace as she tore at the itchy scab.

Kane crouched on his haunches, bringing his hidden eyes to roughly the same level as the girl's. "Abigail? I need you to come inside now," he said, his voice sincere.

The girl looked at him, her jaw set defiantly. "Are you going to shoot me?"

Kane returned the Sin Eater back into its wrist housing and shook his head. "No, I'm not going to shoot you," he assured the blond-haired girl.

Abigail picked at the scab, her nails turning red with dried blood. "Are you going to shoot Auntie Brigid?" she asked.

Kane held his hand out to the girl. "Come inside," he told her.

Abi looked up, seeing her aunt standing against the wall of the apartment. Brigid was trembling and there were tears rolling down her rosy cheeks, but when she caught

Abi's eye she nodded firmly. Abigail walked forward and took the Magistrate's gloved hand. Kane stood up and closed the door behind the girl, leading her back into the apartment and placing her on the couch. She sat there, swinging her legs and watching him warily, her hand still fidgeting with the scab on her arm.

"How did you do that?" Kane asked the girl, pointing to her scabbed arm.

"Lauren pushed me off the stage at school," Abigail told him. "It was deliberately on purpose. Are you going to shoot her, Magistrate?"

Kane smiled just slightly at the girl's hopeful request. "I'm not going to shoot anyone," he assured her. "I'm just going to talk to your aunt for a while, okay?"

Abi nodded very seriously, as only children did.

"You have some gauze?" Kane asked Brigid. "Something we can use to stanch the blood?"

Brigid looked at him, fear in her eyes. "Please don't take her from me, Magistrate Kane," she said, her thoughts racing, confused and muddled. "Please, I implore you."

Kane stood before the woman, looking her up and down and feeling increasingly as if he had made a big mistake. She was babbling, afraid of him, of what he would do, and her fear threatened to overwhelm her. He needed to break down that barrier if he was to figure out what was really going on, why he knew her and how she connected to the tattooed woman who had attacked him. Kane looked from Brigid to her niece, seeing their fear so palpable, and then he did a very unusual thing for a Mag.

He raised his hand to his face and he removed his dark shades, folded the arms and placed them in the inside pocket of his jacket. He looked at Brigid with his steely blue-gray eyes. "I'm not here for your niece," he assured her.

Brigid looked at him, flinching for a moment from his penetrating gaze. "I...I know I shouldn't have hidden…"

"I'm not here for her, Baptiste," Kane said. "I'm not here to take her away and I'm not here to hurt her. Now, why don't you go sit down while I look in your bathroom cabinet?"

Brigid looked perplexed. "My bathroom…?"

"Sit," Kane instructed, gesturing to the couch.

Brigid let out a long breath that she didn't realize she had been holding, and then she walked across the little room and sat with Abigail. As Kane disappeared into the bathroom, Brigid examined the wound on her niece's arm, telling her that she shouldn't scratch it.

"Is the Magistrate man going to shoot us, Auntie?" Abi asked, her voice a whisper.

"He says he won't, munchkin," Brigid assured her, though she wasn't nearly half as certain as she tried to sound.

The Magistrate returned with a package of gauze pads, a bottle of disinfectant and a roll of tape. He handed them to the redhead and stood over her as she cleaned the girl's wound and dressed it once more.

"So, why are you here, Magistrate Kane?" Brigid asked as she blotted disinfectant around the wound.

"I saw you in the market," Kane began. "Did you see me? I saw you and I felt something, like déjà vu."

Brigid looked up at him and smiled, her face still wet with tears. "Are you… You're not trying to come on to me, are you?"

"Shit, no," Kane answered, looking a little embarrassed.

"It's…it's hard to explain, but I think that maybe you and I know each other. In another life, somehow."

"Abi, stop squirming," Brigid said, and she didn't bother to look up as she carefully dressed Abigail's wound. "With the best of respect, Magistrate, that does sound a lot like a come-on."

Kane ignored her, knowing that the only way to really explain what he meant was to give her all the facts. If she was the enemy, he would know, wouldn't he? "I was attacked," he told her, "by a girl, but something strange happened. I was attacked in the street by a girl who wasn't there."

"I recall a poem about a man who wasn't there again today, and the narrator wishing he'd go away," Brigid stated.

"What's that?" Kane asked.

"It's a sort of nonsense poem."

Kane nodded and sighed. "So this girl attacked me, maybe eighteen years old, and she was like nothing you've ever seen. Her body was covered in tats, weird stuff like circuitry, and her clothes—they were so strange."

"This is very interesting, Magistrate," Brigid said, "but I'm not really seeing how it connects to me."

"We fought, me and this strange-looking girl, and then she disappeared," Kane said. "I was standing there and she just went, like she'd never even existed. And if she doesn't exist," Kane said thoughtfully, "then neither do you, Brigid Baptiste."

"What makes you say that?" Brigid asked, scoffing.

"Because I got the same vibe off her as I did off you when I first saw you in the Market Square," Kane told her.

"So I don't exist," Brigid said. "That's just great. Thanks

for dropping by and scaring my niece and wrecking my apartment, Magistrate."

"Stop calling me that," Kane said quietly. "Stop calling me Magistrate. It's Kane."

"Well, Kane," Brigid told him, "I'm not really following any of this. I think perhaps I should call your superiors."

Kane scratched his head, felt the pressure of his conflicting emotions, his strange, nonsensical thoughts. "The thing of it is," he said, "what if she did exist? What if she exists and you exist and I exist, but we're it? What if everything else here is…a trick?"

"What?"

"I have this idea," Kane told her, "that maybe we're all Magistrates stuck in some big prison. At first I thought that maybe you were the jailer, but I'm pretty certain that's not the case. I think you're a prisoner, too, and that's why I know you."

"You don't know me," Brigid said, "and I think you need medical attention. You're deranged. I thought you were going to…to take Abi from me."

Kane looked at the beautiful woman, her pretty little niece, and he cursed himself. He had come in here and terrified them and made things worse for everyone and he had proved nothing, solved nothing. He drew the dark glasses from his pocket, placing them over his eyes once more as he turned to leave. "I'm sorry," he said. "I won't say anything about your niece in this one-person apartment, okay?"

"Thank you," Brigid said, "Kane."

As Kane reached the door the old question came back to him. He turned and looked at Brigid Baptiste as she watched him. "Baptiste, what is Cerberus?"

The color drained from Brigid's already pale face and her jaw dropped. "What?" she asked. It was the island. The island in the report, the island that looked like a three-headed dog. And the dog. The lazy dog. The lazy dog that the quick brown fox never jumped over. But why wouldn't he jump over a lazy dog? It made no sense. It was like the man who wasn't there, and he wasn't there again today, I wish, I wish…

"Close the door," Brigid said in a hushed voice, feeling nausea rising in her gut. "Close the door and come inside."

Kane did so, pushing the door shut. "What is it?"

"Kane," Brigid began, standing up from the couch, feeling suddenly woozy, "I'm going to show you something that would get me arrested and locked away for a long time. But if you're right, I think it holds the answers."

"I'd already have you on the illegal child, if I wanted." Kane smiled sympathetically. "I think we're past all that now."

Brigid told Abi to sit quietly as she led Kane to her bedroom. Kane looked around him, seeing the jumbled clothes and the chair that had been shoved against one wall. Brigid reached for the wardrobe doors and opened them. Inside, Kane saw the old DDC computer on the little shelf-cum-desk, its screen still glowing where Brigid had been working on it before he had arrived.

"That," Kane stated, "is the kind of violation I can't turn a blind eye to. It would mean my badge."

Brigid ignored him. She was in deep already; there was no turning back now. "Read the screen, Kane," she said.

Kane leaned over her shoulder, looking at the glowing words through his dark lenses: "The quick brown fox never jumps over the lazy dog."

"Is this another of your nonsense poems, Baptiste?" he asked.

"It's a mnemonic," she told him. "An old-fashioned way to test the keyboard of a typewriter. The phrase uses every letter of the alphabet."

Kane read the screen again, then looked at Brigid. "Nice, but what am I looking at?"

Brigid was calculating it in her head then, but she already knew the answer. "Why does the quick brown fox never jump?" she asked. "Why 'never'? It's pointless."

"It's just a phrase," Kane said. "All the letters, right?"

Brigid shook her head. "You don't need *never,*" she assured him. The *n*'s in *brown,* the *e* in *the,* and so on. The word is redundant."

Kane looked at it, realizing that she was right. The *v* and *r* were already present in *over.* "Your point being?" he prompted.

"I think you're right, Kane," Brigid said thoughtfully. "I knew it all along, and that phrase proves it."

Nurse Elaine was plumping the pillows behind Grant's head, leaning over him, all curves and swells beneath her starched white uniform.

"Do you know," Grant said, "you must be just about the most perfect woman I ever saw."

Elaine blushed, shaking her head in denial as she eased him back down onto the bed.

"No, I mean it," Grant assured her. "I mean, if you asked every man on this ward to describe his dream girl, I'm pretty sure they'd all say it's you."

"Grant, please," Elaine whispered, moving closer to

him, "you're embarrassing me." She bent at the waist, leaning close to his face. "Someone will hear," she said, that mischievous twinkling in her eye.

Grant closed his eyes in a long blink, and behind the lids he saw the thing he had seen in the theater, the beast that she had been overwhelmed by. He opened his eyes and she was still there, hot breath brushing against his face.

"What is Cerberus?" Grant asked, his eyes never leaving hers.

"'THE QUICK…BROWN…fox…'" Kane read the phrase aloud, shaking his head. "I don't get it, Baptiste, what does this mean? Who is the fox?"

Brigid smiled indulgently as she explained. "There is no fox and there is no dog. It's just a phrase used by typists in the Beforetime to ensure that the keyboard worked. You see?"

Kane glared at her. "I see nothing."

"You don't understand how my mind works," Brigid began.

Kane cut her off. "Don't start believing that that makes you special," he advised her. "I don't understand how any woman's mind works."

Brigid laughed and shook her head. "I have this incredible memory," she said. "I mean, I can remember details that other people never even noticed. I can recall everything. It's called an eidetic memory."

Kane looked at her blankly. "Okay, and so this proves…?" he prompted.

"Let's say that we've been tricked somehow, fooled into believing that we belong here, in Cobaltville," Brigid proposed. "We'd remember coming here, right?"

Kane nodded. "Unless someone did something to our heads," he said, beginning to follow her line of reasoning.

"Exactly," Brigid cried. "And, you see, you can fool some of the people all of the time, but you are trying your damn luck if you think you can fool someone with a photographic memory."

Kane laughed. "Go on."

"They changed our brains," she said, "our very way of thinking. Fooled us into believing what we see, what we feel. But I knew. From the very start, I knew. I just didn't realize."

"And the quick brown fox…?" Kane asked.

"He jumps over the lazy dog, always has, always will," Brigid explained. "Those bastards thought they could fool me, but my subconscious knew all along."

"I still don't get it," Kane admitted after a few seconds.

"Every letter of the alphabet is contained in the sentence 'The quick brown fox jumps over the lazy dog,'" Brigid told him. "By inserting the word *never,* my subconscious was telling me not to trust the alphabet, words, the very device through which we comprehend the world. To not trust what I saw, what I felt. Everything we are told here is a lie."

Kane nodded slowly. "But if that's the case, if you're so smart, why did you need me to bust in here and point it out to you?"

He wasn't mocking her, Brigid knew; it was an entirely reasonable question in the circumstances. "They distracted me," she realized. "They put something in my way that I couldn't see past, like a wall or a blind or…" Suddenly, Brigid stood up and stepped away from the computer nook.

"What is it?" Kane asked as she pushed past him, exiting the bedroom as though sleepwalking, oblivious to his questions. "What's wrong?"

Brigid ignored him as she walked into the apartment's lounge and looked at the little girl sitting on the couch, gazing into the three-dimensional diorama of the fume. "Abigail," she said, her voice trembling, "come here, please. Come give your aunt a hug."

Abigail looked confused as she got up from the couch, placing the fume to one side and walking across to Brigid. "Did I do something wrong?" she asked.

Brigid shook her head and pulled Abi close, holding her tight. "Oh no, munchkin," she said, "you didn't do anything wrong."

Kane watched the scene from the bedroom doorway, feeling confused and irritated. "Baptiste," he called. "Do you think you can explain this a bit more clearly?"

Brigid let go of her niece and held her out before her, looking at her familiar features, those emerald eyes that matched her own. "Go play with the fume, Abi," she said quietly. "I have to work in my room for a little while. Okay?"

Abi turned and leaped onto the couch, picking up the fume and immersing herself into its virtual world.

Brigid turned and walked back to the bedroom, pushing the door closed once Kane had joined her. "It's Abigail," she told Kane. "She's my emotional center— she holds me here in this world. But I don't think that she's real, Kane. I think she's just a cruel trick to stop me from seeing what's going on all around me. All around *us*."

"That little girl?" Kane asked. "She seems so innocent…"

"She is," Brigid said. "She has my eyes—did you notice that?"

Kane nodded. "I thought maybe she was your daughter when I first saw you."

"That wouldn't have been enough," Brigid said. "My sister died in a crash and so I took care of her only daughter. She's like my daughter with added guilt layered in. I look at her and I feel so guilty, Kane, that I never spoke to Bronwyn for years and years."

"Your sister?" Kane asked.

"Ye—" Brigid began and stopped herself. "Probably no, probably just another, carefully constructed lie. I believe you now, Kane, but do you have any idea what you've stumbled on?"

# Chapter 15

Domi's eyelids shot open, and her twin crimson orbs took in her shadowy surroundings. She lay in her familiar place, the right-hand side of the double bed that she shared with her lover, Lakesh. She turned to him in the darkness of the room, her eyes piercing the gloom until she made out his shape. He lay on his side, his breathing slow and deep, a slight snort at the end of each breath. Asleep.

Domi raised herself on one elbow and her eyes searched the room, peering into the darkness. There was no one there, nothing out of place. And yet she could feel it; something was wrong. Pushing the covers from her body, she sat up in bed and looked more carefully about her, ears straining to pick up the slightest noise. Nothing. Just the faintest buzzing of the electricity that powered the sockets and lights, the deep, almost subliminal humming of the air-conditioning.

Domi felt a cold shiver run down her spine and reached behind her, touching the back of her neck. It was clammy with sweat and, when she ran her hand over her shoulder, she found her back was slick with a sheen of sweat, as well. Cold sweat.

She was alert now, conscious of everything around her, her senses checking the information that came to them. Domi was a child of the Outlands, used to surviving by wits alone. Her spatial awareness, her sense of a place, of an environment, often came across to others as uncanny. It wasn't. It was merely that she had trained herself to pay the closest attention to the smallest of details—often her life had depended on it.

She sat up in bed, feeling the cool breeze playing across her sweat-damp back, across her chalk-white arms, her bare, alabaster breasts, her bone-white torso, feeling the way her heart was thundering against her ribs. She calmed herself, taking a deep breath through her nostrils, sucking in the sweet, purified air that was fed to the whole of the Cerberus complex from the subterranean air-conditioning units. As she drew the breath, her nostrils flared and her lips pulled back, showing her gritted teeth, and a snarl emerged from low in her throat.

"Wake up," she told Lakesh, tapping at his shoulder with her hand.

Lakesh's body shifted, and he grumbled something unintelligible.

"Wake up now," Domi urged, pushing Lakesh by the shoulder, rocking him back and forth.

Lakesh turned. "What is it, dearest sweet?" he said, the words coming out in a muddle between the slow, heavy breaths he expelled.

"Thing wrong," Domi said, slipping into the abbreviated language of the Outlands. "Very wrong. Wake and dress. Quick-speed."

Lakesh began to move then, despite his body's protestations. The chron by his bed read 3:08 a.m. and he had no idea what was going on. All he knew was that he wanted to sleep and that Domi would never wake him for anything less than a critical reason. "Lights," he stated, the word sounding loud to his ears. Immediately, the bedside lamps automatically switched themselves on at their dimmest setting.

Lakesh sat on the bed, shielding his eyes and blinking away the muzzy, heavy feeling of sleep as he gathered his wits. He could feel Domi behind him, a still presence in the bed, taking in her surroundings in that incredible, almost trancelike way she would when she felt intimidated or in danger.

"What is it, Domi?" Lakesh said, his voice clearer now as he shook away the last vestiges of sleep.

Sitting atop the bed, Domi took in another breath through her nostrils, concentrating as she slowly inhaled. "Something in air," she decided. "Something foul."

Lakesh turned to his ashen-skinned lover, concern drawn on his face. "Darling, you're forgetting yourself," he said gently, "talking in Outland."

Domi's eyes were narrowed slits, and the fierce red irises turned to Lakesh, watching him for a second. "Sorry. Old feels," she said, trying to bring herself out of it.

Lakesh leaned on the bed, gently placing his hand on Domi's shoulder, stroking her sopping-wet back. "What is it that you feel, dearest one?" he asked in a soft, gentle tone.

Domi turned to look at him, then suddenly she leaped from the bed and rushed to the wardrobe. In a moment, she was tossing a bundle of clothes to her lover. "Get dressed quickly," she said as she stepped into a pair of panties, "and don't breathe."

Lakesh looked at her, incredulously, for the duration of

five seconds or more. Then, knowing better than to question the strange, wild girl, he stood up and began getting dressed.

WHEN THEY LEFT their quarters, Domi and Lakesh found the corridor empty. Lakesh was dressed in his usual jumpsuit and had, on Domi's insistence, tied a kerchief over the bottom half of his face to act as a filter for the air. Domi wore a pair of camo pants, flat boots with twin knives held in sheaths on the inside leg and an olive vest top. Like Lakesh, she had placed a kerchief over her mouth and nose, but she pulled it away to sniff the air.

"It's out here, too," she told Lakesh as she slipped the kerchief back in place over her nose. "There's something in the air."

"I can't smell anything," Lakesh said, though he didn't doubt Domi.

"It's not a smell," Domi told him, "it's a weight, a heaviness. There's a density to the air that shouldn't be there."

Lakesh made his way down the corridor, passing the closed doors of the personnel sleeping quarters until he reached an equipment locker that had been molded into the wall over the nook holding a fire extinguisher. He opened the cabinet and pulled out two breathing filters, small gas masks that could be strapped or held over the bottom half of a person's face. He passed one to Domi as they continued down the corridor toward the fire door that led to stairwell D.

Once they were in the concrete-walled stairwell, Lakesh pushed down the kerchief, letting it hang around his neck, and held the mask over the lower half of his face. "What's going on, Domi?" he asked, his voice now muffled behind the mask.

Holding her own rebreather to her mouth, Domi checked up and down the concrete staircase before she answered Lakesh's question. "I'm not sure, but there's definitely something coming through the air vents. Could be a malfunction."

Lakesh nodded. "Sounds like a glitch. Let's check out the machine room," he said, leading the way down the staircase to the lower levels of the Cerberus redoubt.

Warily, Domi followed, her senses on high alert.

SHIZUKA COULD HEAR a loud banging and there was a drumming pressure at the back of her skull. She opened her eyes slowly, wondering where the noise was coming from.

She was lying facedown on a bed of something soft, and whatever it was, it reeked. She pushed herself up from the sliding ooze, still feeling the bashing at the back of her head, hearing the crashing noises around her.

The room was dimly lit, but after a moment she made out the walls, stained and smeared, and the piles of garbage all around her. The banging noise seemed to be coming from off to her right, and when she looked there she saw that the platform of trash she lay on ended, dropping off like the edge of a shelf. She could feel the shuddering beneath her as heavy machine parts moved. But there was something else, too.

Kneeling amid the trash, Shizuka calmed her thoughts, focusing her mind inward as her samurai training had taught her. The thrumming and the noise was not just from her exterior, she realized; it was within her. There was pain, a pounding ache like a hammer against her head, and the noise was coming from inside her head, too, the pounding of rushing, angry blood. Carefully, she reached up and delicately touched the back of her head. There was a lump forming there, another to the left side of her face, and some cuts across her face, dried blood in her hair.

She had suffered a beating, she realized. She thought back, pushing through the heavy curtain of unwilling memory, recalling Brigid turning on her, Grant grabbing her wrist as she tried to defend herself. She remembered how Grant had turned on her in the bedroom, mocked her, tried to—

She scrunched her eyes shut tight for a moment, wishing away the memory, bringing her mind back to the present. There was a shunting noise, the sound of some kind of lever moving, like a brake being unlocked, and then Shizuka felt the rumbling beneath her. She opened her eyes and looked at the wall ahead, feeling the thrumming force against her knees, even through the soft bed of discarded food and waste that she rested on.

Ahead of her, the wall was moving. No, not the wall, she realized. It was her. The platform beneath her was moving gradually along the wall, heading toward the right where she had noticed the drop-off edge.

Worried now, Shizuka hauled herself up, flashes of pain burning through her muscles like acid as her body moved. She stood on a moving conveyor belt, feeling nauseous. She was in some sort of recycling plant, she realized now. Standing, she could see the grinding metal teeth at the end of the conveyor belt, whirring around at a fantastic speed as they devoured food scraps, the remains of a broken chair, a dented metal plate that had formed part of a shelving unit.

With only the flat wall ahead, Shizuka looked around her until she spied the walkway with its thin safety rails, a gap where things were tipped onto the slow-moving belt. Sizing it up, she guessed that it was ten feet above the surface of the conveyor belt. With effort, she should be able to reach it. As she took a step forward, her bare foot sank into the mulch of the food detritus. She fell forward, landing on her face in the gloop.

She turned then, and a glint caught her eye. There was her *katana,* its hilt and the first two inches of blade sticking up from a pile of trash a few steps closer to the whirring, grinding wheels of the trash compactor. And, next to it, half-sunken into the mush, she saw the operations worker Trent, face pale, eyes closed, tongue sticking out of the corner of his mouth.

"What have I stumbled onto?" Shizuka whispered to herself, a growing sense of dread encroaching on her mind.

THE STAIRWELL D LED into the corridor to the machine room's south entrance. As she pushed through the heavy fire door into the corridor, the overhead lighting dull, Domi held up a hand and signaled for Lakesh to hold back while she investigated. Lakesh watched from the ajar fire door as the albino girl moved forward in a semicrouch. At some point, she had reached down and unsheathed one of the six-inch blades that she wore strapped to her boots, and its burnished-steel edge glinted occasionally as she walked beneath the lights that were affixed to the cold concrete walls.

The corridor was empty, and Domi walked across to

another fire door at the far end, pushing it ajar and peeking into the stairwell within. Satisfied that that staircase was empty, she edged back until she stood before the plant room door. Her chalk-white hand moved through the air like a dove taking flight, gesturing to Lakesh to join her. Right now, Domi didn't like the idea of the man being too far from where she could protect him.

"Follow me in," she whispered, "and wait immediately inside. 'Kay?"

Lakesh nodded, still clutching the rebreather to his face.

In silence, Domi counted down with the fingers of her free hand before pushing open the door and stepping inside, Lakesh directly behind her. Lakesh walked quickly to the side wall closest to the door, backing himself against it to provide the maximum view of the room with minimal exposure to himself. Domi remained at the door for a moment, hunkering down, the knife held out before her. The atmosphere was noticeably heavier here, despite the air being completely clear to the eye.

As the air-conditioning units clanked and grumbled, the cooling pipes gurgled and whined, Domi's crimson eyes scanned the large room, searching for a foe. She crouched lower, placing one hand on the floor as she looked for the telltale appearance of feet beneath the wide pipes. Still bent over, she moved swiftly, like a rabbit, scampering across the room as she checked left and right for any sign of enemies.

Lakesh watched, amazed at Domi's speed, the economy of movement as she covered the main walkways of the room, any noises she made masked by the groaning, huffing, wheezing machinery. In less than a minute she had rejoined Lakesh at the door, and she slipped the knife back into its sheath as she spoke to him.

"No one here," she said, "except a corpse."

Lakesh felt his breath catch in his throat, and he struggled with the urge to cough inside the rebreather mask. "A corpse," he repeated, repelled by the thought.

"Engineer, I think," Domi said curtly, "tucked underneath pipe by big machine."

Lakesh nodded. "The main intake unit?" he realized. "Can we take a look? Is it safe, dearest heart?"

"We can take a look," Domi replied after a moment's consideration. "Safe? Not so sure."

Lakesh walked beside Domi across the vast room, ducking beneath hissing pipes as they made their way to the main intake unit. As he approached it, Domi pointed across and down, and Lakesh saw the glint of something on the floor, sticking out from one of the wide pipes that traversed the room. He bent closer, and saw that it was a gold ring on the stubby finger of a man's hand. The wrist and arm disappeared beneath the thick pipe, and Lakesh knelt to peer more closely.

The hand belonged to Benjamin Michaels, an unassuming engineer who had been with Cerberus since the influx of personnel from the Manitius Moon Base. The man had been a thoughtful, diligent worker, Lakesh knew, but he couldn't say much more about him than that. Now he lay beneath a cooling pipe, a wound in his skull and streaks of blood dried across his face. He just did his job, Lakesh thought, and it looks very much like that was enough to get him murdered.

As Lakesh knelt there, staring sorrowfully at the corpse, Domi called him over with a persistent whisper. Lakesh turned and saw that she was standing beside the front panel of the tall intake unit.

"What is it?" he asked, both keeping his voice low and trying to be heard over the machinery and the muffling effect of the breath mask.

"Look," Domi said, pointing to the front panel and drawing a rough circle in the air with her finger.

Lakesh peered more closely, cursing that the lighting in this room was not better, and then he saw the indentation. It looked as if something hard had been hammered against the side of the unit, and that someone had taken it upon themselves to provide a quick, makeshift repair to the metallic fascia.

"Any idea what happened?" Lakesh said, but he realized immediately what a foolish question it was to ask of his colleague. "Belay that," he said, straightening his legs and walking across to the dented front panel.

Lakesh ran his fingertips along the sides of the panel, where rivets held it against the churning ventilation unit.

"Someone's tampered with this," Lakesh said thoughtfully. "The front panel has been removed and replaced. And they weren't delicate about it, either—this was a quick and dirty job." He looked at Domi, his clear blue eyes full of sorrow. "Michaels over there probably stumbled upon this unauthorized bit of maintenance and whoever was doing it was thoroughly ruthless in keeping him quiet."

Domi was kneeling beside the body of Michaels now, and she touched his hand with her fingertips for just a moment. "He's cold," she said. "Must have been some time ago. Fingers are stiffening."

Lakesh looked at the dented front plate of the processor. "We'll need to get this open," he decided. "Whatever you can sense is very likely inside."

Domi nodded, stepping away from the corpse beneath the pipes to help Lakesh.

WITH HER FEET SINKING into the food waste beneath her, Shizuka gradually made her way across the shuddering conveyor belt to where Trent's body lay. It was an effort moving through the piles of trash, like walking in quicksand, her every step sinking into its mass, the trash oozing around her, trying to lock her feet in place.

Shizuka's nose wrinkled as she knelt on the trash, feeling the sticky gunk push against the bare skin of her exposed legs where the brief length of the silk dressing gown ended. "Trent?" she called to the man lying beside her, repeating it a moment later, just a little louder.

Trent didn't react. The man looked to be dead, but Shizuka couldn't be sure. Girding herself, Shizuka's long fingers brushed the skin of the man's cheek, feeling the warmth there, seeing his body flinch in reaction. She closed her eyes for a moment, inhaling a long, slow breath to stanch the rising sense of nausea in her gut. Then she opened her eyes, reached forward and shook Trent by the shoulders, but still the man did not react.

"Please wake up," she muttered, the words lost amid the clanking and groaning of the conveyor belt. "We have to get out of here."

Shizuka shifted her position on the pile of trash, reaching across to pull her *katana* from where it was embedded in the foul-smelling detritus. Still kneeling, she eyeballed the metal of the blade. It looked fine, sharp and true despite the caking of discarded food that had adhered to it. Shizuka took up a corner of her short dressing gown, carefully ran it along the razor-sharp blade to clean the worst of the debris from its surface. She took a moment to hold the shining surface of the blade before her and inspect her reflection. Like the blade, she was speckled with splashes of blood and food. She brushed gunk from her face, watched it smear across her cheek. She could clean the blade—and herself—properly later; right now she had work to do if she and Trent were to get out of here alive.

Shifting her weight amid the stinking garbage pile, Shizuka pushed herself to a standing position and looked across to the high walkway once more. Ten feet above her—that was all. Nothing she couldn't reach with a little jump. She held the familiar weight of the sword in her right hand, pointing outward like a tightrope walker's pole to help her balance as she made her way across the slushlike mounds of litter toward the side of the conveyor belt where it abutted the filth-stained wall.

As she took another step, the conveyor belt rumbled on, dropping lumps of discarded food, packaging and a broken serving tray from the canteen into the grinding metal wheels. Shizuka winced as the tray fell into the grinder, clattering for a few moments before being reduced to so many sharp, gray, plastic splinters. Within two seconds it was unrecognizable as a tray.

"Damn it, Trent," she muttered, "wake up."

STILL WEARING THE GAS mask rebreather, Domi went over to one of the exit doors of the machinery room, where a fire ax with a red handle and a red stripe of paint across its blade resided behind the window of a glass cabinet. She pulled at the door for a few tries, finding the old cabinet either locked or sealed with old age—like almost everything else in the redoubt, the Cerberus fire-safety equipment had waited patiently for more than two hundred years until being called upon.

Domi removed one of the blades that she wore against her shin, reversed it and used the blunt end of its handle to smash the glass in the cabinet. As the glass fell away from the cabinet door, Domi reached inside and plucked the ax from the brackets that held it there. The ax featured a small, heavy head atop its long handle, and it struck Domi as a poorly balanced tool, certainly of no use in combat. The handle stretched almost the full height of the petite woman's torso, from shoulder to groin, and, having sheathed her knife, she held the fire ax in a two-handed grip as she made her way back to where Lakesh waited beside the large intake unit that dominated the room.

"Can opener," Domi explained as she handed the long-handled ax to her lover.

Lakesh took the ax, adjusting his grip as he familiarized himself with its weight and heft. Standing before the dented metal plate at the front of the air-filtration unit, Lakesh swung the ax in a long arc from behind his shoulder, over and into the point where the back of the panel touched the boxlike unit of machinery itself. A flash of sparks erupted as metal struck metal, and Domi applauded briefly as she saw the front plate pull away from its housing. Drawing back the ax, Lakesh swung again.

THE CONVEYOR BELT rumbled, moving Shizuka another few feet toward the grinding wheels at its edge, and she steadied her balance, bending her knees a little to ensure that she wouldn't fall. After a few moments, the shaking stopped and the conveyor belt came to a halt.

Once the belt was still, Shizuka stood at the side nearest to the overhead walkway, the same one that she had been tossed from by the counterfeit Grant just a few hours before. Her head was still pounding, ears ringing, but she focused her concentration, ignoring the pain and considering how to reach the platform.

It was just ten feet above the surface of the conveyor belt, less than five feet above the top of her head. Shizuka reached up, stretching her left arm, the empty hand straining against the grimy wall. The wall was smooth, its surface slimy with the remnants of discarded food and drinks. Shizuka staggered for a moment, wavering in place as something within the trash pile beneath her burst, feeling its oozing contents trickling over her bare foot.

It shouldn't be difficult to make the climb. She would just need a little run up, so that she could kick out and jump. Once up there, she could assist Trent, find a rope or work the controls to shut down the system. She was a highly competent athlete, a phenomenal fighter—she had achieved more demanding jumps than this.

Shizuka stepped back a pace, her heel dragging through the oozing junk beneath her, and she foresaw a problem. With the unsteady surface below her, the sinking, clinging, quicksandlike mounds of trash that supported her and threatened to engulf her, getting any kind of run up for a jump would be next to impossible.

She tried pushing down against the trash below her, feeling it compact a little as she sank into it, past the height of her left ankle and then midway up her slender calf. If she kept pushing, the trash would keep giving, she realized; it could be another three feet before she reached the actual surface of the conveyor belt itself. It may be five or six feet—more than Shizuka's height—and if that was the case she would end up burying herself before she ever got the chance to make the jump.

Shizuka pulled her sinking foot from the trash, feeling the squelching mass writhe around her as she extricated herself and took a step backward onto slightly more solid ground. She stood there, eyeing the overhanging walkway once more. There was a very real possibility, she realized to her horror, that she simply would not be able to get up high enough to reach it.

ONCE LAKESH HAD loosened the front panel using the fire ax, Domi helped him remove the panel so that they could properly look inside the processing unit.

Even in the dim lighting of the shadow-filled machine room, Lakesh spotted the first canister immediately, tucked a little way back among the network of cooling pipes, the yellow transfers on its side designed to catch the light despite the shadows all around. His hand went automatically to the rebreather mask that he had strapped across his mouth and nose, ensuring it was secure as he poked his head amid the pipes to look more closely at the canister. Beside his ear, the sound of water rushed through the cooling pipes as the processing unit continued to pump cooled air around the building.

"Phosgene," Lakesh read aloud, his eyes fixed on the instructions on the side of the bucketlike canister. "This is a pulmonary agent."

"Not good?" Domi asked, smelling the change of atmosphere even through the gas mask she wore. There was a strange smell in the air now, like fresh hay or cut grass, a freshness but also a pressure, something that clung to one's air tracts like a heavy fog.

Lakesh looked over his shoulder, addressing Domi. "It's a choking agent. They used it as far back as the trenches in World War I," he said.

Domi shrugged, the reference meaningless to her.

Lakesh looked across and spied the second canister, shoved a little way back into the processing unit, its lid also removed. "There are at least two of them," Lakesh stated, "and we have to prepare ourselves for the very real possibility of more."

"This stuff travels through the air," Domi pondered. "How much would it take to kill someone?"

"Not much," Lakesh replied, turning the closer canister around so that he could read the warnings on its label.

"Where would someone get this from? How did they get it here without anyone noticing?" Domi asked, trying to comprehend how such a breach in security had occurred.

Lakesh ducked out of the unit, lugging the first phosgene canister with him, bringing it away from the pipes and into the light. "This has come from our storeroom," he told her, recognizing the storage bar code on the side. His mouth was hidden by the rebreather, but Domi could see the concern in his wide eyes. "This is an inside job. Somebody on our team is trying to kill us."

Domi's eyes focused on the canister that Lakesh had brought with him before she spoke. "So what do we do now?"

"It's already in the ventilation system," Lakesh stated. "We have to evacuate Cerberus."

# Chapter 16

Brigid held Abigail's hand tightly as they followed Magistrate Kane along the corridor of the Cobaltville medical hub. Abi's movements were sluggish, and she had yawned several times on the way over. Brigid tried her best not to worry herself about the girl. If she and Kane were right, then there were much more significant things to occupy her mind right now than how tired her niece was feeling.

Kane stopped outside a door marked 17. "This is it, Baptiste," he said, and waited to see what she wanted to do next.

Brigid looked up and down the corridor until she saw a grouping of comfortable chairs a little way down from the next door along. She turned to Abi and instructed the girl to go sit there quietly until they came to get her.

As Abi walked off to the chairs, Kane spoke to Brigid in a quiet voice. "Seems like a good kid."

"She is." Brigid nodded. "I hate for her to get mixed up in all this. She's scared enough already."

"It isn't going to matter if she hears, you know," Kane reminded her, "not if we're right."

Brigid nodded slowly as she watched Abi climb onto the chairs and sit down. "I know," she said, "but old habits die hard, and I love her, Kane."

Silently, Kane pushed open the door and ushered Brigid inside the room.

Within, Brigid saw a hulking, dark-skinned man lying faceup on a high bed, gazing up at the ceiling of the darkened room. The shades had been left open and the night lights of Cobaltville played across the room through the window. Brigid looked at the man, unfamiliar as he was, saw the mound of his body that was hidden by the sheets, and flinched when she realized how its length ceased just past his waist.

"This is my partner, Magistrate Grant," Kane explained. "Grant, meet Brigid Baptiste."

"Baptiste," Grant repeated, not taking his eyes from the ceiling as he rolled the name over his tongue. "I don't remember any Baptiste." He turned to look at her then, and saw the vibrant red hair, like flames framing her porcelain face. "Ah, the redhead," he muttered, nodding.

Brigid smiled, holding out her hand to shake Grant's. "You two have spoken about me, I guess."

"A little," Grant told her, a wide smile on his own face as he shook her hand. "Kane tell you his theory?"

"We discussed it," Brigid said.

Kane stepped closer to the bed, acknowledging his longtime partner with a brush of knuckles against knuckles before he continued. "Baptiste has some insight into this that may help us," he explained.

"I've been thinking about it myself," Grant said, "but why don't you kids go first."

Brigid pulled a seat over and sat beside Grant's bed while Kane paced the room, glancing out the window from time to time as though anticipating something bad coming from the skies or the other buildings.

"I have a very specific memory trait," Brigid told Grant, "known as eidetic. You'd probably know it better by its popular term—a photographic memory."

"I didn't think that really existed." Grant laughed.

"It's rare but not unheard-of," Brigid assured him. "Statistically, young children are especially prone to display the ability of perfect recall, but most of them lose that talent as they get older. I happen to be the rare exception."

"And this helps us how?" Grant encouraged.

"This is the only world I've ever known," Brigid stated, gesturing to the view of the skyline through the window. "It seems real and solid. It fits every memory that I appear to have. But my subconscious has been sending me messages for the past two days. Messages that suggest that the whole thing is a lie."

*"The whole thing?"* Grant mimicked, unsure what the woman meant.

"The structures of perception have broken down, Magistrate Grant," Brigid told him, "and it is my belief that our interpretations of the world about us can no longer be trusted."

Grant nodded. "Kane thinks we're in a prison—he tell you that?"

Brigid nodded. "He had me pegged for one of the jailers. But I'm not. Not so far as I know, at least."

Grant looked at Kane, then back to Baptiste. "So, here's what I've been thinking," Grant began. "There's a woman here, a nurse called Elaine and she's—" he shrugged "—very attractive. I mean, she would be any man's dream. The woman practically threw herself at me, a messed-up, crippled Mag with bad attitude. Threw herself."

Kane looked impatient. "Your point, partner?"

Grant's eyes narrowed as he looked at his partner. "Dreams, Kane. The dream girl. The whole thing. I think we're dreaming."

"Crazy," Kane spat.

"No, it's not," Grant told him. "The whole setup works with dream logic. Me and the nurse, the job. You and— What, Kane?"

"His mother," Brigid stated, when Kane failed to answer.

"Ms. Baptiste here and…" Grant encouraged.

"Abigail," Brigid responded immediately. "My niece."

"Dreams and desire," Grant said. "We all get what we want."

"But how do we all dream the same dream?" Kane asked.

"It is impossible for two minds to dream the same dream," Brigid prompted.

"It's not *our* dream," Grant said. "We're players in someone else's dream, and we're being played, too."

"Whose dream?" Kane asked.

"Right now," Grant said thoughtfully, "the dreamer is the closest thing to a supreme being—to God—that we have."

"Trapped in the God dream," Kane muttered incredulously, shaking his head. "This is not good."

"We can't see the waking edges of the dream," Grant continued, "but we know they must be there. We just need to find them."

In silence, the three of them considered Grant's speculations. As they quietly pondered, turning the idea over in their heads, the door to the room opened and Abigail stood there, slouching her shoulders.

"Auntie Brigid," Abi moaned. "Can we go home yet? I'm really yawny."

Brigid looked at the cherubic girl as she came over to rest her head on her lap. "I know, munchkin," Brigid whispered, stroking Abigail's hair. "We're all tired. Won't be very long now, I promise."

Abi rested against Brigid's legs and gazed at the man in the bed. Then she let out a little shriek and turned away. "What happened to that man?" she squeaked, screwing her eyes shut tight.

Brigid pulled Abi closer. "Shh, Abi," she said, "it's okay. This is Grant. He's our friend."

"What happened?" Abi asked again.

"We're not sure," Brigid said, not really thinking about Abigail's question so much as the question that underpinned it, a scholar once more.

At the side of the room, Kane pushed the remaining two chairs together and suggested that Abigail lie down. Brigid sat with her, silently watching the lights twinkling through the window, stroking Abi's hair until the girl fell asleep.

Finally, Kane broke the silence, keeping his voice low. "What are we going to do?" he asked.

Brigid looked up at him and Grant, her sleeping niece's head resting on her lap. "I don't want to leave," she said.

Kane almost choked with surprise. "Are you crazy, Baptiste? What the hell do you mean, you don't want to leave?"

Brigid let her breath out slowly before she spoke, her voice steady. "I have everything I could ever want right here," she said, stroking Abi's blond hair gently. "Why would I leave?"

"Because it's a trap," Kane whispered harshly. "Because we've been stuck inside a dream cage."

Brigid looked at him, then at Grant, her expression serious. "But what if this isn't a prison? Maybe this is our reward," she said, "for everything we've done in that other world. Maybe this is Heaven. Did you ever think about that, Magistrate?"

Fury bubbling within, Kane began to say something but stopped himself, looking at the angelic girl resting her head on the archivist's lap. "Maybe you're right," he allowed.

The three of them remained in silence in the darkened room as Brigid's words sank in. Finally, Grant spoke up. "But it's not real," he pointed out.

"Does that matter?" Brigid asked. "It feels real enough. Your mother feels real, right, Kane?"

Kane was silent.

Grant's eyes fixed on his partner. "Kane?" he prompted.

"I need to think about this," Kane admitted.

"What's to think about?" Grant challenged. "If we're right, then it's not real—it's just smoke and mirrors."

Kane looked at the crippled man lying in the bed. "Did you ever regret waking up from a dream, Grant? Ever find yourself wishing you could just go back to sleep and return to it?"

Grant breathed through clenched teeth, trying to work out the argument in his head. "Now, Baptiste here I get. She's got her daughter—"

"Niece," Kane corrected automatically.

"Niece, then," Grant continued, waving it away. "But you? What do you have here, Kane? As long as there's a never-ending supply of perps to catch and you can have lunch with your dead mom every now and then you'll be happy as a fly in shit? Is that really what you think?"

Kane looked at Grant, vexation lining his brow. "What did we come from, Grant? What did we...*escape* from? War? Plague? Something worse? What if we chose to come here? What if we're not the only ones who chose this life? What if we're the only ones who suspect there was ever anything else?"

"What if we break down the gates of Heaven and find we can't get back in?" Brigid added.

Grant lay back on the bed, feeling his thoughts churning. "You came to me with this, Kane," he said patiently. "You came to me with your suspicions and you made me doubt everything."

"I'm sorry," Kane whispered. Then he turned and left the room, pulling the door closed behind him.

Brigid looked at the Magistrate lying in the bed before her. "I'm sorry, too, Magistrate," she told Grant, lifting Abi's head and extricating herself from beneath it. "I think I should be going. Abi should be in her own bed."

"Yeah," Grant said. "We all should. But unless we fight this, we'll never get to be in our own beds ever again, Ms. Baptiste. Isn't that the point?"

"I know." Brigid nodded, carefully lifting Abi from the chairs and cradling her in her arms as she made her way to the door.

Grant watched the door close behind Brigid Baptiste, and then he cursed, over and over, feeling all the tension in his broken body. "This whole place is wrong," he said finally, speaking to nothing but thin air.

In Realworld, in another cave within the vast complex of the Original Tribe, Cloud Singer stood before the council elders as they listened to her plea from behind their battered and worn wooden table. Many years before, the long table had served in a bar, and its rich, dark surface still showed the rings where wet glasses had been left upon it for too long.

"Everything is in place to destroy Cerberus," Cloud Singer told them, an arrogance to the way she held her head high in such exalted company.

The elders looked at her with piercing eyes until she shrank a little, taking a half step backward. Behind her, Broken Ghost waited in the shadows, having agreed to listen to the plea but making no promises to contribute. Broken Ghost considered this an irrelevance. The campaign was already in motion, the endgame approaching fast; they did not need their movements to be sanctioned by the elder council now. It was a warrior's right to avenge his or her war brothers.

The eldest of the council, a man with an age-lined face and a patchy gray beard that fell down to his little pot belly, spoke in a voice like crinkling autumn leaves. "The tribe must always strive to remake the world, to better it for everyone, Cloud Singer," he said. "Can you assure me that your actions will do this?"

Cloud Singer nodded. "Cerberus stands in the way of that goal," she said. "They have interfered before in our plans—"

"The council is aware of this," a white-haired woman at the end of the table interrupted.

"They stood against my field team when we went to

retrieve the Death Cry," Cloud Singer continued. "We lost our best warriors and we failed to secure the weapon itself."

"Which makes this sound like a revenge mission," the council leader stated. "The Original Tribe must hold themselves above such things, girl."

Cloud Singer stood still, aware that all eyes were upon her, unable to think of what to say.

And then the assassin, Broken Ghost, spoke from the rear of the cave. "The actions of the Cerberus personnel on that day infected the Dreaming. In six weeks it will be unusable."

"The council recognizes the wet worker—Broken Ghost," said the secretary of the board as the pale-skinned assassin stepped forward.

"They are like a rabid dog, snapping at the tribe's heels without any comprehension of the damage that they do," Broken Ghost elaborated. "If we do not put the dog out of its misery, it will become an insurmountable obstacle to our happiness, and to our overall mission—the betterment of man."

The bearded council leader nodded once. "Your point is well made, wet worker," he said in his frail, ancient voice. "We wish you success in your endeavor, Cloud Singer."

"Thank you," Cloud Singer said quietly, bowing once to the council. Then she turned on her heel and joined Broken Ghost as the assassin led the way from the cave. "And thank you, as well, Ghost," Cloud Singer added as she caught up with the older woman.

Broken Ghost looked at her, the skull face drawn over

her own like a specter. "Whatever they had said, the project is too near completion to halt now. I said what I said to smooth things over, for when we return. Nothing more. You walk the assassin's path now, Cloud Singer."

"But you accepted the task from me as soon as I approached you," Cloud Singer said as they paced through the tunnels, past the flickering torches that lit the passages within the rock. "Why?"

"When Bad Father died I lost my mentor and my patron," Broken Ghost stated simply. "The council has always feared me, but he did not. Thus, without him, I have no mission."

"Then why didn't you join us when we went to the mountain range in Russia to retrieve the Death Cry?" Cloud Singer asked.

"Because if I had gone, I would have done so alone," Broken Ghost replied simply.

BRIGID BAPTISTE STOOD in the lounge of her apartment, replacing the ornaments that had fallen from the shelves during her struggle with Magistrate Kane just a few hours before. Abigail was fast asleep in Brigid's bed, the door pulled closed not so much to allow the girl her privacy as to prevent Brigid's anxious movements keeping her awake. Not likely, Brigid thought. Abi's dead to the world now.

It was strange, she realized, walking about an apartment that may not even exist. She knelt, picking up the shattered pieces of a vase that had skittered under the couch during the fracas. I remember Helen, my fellow worker, giving me this when she left the Historical Division, Brigid thought. Did she really give it to me? Is it really broken? Or is it all just make-believe? The pattern on the vase was familiar—a dog, its face now split in three pieces.

Brigid took the pieces, placing them carefully on her open palm. Then she walked across the small apartment to the trash receptacle in the kitchen area and tossed the colored shards inside.

"I don't know what's real anymore," Brigid whispered, frightened by the words coming out of her mouth. "I don't even know if *I'm* real."

She leaned forward and pressed the green button marked Trash on the receptacle, watched as the vacuum activated and the shards of the vase disappeared, swept away into the Cobaltville trash system to be dumped in the Epsilon Level storage area before final destruction.

KANE ENTERED HIS apartment and pressed the play button on his comm unit before he made his way to the fridge.

"Good morning, Kane." The answer unit on the comm spoke in its artificial voice as Kane peered into the fridge, wondering what he wanted. Morning? Kane thought, checking his wrist chron automatically and seeing it was almost 2:00 a.m. It had turned into a hell of a long day, he thought as he reached for the jug of cooled fruit juice in the refrigerator.

"You have no new messages. You have one old message, received yesterday at 10:07 p.m. Playing…"

A woman's voice came over the speaker then, the familiar voice of Kane's mother, and her face appeared onscreen, those smiling eyes, so full of life, peering from beneath the curtain of brunette hair. "Kane, darling," she began. "Are you there? No? I guess you must still be working. I was just calling to see if we could move our lunch date an hour forward tomorrow. Nothing important, just some new shipment coming to the gallery that Jeff wants me to evaluate, so I need to be back for three o'clock."

Balancing the jug of fruit juice, Kane walked over and peered at the tiny screen of the comm. The beautiful woman was shrugging, as though the whole thing was ludicrous. "Well, anyway," she continued, "I'll be at the café at twelve-thirty, okay, honey? I'll see you there, I hope. Let me know if it's a problem, okay?" She paused then, and Kane watched as her hand reached toward the screen to disconnect the communication. She stopped and looked back at the screen, her beautiful, chocolate-rich eyes peering into the camera lens that captured her image. "Don't forget how proud of you I am, okay? I couldn't ask for a better son."

Abruptly, the picture disappeared and the machine's mechanical voice spoke once more. "Message ends. No further messages."

Kane stood by the comm, still clutching the jug of juice as he peered at the blank screen. "Maybe Baptiste is right. Everything we want is here," he muttered to himself.

Sitting on the dilapidated couch, Kane poured a glass of juice from the jug, considering his words. But it's not enough, he realized as he pressed Play once again on the answer comm, feeling empty inside.

# Chapter 17

Lakesh felt his hot breath panting against the rebreather mask as he rushed up the concrete stairs after Domi. In front of him, the agile albino girl took the stairs two at a time, moving with dazzling speed, reminding Lakesh of a rabbit bounding back to its warren. Swiftly, the pair made its way to the main floor of the Cerberus redoubt, and Domi led the way through the stairwell's heavy fire door and into the wide corridor that led to the operations room.

When Lakesh exited the stairwell, Domi was well ahead of him, hunkering down, knife in hand, as she checked the doorways and junctions that peeled from the main thoroughfare. "It's safe," Domi called back to him, "but it's empty. There's no one about."

Lakesh checked his wrist chron as he strode rapidly along the corridor in Domi's wake. It was almost 4:00 a.m., so the lack of personnel was not especially remarkable. The facility was supposedly enjoying some downtime between operations, and Lakesh had seen no reason to keep the facility staff on high alert. In light of the discovery in the air-conditioning unit, Lakesh was beginning to curse that laxness. But if, as he suspected, it was an inside job, then no amount of vigilance would have protected Cerberus.

The dead body of Michaels proved that their enemy or enemies were ruthless and utterly without mercy.

First things first, Lakesh reminded himself as Domi waited at the door to the main operations center—evacuate the redoubt and access the mainframe to shut down and cleanse the ventilation system before it became riddled with the phosgene. Domi had helped him remove the deadly canisters from the air conditioner, but it was impossible to guess how much had already leaked into the system, was even now being inhaled by his staff.

Domi held up her hand, silently instructing Lakesh to wait once more as her bloodred eyes scanned the corridor before she peered into the ops room itself. Inside, the room was illuminated with a warm, cozy glow from the subtle sidelights. Two staff members sat at their desks, monitoring the incoming feeds and checking that the systems remained working as normal. Domi turned back to Lakesh, encouraging him inside.

Farrell, a shaven-headed man wearing a neatly trimmed goatee beard above a wide mouth and a single gold hoop earring, turned as the pair entered. His eyes widened when he saw that the two of them wore rebreather masks, and he pushed back from his desk and rushed over to talk with Lakesh.

"What's going on?" Farrell asked, indicating the mask that Lakesh wore across the lower half of his face.

"There's a chemical agent in the atmosphere, Mr. Farrell," Lakesh explained briefly. "I want you and—" he peered over, recognizing the blond-haired woman at the communications desk "—Delaney to clear out and head straight to the main exit immediately."

Beth Delaney looked up at the sound of her name, and realized that something odd was going on. "What's happened?" she asked, removing the earpiece she wore to monitor incoming signals.

"Evac protocol," Lakesh told her. "I'm issuing the order now." Even as he said it, he pulled the tiny earpiece-and-mike headset from his desk and flipped on the public-address system. A green light glowed, and Lakesh pulled down his gas mask and issued the evacuation order. His voice echoed through the public-address speaker system of the redoubt, waking all personnel and instructing them to evacuate immediately. "This is not a drill," Lakesh concluded sternly into the mike pickup. "I repeat, this is not a drill." His finger jabbed at the PA control once more, and the green light faded back to a dull amber as he tossed the headset back onto his desk. Lakesh tapped out a brief security code on the master control on his desk, and then an alarm bell could be heard from the main corridor as the lights in the ops room switched to a reddish orange.

Domi stood by the door, watching as Farrell and Delaney walked swiftly out of the ops room and briskly made their way down the main corridor. The corridor, like the ops room, had switched to red lighting, and pulsing white lights lit the edges of the wide walkway, indicating the direction of strategic withdrawal.

"You too, Domi," Lakesh said, as he noticed her waiting for him.

"Uh-uh," Domi said, shaking her head.

Lakesh looked at her, the rebreather hanging around his neck. "Whatever's happened here, I need everyone out of the facility, and that includes you."

"I'll leave when you do," Domi told him, her strange eyes staring fiercely into his.

"Domi, dearest," Lakesh said gently, "this is an order. I have to be the last to leave, basic protocol, but I want to be sure that you are safe."

Domi tapped a chalk-white nail against the rebreather she wore over her features. "Right now I'm safer than you are," she told Lakesh, "and I'm not going anywhere unless you're with me. One—it's no more dangerous for me to be here than it is for you. Two—I just know you'll get yourself into a wagload of trouble if I'm not watching your back."

Lakesh began to argue, then he stopped himself and reached his hand out, clenching hers. "Thank you," he said. "Now, if you're staying, perhaps you can run a diagnostics check on our HVAC system, see how much phosgene has infiltrated it and whether we can flush it out."

Stepping across to the nearest computer terminal, Domi tapped the keys that brought it to life, and got to work. Lakesh was quietly surprised to see her work at the computer without a word of complaint—it certainly wasn't her preferred modus operandi.

Taking his seat at his own terminal, Lakesh tapped out the security code that would grant him access to the mainframe.

After a few moments, Domi peered across to him, her brow creased with worry. "I can't get access," she stated.

Lakesh glanced up at her, struggling not to show his frustration. Domi wasn't an ideal operative to have for computer work; her expertise was in the field. Even now, he could see some jumble of figures on her screen where he had hoped she would access the redoubt plans.

"Allow me," he said, wishing Brigid Baptiste or Donald Bry were here to employ their remarkable computer skills to the required analysis.

He tapped out several commands, rushing past the sub-routine menus and bringing up an as-live monitor feed of the air-filtration system. An alien contaminant was clearly identified on the three-dimensional map of the ventilation system, its illuminated tendrils emanating from the central processor and reaching out to…

Abruptly, the screen went blank and, after a second's delay, a stream of data made up of apparently random numbers and letters rushed before Lakesh's eyes. "What—" he began, watching as the figures raced across the terminal screen.

"Same thing's happening here," Domi said, and Lakesh saw that she had moved across to the next terminal from the one she had initially been working at. "Something's wrong with the system."

"Bother," Lakesh muttered as he felt the sinking feeling in his stomach. Whoever their mysterious enemy was, they had done something to the Cerberus mainframe.

BELOW THEM, in the recycling room, Shizuka stood on the conveyor belt, glaring at the walkway above her. She had made several unsuccessful attempts to clamber up the side of the wall to the overhanging walkway, and all of them had ended with her sinking back into the festering trash. The walkway was so close, and yet remained frustratingly out of her reach.

She needed something sturdy that would act as a scaffold, a climbing frame. If she timed her next attempt between the erratic movements of the conveyor belt, the frame should stay in place long enough for her to be free of the relentless recycling operation. She looked around, her eyes scanning for something solid amid the mulch. Trent's body still lay, faceup, eyes still closed. The unfortunate man was sinking into the trash, Shizuka realized—the back of his head had already disappeared and the trash had almost reached to his earlobes.

As Shizuka watched, the hum of machinery started up again, and the conveyor belt began to move, edging Trent's unconscious form ever closer to the grinding blades. This was it, Shizuka realized suddenly. With this push, the conveyor belt would toss Trent's sleeping form over the edge, where the screeching blades would begin their butcher's work. The man deserved better than that.

On light feet, Shizuka dashed across the moving, sludgelike mess, reaching for Trent's sinking hand.

LAKESH'S PRIMARY discipline was cybernetics. Domi watched as his fingers tapped at the keyboard, employing all of his skills as he accessed the Cerberus operating system and hunted down the cause of the system-wide error.

"Somebody's set up a rootkit," Lakesh explained, not bothering to look up from the screen as the data refreshed. "It's taken control of the mainframe and is aborting any conventional attempts to access our hardware."

"That's bad," Domi said through the filter of her rebreather mask.

"Given time, I can work around it," Lakesh said confidently. "If I hadn't just given the evacuation order, I'd ask Donald or Skylar to help, perhaps Brigid."

Domi moved to the main door of the room and peered at the evacuating personnel as they trudged along the red-lit corridor. There was no pushing or shoving, no sense of panic—the Cerberus staff understood the need to evacuate in an orderly manner. "Donald's up front," Domi said. "Looks like he's counting people off on a chart."

"Good old Donald," Lakesh acknowledged.

"Should I go grab him?" Domi asked.

"No," Lakesh told her, "let him get on with his job. The personnel come before the facility, Domi. Computers can be replaced."

As Domi watched the crowds marching through the corridor, a side door opened at the emergency stairwell and Brigid stepped out, her red-gold hair seeming to glow in the altered lighting. Domi saw the woman watch the exiting crowds for a few moments before turning to look in Domi's direction, a grim look on her face.

"Brigid," Domi called. "Come here, we need you."

A moment later, Brigid began walking toward the ops room.

"Domi, Lakesh?" Brigid panted. "What's going on? What's with the masks?"

Lakesh glanced up from his work at the terminal, his face set in a frown. "Brigid, thanks for joining us," he said. "I could use your assistance right now."

Brigid stood beside Lakesh, peering at his screen while Domi pulled a spare rebreather mask from one of the room's equipment lockers and passed it to her.

"Someone's attacking Cerberus," Lakesh explained. "The attack is coming from multiple angles and, more worryingly, it appears to be an inside job."

Brigid slipped the mask over her face, adjusting the straps as she asked Lakesh what she could do to help.

"They've put a pulmonary agent into the ventilation system," Lakesh said. "We should be able to flush the system clean once the personnel are evacuated, but right now I can't access any of the commands. Someone has set a rootkit program on the mainframe. It's acting as administrator, overriding anything I try to do. Right now I can't even get a status report."

Brigid rushed across to a nearby terminal, pulling a chair over as she sat before its glowing screen. "I'll see what I can do," she assured Lakesh.

"THE GATEWAY'S SECURE," Decimal River confirmed, checking through the readings that were scrolling across his computer screen.

Grimly, Broken Ghost turned to Cloud Singer and smiled, a hideous thing within the skull-like makeup of her face. "It is time to go," she said.

Cloud Singer felt elated, but she simply nodded once, hiding her joy from the older woman. It seemed, right then, that she had been waiting forever for this moment, when she would finally see Lakesh dead. She watched as Broken Ghost stripped off the loose shirt she wore, revealing her toned body.

Broken Ghost reached down and unclipped the bull roarer from its place at her belt, judging its weight in her hands. Without a word, she strode out of the cave, and Cloud Singer followed her into the bright moonlight that lit the arid plains of the outback, feeling the weight of the boomerang that she had strapped to her own waist, ready for the coming battle.

AS SOON AS Lakesh had given the evacuation order, the Cerberus personnel had been awakened from sleep or alerted at whatever task they were doing, and all of them made their way to the main corridor to exit the structure by the large, accordion-style door. Shock-haired Donald Bry had brought a list of personnel with him, and he counted people as they passed him on their way to the exit, ticking them off to ensure that everyone escaped unharmed. After the main evacuation was finished, Bry would head back to the operations room and see who remained—he didn't doubt that Lakesh would be the last to leave.

The general hubbub from the throng rose, and Bry looked up from his checklist to see what was going on. He could see that the door at the far end of the corridor was still closed, despite his issuing the order almost three minutes ago that it be opened to its widest extent. Bry strode forward, urging people aside as he went to see what was going on.

A well-muscled ex-Mag called Edwards peered up from the control panel. Edwards had styled his hair into a severe crew cut that showed off a bullet-bitten right ear, and he wore a tight undershirt that left his powerful arms exposed. Bry noticed the concern on the ex-Mag's face immediately. "What's wrong?" he asked.

"I can't get it to open," Edwards explained, flipping the little door that hid the controls wider so that Donald could peer inside.

Donald tapped at the open button several times, before entering the unlock code and trying again. Nothing happened.

"You see?" Edwards said.

Pushing his thumbnail into the groove at the bottom of the little panel, Donald flipped off the fascia and peered inside. "The wiring appears to be intact," he mused. "I wonder what's stopping it?"

"You want to wonder a bit quicker, brainiac?" Edwards encouraged. "I think the natives are getting restless."

Peering over his shoulder, Bry saw the waiting people watching him peering at the control panel. Curiously, he couldn't help noticing that a few of them were coughing over and over. "No need to panic, folks," he said in a loud voice, "just be a minute." He turned back to the controls, wondering what on earth he was going to do.

Standing amid the crowd, Kane smiled as he watched the concerned faces around him as Bry took a tiny screwdriver to the security plate and began dismantling the unit.

THE CONVEYOR BELT trundled onward, dumping its next load of trash over the edge of the rollers and into the whirring, grinding blades below. Shizuka was beside Trent now, and she pushed the sleeve of her ruined silk dressing gown back as she reached for the man's arm, grabbing him just above the wrist.

"Wake up," she urged, raising her voice above the clanking moan of machinery.

Then she yanked, trying to pull Trent free of the sludge-like detritus that his body had sunk into. He was stuck fast, and Shizuka knew she would need both hands to pull the man loose. As the conveyor belt moved relentlessly onward, Shizuka turned the *katana* in her hand so that it faced downward like a walking stick. Then she rammed the blade hard into the festering trash, until it sank to halfway along its length, hilt plus ten inches of steel sticking from the foul-smelling pile.

With both hands now free, Shizuka took a firm grip on Trent's arm and tried to pull again, but it was no use. The man was sinking deeper into the trash, and, Shizuka realized, so was she. The more she tried to secure her footing, the more force she exerted and the farther she sank into the gunk beneath her.

The conveyor belt trundled on, slow and inevitable, tossing the slush of trash over the side and into the waiting blades.

Shizuka's breathing was coming harder, and she gritted her teeth, trying once again to pull Trent free, this time placing a strong two-handed grip on his right ankle. Again the same thing happened—the difference that her actions made on the position of the sinking man was negligible, and meanwhile she was sinking farther into the gunk beneath her feet. Already the damp, slimy trash was oozing over her ankles, washing against the bottoms of her shins.

Shizuka let go of the man's leg, and fell back as she tried to pull her feet free. The clump of food waste before her, where Trent's unconscious body was embedded, reached the rounded edge of the conveyor belt, and Shizuka turned her face away as she waited for the inevitable. She heard the network of blades swishing as they chopped at the trash, dicing it into smaller and smaller chunks. Then the mechanical whining of the blades increased, their rhythm changed, as they met with something far more solid than potato peelings and this morning's discarded pastries. Shizuka clenched her eyes tight as she heard the blades thunking against the solid object, banging at it like hammers against a wall. A man's screams came to her then, Trent finally waking up from his stupor, unable to comprehend what was happening to him. The awful noises continued for more than ten seconds until the screaming ceased and the whirring, grinding noises returned to normal.

Shizuka opened her eyes and peered at the rolling edge of the conveyor belt as the lip came trundling toward her. Trent was compost, and she was next.

THEY WALKED, just the two of them, for a few minutes, Broken Ghost's hands holding the dreamslicer, wrapping its cord over her knuckles, familiarizing herself to its weight once more. They passed the huts of the tribe's village, continued to the edge of the settlement, to the special area that had been marked out in pebbles. The area showed two rings, one large and one small, and Broken Ghost walked across to the center of the larger ring and stopped.

"Do you need me to go into the other ring?" Cloud Singer asked, confusion in her voice. Normally the leader of the dream journey would take point in the small ring, and the strike team would be lifted into the Dreaming from their positions in the larger circle.

"It's just ritual," Broken Ghost muttered, her eyes now closed. "Stand where you will."

Dressed in her blood-dyed strips, Cloud Singer stood across from the assassin, placing her arms around herself to stave off the night's chill. "I'm ready," she said, her voice little more than a whisper.

Without a word, Broken Ghost began spinning the bull roarer, raising it above her head as its droning, ugly song began. In the back of her head, at the top of the spinal chord, Cloud Singer felt the bubbling, brushing sensation as the dreamslicer's song engaged her subcutaneous implant. In an instant, she and Broken Ghost were in the Dreaming World.

SHIZUKA SQUIRMED amid the stinking, rotting trash, desperately trying to free herself as the conveyor belt unstoppably headed for the drop that would toss her fragile form into the crushing blades. Her own weight, light though she was, was acting against her, dragging her down into the quagmire of decaying garbage.

She kicked her feet out, watching as, just three feet from her bare toes, scraps of food fell over the curve of the moving belt, plummeted into the whirring blades that waited below. Shizuka clawed at the moving, spongy mound beneath her, digging in with the heels of her hands as she tried desperately to pull herself free. With a squelch, her sinking legs were pulled out of the gunk, and she dived forward, her face brushing against the foul slop that oozed all around her.

Free now, the samurai warrior shot forward, rising from a crawl to a crouched walk as the conveyor belt shook beneath her. Her right hand reached back, clasping the long hilt of her *katana* where she had left it buried in the trash, and she whipped it free as she hurried ahead, creating more and more distance between herself and those relentless, grinding blades.

Moving swiftly, her tread deliberately light, Shizuka trotted over the mounds of trash that threatened to pull her under. Then, with a sudden thump, the machinery powered down and the conveyor belt stopped moving.

Standing with sword in hand, Shizuka steadied herself as the floor beneath her ceased vibrating. She had been granted a reprieve, albeit a temporary one. She needed to find a way out of there, and quickly, before she ended up as much minced meat as the unfortunate Trent.

Once again, Shizuka stared at the stained, grease-slick and seemingly insurmountable wall and wondered what she was going to do.

CLOUD SINGER AND Broken Ghost stepped into the void, walking the in-between. To Cloud Singer's eyes, the Dreaming was as beautiful as ever, with its fresh fields and verdant valleys, a map of Australia that teemed with life, with energy and excitement so unlike the outback of Real-world, with its poisonous creatures that lurked beneath the dust, ready to pounce on their unsuspecting victims. Above them, the white clouds swirled through the sapphire-blue sky as Cloud Singer and her colleague walked away from the two rings that had been marked out in pebbles on the ground.

Her eyes slits, the assassin looked back at the girl, her hand rocking back and forth above her head as she whirled the bull roarer in an almost negligent rhythm. Cloud Singer felt the tingling pull at her nape, the implant firing again and again, holding her in the Dreaming, that world of secret pathways that only the Original Tribe knew.

The Dreaming was the world wrought in imaginings, carved from belief. It was a place to visit, as their ancestors had visited it for more than a thousand years. When Good Father and Bad Father were young, they had been explorers and thieves. They had found an old Australian military facility, long abandoned, much of it wrecked. Within they had found the singing circuit that allowed access to other places. It was a similar system to the mattrans that had been developed in America, a teleportation system that allowed personnel to travel vast distances in the blink of an eye.

When Good Father and Bad Father stepped into the teleport warp, however, they realized that it was something more—this was not merely a device to go from A to B, but here was something to access the places in-between, the places that their ancestors had explored again and again in their ritual dreams. Accessing the portal to slice the dream required a receiver unit, implanted into a traveler's spinal column. This circuit acted in conjunction with the ululating note of the dreamslicer to allow an individual access to the Dreaming World. Once in the Dreaming, that individual had access to everywhere else. Or, that was the way that it had worked, until Cerberus, in its jealousy, had unleashed the Death Cry into the Dreaming, eating it from the inside out.

There had been other technologies, too, things grafted onto the warrior caste to make them stronger, faster, to allow them night vision and swifter reactions. Cloud Singer had first undergone surgery at age five, and she could still remember the burning sensations that had run through her body as it had been laced with the first traces of circuitry. Once one had experienced pain of that nature so very, very early in life, it was hard to imagine a life without pain.

The Original Tribe, the peoples who had once been called Aborigines by the settlers, had a need for warriors now, because of their responsibility. They saw that humankind had almost destroyed itself in a suicide pact between nations two hundred years ago. The vast majority of the population had been killed, and the survivors were left as tiny clusters across the globe, desperately eking a living from the radiation-spoiled soil. The Earth itself had turned against humankind then, tossing up mutant creatures and freakish weather patterns, toxic clouds filled with radioactive rain and new predators to hunt any who survived. Someone with a firm sense of the dramatic and the macabre had renamed their world Deathlands.

Observing this, the Original Tribe, long dismissive of the affairs of the world at large, had seen the need for firm leadership, for a clear and beautiful path for humanity to follow. The portents were clear, the fates unmistakable—the Original Tribe had survived to lead humanity into a glorious new era, a golden age. They had embraced their responsibility with willing hearts, and spent their days organizing the remaking of man. Scout teams searched the globe, looking for all the things that could either help them or destroy them, which was how the incredible technology of the dreamslicer had found itself in the hands of the Original Tribe.

Broken Ghost took a step backward, feet crossing as Cloud Singer watched. Then, in the blink of an eye, the assassin who moved like a ghost disappeared, a cloud of dust all that remained of her passing. Cloud Singer stretched her arms out to her sides, opened her mouth and unleashed that beautiful, all-enveloping note from which she earned her warrior name. It was a note so pure that it made the heart ache to hear it, but it would only ever be heard—*could* only ever be heard—within the Dreaming itself. It was a note drawn from the soul, constructed only of belief. As the note exuded from her vocal cords, Cloud Singer rose from the ground, arms outstretched, head up and facing forward, her body held at a thirty-degree angle with the long, outstretched beauty of a swan's neck. And then, holding the wonderful note, she rocketed through the sky, chasing Broken Ghost across the multicolored dreamscape.

As HENNY JOHNSON was jostled about among the crowd, waiting for Donald Bry to open the main door, she spotted Kane close to the stairwell. He was a tall man, and his years as a Magistrate had instilled in him an erect posture, so that he seemed to loom over the other Cerberus personnel as they waited, babbling in conversation. Standing on tiptoe, Henny waved to the man, but he seemed oblivious, watching the progress at the door with narrowed eyes. Running a smoothing hand quickly over her blond bob, Henny pushed her way through the crowd.

"Hi, stranger," she began, suddenly feeling like a slob, very conscious of the fact she had gotten dressed in a hurry when the alarms had started ringing. "Any idea what's going on?"

Kane's blue-gray eyes flicked to Henny, and she saw him smile. "Johnson," he said, recalling her name. "Henny Johnson. How are you?"

"Just about awake," she groaned. "What is with this 4:00 a.m. evac?"

Kane's eyes went back to the action at the far end of the corridor, where Bry and Edwards were dismantling the keypad. "Darned if I know," he replied. "Looks like there's a glitch with the lock."

"So we're sealed inside?" Henny reasoned, a trace of concern in her voice. There was something else in her voice, too, she realized—a throaty tickling, as though she had a cold coming on.

"Could be," Kane agreed.

Henny looked at the broad-shouldered man ponderously for a moment, wondering what was going through his mind. "And that doesn't scare you, Kane?" she asked him.

"A man shouldn't be scared of dying, Henny," Kane assured her, "not if it's for the right cause."

With those words, the ex-Mag made a path along the wall, heading back toward the ops room. Henny began to cough as she watched him go, wondering why he seemed so sure of himself, pleased while the other members of the Cerberus personnel were becoming increasingly restless.

LAKESH PEERED across to the terminal where Brigid Baptiste worked, hoping she might have found a way to bypass the rootkit. Her fingers played across the keyboard, tapping out new sequences, punching at the enter button.

"Anything?" Lakesh prompted.

Brigid's mop of red hair swung back and forth as she shook her head. "Nothing yet," she explained. "The whole system is riddled with this thing like a cancer. It's taken control of the administrator functions, which means it instantly overrides anything I try to do. Sorry, Lakesh, but I think this one's beyond my computing skills."

"You're right," Lakesh said as though to himself. "We need one of the IT experts in here right away." He turned to Domi, instructing her to find Donald Bry or Skylar Hitch. "Or preferably both of them!"

Domi pushed through the door once more and was surprised to see that the crowd was still waiting there. The corridors of Cerberus always felt cool, but she detected no breeze coming from the large entrance door at the far end. That was strange, Domi thought as she padded into the vast corridor and headed toward the milling crowd.

As Domi walked along the corridor, she saw Kane striding directly toward her, head down, determined. "Kane," she said, catching the man's attention. "What's going on? Why are people still inside the building?"

"Door's broken," Kane told her simply.

"Shit," Domi cursed. "Look, there's something in the air, some contaminant. We need to get these people gas masks if they're staying inside. Right away."

Kane nodded. "I'll get some from the ops room," he told her.

Domi watched as the broad-shouldered man continued striding along the corridor in the direction she had just come from. "Be careful," she called to him. "Something's going on, Kane. Something bad."

SHIZUKA'S EARS WERE still ringing, and the ache at the back of her head nagged at her from the beating she had suffered at the hands of the phony Grant and Brigid, but the throbbing was gradually subsiding. At last she was finding that she could think more clearly. The stench in the vast recycling room beneath the Cerberus redoubt assaulted her nostrils, and the heat was close, oppressive. She wished the air-conditioning in the room would kick in, little realizing the irony of such a desire.

Sword in hand, she walked across the uneven surface of trash that congealed on the conveyor belt, sure that there had to be some way of scaling the slick wall if only she could keep her thoughts clear enough to see it. The wall was pitted here and there, but the notches were small, hardly enough to act as proper hand- or footholds. No, that was a dead end—she had tried that three times before and had run out of grip long before she had scaled the mere five feet in height she would need to reach the overhanging walkway.

The trash mound beneath her had too much give; if she applied pressure she just sank deeper into it and lost height rather than gaining it, pushing her target farther away like something from a bad dream.

There was nothing in the piles of rotting garbage that she might use, either to stop the whirring blades or to act as a ladder. Not even something to provide her with just a single step up so that she might spring to safety. As the thought struck her, the corners of her mouth raised in an enigmatic smile, and Shizuka stepped back once more, gazing at the walkway that ran above the conveyor belt along the side of the wall. *Of course!*

She heard the mechanics of the conveyor belt sigh once more, and felt the rumbling as the system powered up and the belt began to move again.

As the conveyor belt trundled forward, Shizuka walked in the opposite direction, her feet sloshing in the rotting food as she kept pace with the wall. Beside it, the walkway moving beneath her, Shizuka thrust her *katana* into the wall itself, driving its sharp point high into the crumbling seam between two greasy, stained breeze blocks. The mortar between them cracked, puffing away as powder, and Shizuka used both hands to push harder on the hilt of the blade, forcing it farther into the wall until it was held fast.

The conveyor belt trundled onward, dropping more trash into the spinning blades below as Shizuka patiently kept pace with the wall, her blade now hanging there, embedded in the old mortar.

With a hiss of steam and a metallic sigh, the conveyor belt stopped moving once more, and Shizuka stopped before the sword that poked out from the wall. The *katana* was embedded to about one-third of its length, leaving almost two feet of steel and hilt sticking out from the wall at roughly shoulder height. Eyes on the blade, Shizuka stepped back, her feet dragging in the sloppy mire of trash. She hunkered into herself, coiling her body like a spring before rushing the three short steps that took her to the wall.

As she reached the wall, her right hand slapped against the hilt of the *katana,* and the flexible blade curved just a little toward the surface of the conveyor belt as Shizuka leaped upward. As the blade sprang back into shape, Shizuka pushed off from it with her right hand, her left striving upward to grab for the edge of the high walkway. The walkway was just five feet above her, and the stretch of her body as she flung herself up was sufficient to grab hold of its teasing edge.

She swung there, dangling from her left hand, all of her weight pulling down on that desperate grip as she kicked with her legs, keeping her momentum going to continue the arc of her movement. Her right hand had left the hilt of the blade now, and it darted through the air, crossing her body and lunging high over her head. Suddenly Shizuka's right arm passed over the floor of the walkway, her spinning motion pulling the rest of her body behind her. And then she was falling again, just for a moment, and her right hand spread as hand and forearm crashed down on the surface of the walkway. Shizuka howled as the impact drove down her arm, her shoulder burning with the sudden pressure dragging at it.

Her legs kicked out, like a beached fish's tail, back and forth, as she struggled to maintain her grip on the walkway. Relentlessly she pulled herself up, her body swinging to and fro as her feet kicked frantically.

In a moment she was over the edge of the walkway, slamming against it with her arms and chest, her legs still kicking out as they hung out over its edge. Below her, she could hear the grumbling moan of machinery as the conveyor belt began moving once more, a hiss of steam as it powered itself up. Shizuka pulled herself forward, dragging herself entirely onto the walkway that hung over the shifting conveyor belt. Then, as the machinery below her groaned onward, she took a moment to gather her thoughts.

As steam hissed all around, Shizuka rolled herself over on the walkway. Securing her left hand on the safety bars that ran around the sides of the walkway, she dipped her body, bending her waist over the edge and reaching far down until she grabbed the hilt of her *katana* where she had embedded it in the wall. With a grunt, she pulled it free and swung herself, blade in hand, back onto the safety of the walkway.

What now? she wondered as her black, steam-damp hair clung to her face. Much as she wanted to track down and dismember the traitorous faux Grant, she knew that her number-one priority was to warn Lakesh so that he could take action against the other two snakes in their midst. Two?

"Kane's one, too," Shizuka said aloud. "He just has to be."

A moment later, the samurai was on her feet, dashing along the walkway and pushing through the scratched-paint double doors into the cool, airy corridor beyond.

THEY RUSHED ACROSS the Dreaming World, Cloud Singer and Broken Ghost, like fireflies dancing across the sky. Broken Ghost moved with long-legged strides, a hop, skip and jump across the ocean's surface. Above her, arms spread, Cloud Singer swooped on the breezes, her song, that beautiful, incredible note, powering toward the empty horizon.

The waters beneath her were speckled with red where the sun painted its reflection upon the waves, and Cloud Singer turned to gaze off at the far distance. Out there, off to the east, the oily black wall was oozing forward, consuming everything in its path. The Death Cry, the end of the Dreaming World.

The American continent loomed ahead of them, and Broken Ghost's toes touched the ground, kicking up sparks as she moved with incredible speed. Cloud Singer swooped low, her black shadow growing larger as she neared the ground. There were settlements here, fishing villages and little trading posts that served the farming communities dotted infrequently across the massive continent. Shining, mighty towers sparkled on the horizon where the former baronies of America stood, pumping thought energy into the Dreaming World.

Beneath Cloud Singer, the assassin seemed almost to

not be moving at all. There was no effort to what she did, just as there had been no effort when she had slain the kangaroos. The world seemed to move for her, as though she had set the globe spinning while she remained in place, its surface kissing her bare feet.

By contrast, Cloud Singer felt the pressure in her lungs as her single-note song pulled from her all that she had to give. She wanted to land now, to recoup. The trip to Montana would be what Bad Father had called a two-dream, meaning that he would expect and plan for a stop-off in Realworld before reaching their final destination. The last time that she had traveled here with Broken Ghost, the assassin had held her hand, had pulled her along in her wake as she powered effortlessly across ocean and land. No matter—Cloud Singer was determined to keep up, to prove her worth as they entered this, the final battle.

Broken Ghost looked up, her lips pulled back in a terrifying smile amid her skull-like face. They were nearly there, less than a minute now.

Cloud Singer looked ahead, forcing her eyes to lose focus, to see the middle distance and the constructions beneath the world, the pulse that hid from normal eyes. There were objects here and there that glowed, sparkled and spun. Cloud Singer looked for the door beneath the mountains, the hidden entrance to the Cerberus tribe's home.

Broken Ghost had slowed, easing the mind-blowing speed from her limbs, pulling back to cover just a handful of miles per second now, the breeze of her passing catching her hair, making it trail behind her like a ribbon. Cloud Singer saw it then, ahead and off to the west. The gateway beneath the soil was there, a rectangle hidden from normal sight, pulsing with an incandescent glow. Not orange now but a shade of gold mixed with green, the color of the flesh of the lime.

It was as Decimal River had promised—the door was open. Brigid Baptiste had been successful.

LAKESH TURNED as the ops room door opened behind him, and he felt relief when he saw the familiar figure of Kane come striding into the room. "Kane," he began, "you need to get out of here—we're evacuating right now."

Kane's steely gaze fixed on Lakesh. "We're not going anywhere," he said. "We're all going to wait right here."

Lakesh was perplexed. "What do you mean?"

Brigid spoke up as she turned away from her computer terminal, tossing her gas mask rebreather aside to reveal a devilish smile on her lips. "We've prepared a little surprise for you, O mighty leader."

Behind his own rebreather, Lakesh snorted an incredulous laugh. "What are you talking about? I don't follow," he said.

"You will," Kane assured him, reaching forward and plucking the rebreather off Lakesh's face in one single, swift motion, "old man."

Without the gas mask filtering his breathing, Lakesh could smell immediately the new scent that was filling the air, subtle and familiar. He turned away from Kane, peering over Brigid's shoulder, across to the antechamber beyond the operations center. The armaglass walls of the jump chamber were misting up, and the howling sound increased in pitch. The four-inch-thick bulkhead that sealed off the operations room from the rest of the redoubt slid into place with a thud.

"'Someone's using the mat-trans,'" Lakesh uttered, unsure if he had actually said the words aloud.

"You bet they are," Kane assured him.

Brigid stood up, stepping close to Lakesh. "It's always nice meeting new people," she added as the grin widened on her face, "don't you find?"

The mat-trans unit powered down, and Lakesh watched two silhouettes step from the swirling mists of the mat-trans unit. They were two women, their skin lustrous, their black hair coarse. The shorter one was dressed in strips of material of the deepest red and Lakesh saw that her bare brown flesh was covered in tattoos of the most intricate designs, circuitry and diagrams. The other's skin was far paler, almost translucent, and it was unmarked. She wore a white strap across her chest, and dangling white skirts flowed below her waist, leaving her legs free to move. Glass glinted in her braided hair, catching the red emergency lights of the operations room, and something was spinning at the end of the cord she held in her hand. But it was her face that Lakesh dwelled upon—the rest he took in with a single glance, but her face was something mesmerizing, a terrifying visage from a nightmare. Even in the deep, red glow of the room, Lakesh could see that the woman's face was colored white with dark patches around the eyes; her face was a skull.

# Chapter 18

Donald Bry had removed the cover to the security keypad, and he stood beside it, fiddling with the pen in his hand that he had been using to keep a record of the evacuees. With a bend and a snap, he plucked the metal pocket clip off the pen. Leaning one arm against the wall as he stared at the keypad wiring, Bry used the pointed end of the broken pocket clip to enter a sequence into what remained of the keypad itself.

There was the sound of a low, metallic thunk as machinery went into action and the huge door shuddered open, letting the cool night breeze into the corridor. Behind him, Donald heard a cheer rise up from the crowd of evacuees.

"Good job, Poindexter," Edwards told Bry out of the side of his mouth before he stepped forward and began ushering people through the widening gap. "On the double, people, let's do this quick and orderly."

Watching the crowd file past him one by one, Donald Bry breathed a sigh of relief. Even as he did so, he felt the ticklish feeling in his chest and, just for a moment, spluttered into his hand. It must be the cold air, he told himself as he joined Edwards to direct the Cerberus personnel outside.

AT THE BACK of the shuffling crowd, Domi stood on tiptoe and examined the faces of the people around her. She could see Donald Bry up at the front of the crowd, standing beside the large door as it folded slowly back and the sea of people flooded through the opening. With the number of people in the corridor right now, it would take several minutes to push her way through and reach Bry. She checked the faces around her, hoping to find Skylar Hitch. She couldn't see the woman anywhere nearby, and the fact that Skylar was only five feet tall meant, Domi realized, that she could easily miss her in this crowd.

She turned back, gazing down the corridor toward the entry door to the ops room, wondering what to do. As she looked, the door to a nearby staircase crashed open and Shizuka came sprinting into the main corridor, clothes and skin covered in filth, holding the gleaming blade of her *katana*.

"Shizuka?" Domi cried, dashing along the corridor to catch up to the warrior woman. "Shizuka, is that you?"

Peering up and down the corridor, Shizuka saw Domi running toward her and her fierce expression turned to a look of relief for a moment. "Domi, what's going on?" she asked.

Domi touched the rebreather that covered the lower half of her face. "We've detected a contaminant in the air. Cerberus is being evacuated. You have to leave."

Shizuka took several steps toward the disappearing crowds, then glanced back at the albino woman. "Where's Lakesh? Where are Kane, Grant and Brigid?"

"It's okay. I think Grant's already evacuated—I haven't seen him. The others are in the ops center together," Domi said. "Lakesh and Brigid are having trouble sending the order through the Cerberus mainframe to purge the air-conditioning, and Kane just went in there to get some gas masks for—"

"Come on!" Shizuka interrupted, dashing down the corridor at full sprint. "Lakesh is in trouble."

Domi ran after the bedraggled samurai warrior, not bothering to question the statement.

WHEN BRIGID BAPTISTE entered Grant's room in the Cobaltville medical hub, she found Kane was already waiting, sitting in one of the comfortable chairs beside Grant's bed. She was soaked, her hair dripping from the rainstorm that was darkening the skies outside.

Kane looked up as the door swung open, surprise on his face. "You decided to join us after all, Baptiste?" he asked.

"Couldn't let you storm Heaven without me," she replied as she pushed the door closed behind her, sweeping a dripping lock of red hair over her ear.

Grant spoke up from the bed, his broken form hidden beneath the sheets. "Where's Abi?" he asked.

"I left her with one of my neighbors," Brigid told him.

"Will she be all right?" Kane asked.

"Does it matter?" Brigid replied, her voice sounding brittle.

The room was quiet for a few somber seconds, and then Grant spoke up, forcing a light tone into his voice. "Are we all here for the same thing? To leave this prison or dream or whatever the fuck it is?"

Kane nodded as Brigid paced across the room to watch the heavy rain slapping against the window. "I don't really want to leave," she said. "But I can't stay here knowing what I know. Knowing that it's all a lie."

"No matter how beautiful," Grant stated, "a lie is still just a lie."

"DR. SINGH?" the woman with the skull-painted face asked as she stepped out of the mat-trans chamber.

Lakesh nodded, feeling fear rise within him.

"I understand that Lakesh is the name you prefer," the woman continued as she strode confidently toward him.

Lakesh wondered if he should run. As the thought crossed his mind, Kane stepped behind him, blocking the route to the exit door while Brigid remained at his side.

The skull-painted, pale-skinned woman spoke again, her voice a hideous whisper. "I am Broken Ghost," she said, "and I am here to bring justice."

Lakesh swallowed, watching the woman approach. The other one, the one in dark red rags, was holding back a little, standing close to the doorway to the mat-trans unit.

Broken Ghost stopped before Lakesh, her dark eyes boring into his own. "Do you believe in justice, Dr. Singh?"

"Yes, I do," Lakesh told her. "Fundamentally."

"Your people are trapped, dead, dying," Broken Ghost said, "and this facility will shut down shortly, never to reopen. For that is simply the way in which I do things—no loose ends. I am here for you, Lakesh. I have come here to kill you."

"I see," Lakesh said, nodding, "but I don't understand. Why me? Why have you targeted my people?"

From beside the mat-trans chamber, the other woman spoke. "Bastard!" the tattooed girl in strips of red spat. "Don't you know who we are? Don't you know who I am?"

Broken Ghost held up one pale hand to still the girl's outburst. "Cloud Singer, please," she warned. Then she reached forward, stroking pale fingers down Lakesh's cheek as she looked into his eyes. "Months ago," she explained, "you sent your people to Russia to execute my tribe brothers. In so doing, you have destroyed the Dreaming. You understand now why you must be punished, why we are here to kill you?"

The Death Cry, Lakesh realized. She was talking about the failed operation to retrieve the Death Cry, that Russian superweapon that promised to put an end to the threat of the Annunaki. The weapon had turned out to be unstable and, to further complicate matters, a second group had arrived in an effort to snatch the weapon. These women, Broken Ghost and the one she had called Cloud Singer, had to be a part of that other group.

"What have you done to my people?" Lakesh asked, inclining his head toward Brigid, then Kane.

"You need not worry yourself with such trivialities," Broken Ghost stated, placing her other hand on the other side of Lakesh's head, pressing against him. "Hold still."

The woman looked at him from the skull-like makeup of her face, pushing her hands against his skin as she took a grip on his head. She planned to twist his neck, break it, snapping the spinal column in a single deadly movement, Lakesh realized. It would be swift and painful, and then he would be dying in agony until the life finally ebbed out of his body. He clenched his teeth as the assassin's hands began to rotate his head.

"Please, stop this. Don't do this," he said. "You have misunderstood the situation."

The assassin ignored him, forcing his head slowly to face to the left, her fearsome power welling.

Suddenly the vanadium-steel bulkhead and door behind it opened, and a white streak blurred through as Domi's arm appeared, throwing one of her knives. Broken Ghost stumbled backward, letting go of Lakesh as the blade embedded itself in her left shoulder with a wet thud.

"Get the hell away from him," Domi warned.

Beside the albino girl, Shizuka rushed into the room, swinging her *katana* through the air. "Lakesh," she shouted, "they can't be trusted. Brigid and Kane aren't working for Cerberus anymore."

"So I gathered," Lakesh said as he stepped backward, retreating to stand with Domi and Shizuka as their enemies spread out. "What's happened to them, do you know?" Then he saw the state of Shizuka's silk dressing gown, the stains of blood and gunk that clung to her skin. "Come to that, what happened to you?"

"Grant attacked me," Shizuka breathed, holding the *katana* high and ready, "tried to kill me with Brigid's help."

Brigid looked at Shizuka, that reptilian, self-satisfied grin on her lips. "I'll make sure this time, midget gem," she stated.

Then Kane turned, and Shizuka, Lakesh and Domi all saw the Sin Eater pistol that was forming in his grip.

"Duck!" Domi shouted as the first stream of bullets blasted across the operations center.

BRIGID TURNED AWAY from the window as heavy rain lashed against it. "How do we get out?"

"We could run," Kane said. "Grant and I were just talking about taking a Sand Cat and driving out of the ville gates, seeing how far we could go."

"Maybe that would just be running away," Brigid observed. "What do we know about the nature of this place?"

"That it's a huge production," Grant stated, "involving perhaps a thousand actors in their roles."

"That our thoughts have been changed," Kane added, "our memories altered so that we don't know how we got here, so that we wouldn't question what we saw."

"Then it's some kind of illusion," Brigid reasoned. "Those aren't actors, they're…creations."

"Robots?" Kane asked.

Grant laughed. "My nurse here is no robot. I can assure you of that."

"It's as real as we think it is," Brigid said, arranging her thoughts out loud. "Which means it works in our heads, plays with our minds to create the illusion. You said yourself, Grant, that it felt like a dream. In a dream you never question, never wonder what the backstory was. You just accept and move forward, and no matter what happens you incorporate it as a part of the dream."

"So we're trapped in a stream of consciousness," Kane suggested, trying to formulate the concept in his own mind. "Could be a psychic behind it."

"Or a psychotropic drug," Grant theorized, "pumped into us without our knowledge."

Brigid shook her head in frustration. "Argh! It's impossible. You can't fight what you can't see. And what does Cerberus have to do with any of it?"

Kane looked at her calmly. "Cerberus stood at the gateway, guarding the path into the underworld."

"Perhaps there was a gateway that we came through to get here," Grant pondered. "Perhaps we're in Hell."

Slowly Brigid's lips curled into a smile. "Of course," she said with a laugh. "That's it."

DOMI PULLED LAKESH down behind one of the desks as the stream of 9 mm slugs zipped all around them. "Keep your head down, lover," she instructed Lakesh through her gas mask.

Shizuka leaped over a chair and landed beside them, crouching behind the next desk along as Kane's bullets continued to fly across the room, drilling into desks and walls.

"This is very disconcerting," Lakesh stated, turning from Domi to Shizuka and back.

"That's not Kane," Shizuka reminded him. "Just get that idea out of your head. It's not Kane, not Brigid and it most assuredly wasn't Grant."

Another stream of bullets pounded against the side of the desk, throwing splinters of wood all around the group.

"What happened, Shizuka?" Lakesh asked.

"Grant…" she said haltingly. "He…attacked me. It wasn't him. It looked like him but there was nothing of Grant in that…that abomination."

"These people are here to kill me," Lakesh told the women warriors. "The two newcomers are called Broken Ghost and Cloud Singer."

"Cloud Singer," Domi repeated, recognizing the name. "I met her, briefly, in Georgia. Crap. These are the bastards who almost blinded me."

"I know," Lakesh said, following Domi in a crouch as the three of them moved to the cover of another desk. "That time, they took control of the satellite feed and the biometric data, fed us false information until it was almost too late."

"What did you do?" Shizuka asked, having not been present during the operation that Lakesh was describing.

"Kane's field team was left defenseless in hostile territory," Lakesh stated. "These people are technological shamen, able to turn our equipment against us, seemingly at will. Donald and his team have spent months repairing the damage they caused to our systems and bolstering the security protocols, and yet they've managed to set a rootkit in the mainframe that's preventing anyone's access but theirs."

"Brigid filed a report, didn't she?" Domi pondered.

Lakesh's eyes lit up as he saw her point. "Of course, dearest. And her bogus report must have unleashed the virus."

The sound of bullets stopped, and Broken Ghost's voice cut through the air. "I thought you were an honorable man, Dr. Singh. I thought that you believed in justice. And yet now you hide from it."

"This isn't justice," Lakesh cried out in response. "This is an execution."

Almost as soon as the words left Lakesh's mouth, another burst of gunfire cut the air, and a cluster of bullets drilled into the desk and floor around him and his teammates.

"We need to fight past them," Domi snarled, looking at Shizuka for confirmation, "and get the hell out of here."

Shizuka held her sword ready.

"Wait," Lakesh instructed them both.

"What is it?" Shizuka whispered.

"You're right," he replied. "It's not Kane, not Brigid. They were changed when they came through the mat-trans. Skylar noticed, but I ignored her when Donald mentioned it to me. It's incredible—that woman is so in tune with computers that she can recognize a corrupted file in any form, even human!"

"So what do we do?" Domi asked.

"If I can get to the mat-trans controls I may be able to backtrack and reverse the damage," Lakesh theorized, working through the complex equations that this would involve in his head.

Domi looked at him blankly, but Shizuka understood immediately and her breath caught in her throat. "Grant," she muttered. "You can save him?"

Lakesh nodded. "Get me to the controls and I will do my very best, Shizuka."


"THERE WAS RUMORED to be a project in the Beforetime," Brigid began, Kane and Grant hanging on her every word, "that experimented with the transfer of matter from one location to another using quantum gateways. An instantaneous transport system via folding space."

"And what?" Kane asked. "You think we're part of that experiment? You think that's maybe how we came here?"

Brigid looked at him, a widening smile on her face. "It's funny, Kane. You see, you're both going to laugh, but the name of the rumored division involved in this was Project Cerberus."

Kane stood, his mouth open, first in shock, then, almost immediately, replaced with anger. "And you didn't think to mention this before?" he yelled, grabbing her by the shoulders and shaking her.

"I didn't remember it, Kane," Brigid told him. "When you mentioned gateways it must have triggered something, something that they tried to hide from me when they put us here. Remember when we met in my apartment, the way we fought? Didn't you feel as though your thoughts were being messed around with then, like you couldn't quite keep hold of them?"

Slowly, his face still flushed with anger, Kane let go of the woman's arms and stepped back.

Thoughtfully, Grant spoke up from the bed. "Then we need to find a gateway," he told the others. "You have any idea what these things look like, Brigid?"

Brigid closed her eyes, trusting her eidetic memory to bypass the blocks that had been set in all their minds and locate the information they required.

BULLETS WHIZZED over the desktops as Lakesh, Domi and Shizuka edged across the ops room. A moment later, the gunfire stopped and they heard Kane's heavy footfalls as he approached their hiding place.

"We're sitting ducks here," Domi realized, her voice coming harshly through the filter of the rebreather. In swift sentences, she explained her plan to the others.

Suddenly, the tip of Kane's gun barrel appeared, poking through the space between desks. Instantly, Shizuka swung her *katana* and the razor-sharp blade knocked the barrel aside, even as Kane pulled the trigger. A burst of 9 mm slugs rushed forth, scattering about the area as Shizuka leaped back. Computer screens burst apart as bullets smashed them, spilling shards of sharp glass across the floor.

As she jumped out of the path of the bullets, Shizuka yelled an instruction to her partners. "Now, Domi!"

Domi and Lakesh didn't need to be told twice. The albino girl pounced from her hiding place behind a desk, her second boot knife clenched firmly in her grip, the blade reversed so that it pointed toward the floor.

Brigid Baptiste laughed as she saw the chalk-skinned woman leap from cover, and she started to run across the room after her, Broken Ghost and Cloud Singer just strides behind.

At the same time, across the room from the leaping figure of Domi, Shizuka was driving the fake Kane back through the aisles of computer terminals with broad swings of her sword. The Sin Eater pistol in Kane's hand had been ruined by Shizuka's *katana*. He tossed the ruined handblaster at Shizuka as she took another step closer, and she batted it aside with her blade.

Domi was at the door now, her knife raised. With a final, sweeping gesture, she drilled the blade into the control panel in the wall. The red emergency lights of the room flared for a moment, the red alert replaced with a dazzling, halogen-bright whiteness, before the control panel began to spark. Then, as Brigid, Kane, Broken Ghost and Cloud Singer blinked away the aftereffects of being dazzled, the lights fizzled, popped and the room went dark.

Domi pounded at the door, urging it to open. The sounds of the alarm Klaxon could be heard whining in the main corridor as she slipped out. "Come on, you sorry-assed Pit scum," she muttered, her voice masked by the rebreather, "let's get it on."

At the same time as the lights flared and dimmed, Shizuka drove her *katana* at Kane's torso, hollering in a release of anger as she pushed the blade into the man's chest. Kane stumbled, the rods and cones popping in his eyes where the flash of lights had surprised him just moments before, and he cried out as he felt the sharp blade slip through his body.

Gripping the hilt of her *katana*, Shizuka began to lift

and turn. She had narrowed her eyes to squints, knowing precisely what Domi planned to do and preparing herself for the change in lighting. Ambient light still cast a glow in the darkened room, emanating from more than a dozen computer terminals that were dotted across the desks. In this light, the broad figure of Kane was reduced to a silhouette, with two white spots in his head where the light glinted from his rapidly blinking eyes. As Shizuka turned the blade, skewering Kane at its end, she saw two new spots of white appear, twin, horizontal slashes across his face where he had opened his mouth to cry out, the diffuse light glinting off his teeth.

Across the wide room, Shizuka could make out Domi's figure standing in the open doorway, framed in the dull orange emergency lighting of the corridor as the others in the room rubbed at their blinded eyes.

"Come on, Shizuka," Domi shouted. "We're getting out of here." With that, Domi disappeared into the corridor.

Broken Ghost blinked, and the night-vision lenses swooped over her eyes on their nictitating membranes. The darkness of the ops room was brought into sharp focus once more, and she saw Kane lying against a desk, teeth clenched, hands clutching at his stomach. Then the samurai warrior was leaping through the air at her, sword held high as Kane's blood dripped down its length.

Broken Ghost brought up her hands in a blur, clapping against the sides of Shizuka's blade and throwing her aim off. Shizuka landed heavily, pulling herself down into a balanced crouch, the sword held before her. Broken Ghost was still holding the blade between her clasped hands, and suddenly she swiped her hands off and to the right. The *katana* spun out of Shizuka's grip, spinning in the air before clattering to the floor tiles.

Broken Ghost stalked toward the samurai, her bold, skull-like, white makeup seeming to glow in the darkened room.

Cloud Singer had brought her own night-vision lenses into play by now, and she scoured the room, trying to see where the other party had gone. "Lakesh isn't here," she told the faux Brigid at her side. "He must have left with the white girl when the lights went out. Quickly, after them!"

Brigid's long-legged stride took her to the door in a fraction of a second, and she and Cloud Singer rushed out into the corridor after their departing enemies.

From a hiding place in the leg space of one of the desks, Lakesh watched the door close behind them, and he smiled. The ruse wouldn't last long, but if Domi could keep them busy for a few minutes he may just be able to retrieve the real Kane, Grant and Brigid from digital limbo. He crouch walked across the ops room, past the bloody, fallen figure of Kane, as the savage battle between Shizuka and Broken Ghost raged on across the far side of the room. In a few seconds he was at the mat-trans terminal, punching in his override password and backtracking through recent arrivals and departures.

His fingers began tapping out a sequence on the keyboard, and a series of indicator tags appeared on the terminal.

"Good," Lakesh murmured. The files on Kane, Grant and Brigid were still alive; their information had not been wiped.

It was pure good fortune that the assassin had chosen to enter the redoubt via the mat-trans. Without that decision, it was entirely possible that the program would have been wiped or corrupted along with the rest of the Cerberus database. The rootkit had hitched itself to so much of the basic programming, and yet a firewall had been built into the viral program itself to prevent it touching the mat-trans system lest it should interfere with the ultimate arrival of the invaders.

Lakesh skipped past the front-end programming screens and accessed the protocols of the mat-trans. His friends were inside here somehow, held in stasis. Whatever had stepped out of the mat-trans just seventeen hours earlier was a strange, warped copy, utilizing the data held in the mat-trans computer. As his fingers tapped at the keys, Lakesh's mind was rapidly running through the steps necessary to free his friends from limbo.

His fingers jabbed at the keyboard in a blur, tapping out algorithms to bypass the system's built-in safety measures.

NERVOUSLY, GRANT AND Kane watched as Brigid closed her eyes and tried to claw at the memories that had been subdued in her brain.

"Lights," she said softly. "Lights and electricity, lightning crackling within the swirling mist. That's all I can recall, that and a howling noise."

"Where do we find all that?" Grant asked.

"Alpha Level," Brigid answered as a dim recollection of a secret chamber in a storeroom on A Level suddenly took shape in her mind.

DOMI SPRINTED along the wide main corridor of the redoubt, its overhead metal struts glinting with the flashing red alarm lights, disappearing into shadow before they reappeared once more. The corridor was empty, and at the far end she could see moonlight seeping in through the gap where the entrance door had finally been opened. She looked over her shoulder, checking on her pursuers. Two of them had followed her.

Damn! She had hoped for all four, hoped to distract them long enough so that Lakesh could get to the mat-trans and do whatever it was he had planned. No point worrying about it now, she chastised herself. Hopefully, Shizuka was maintaining a strong defense for the elderly scientist.

As she ran down the wide, arched corridor, Domi heard a whooshing noise, and something cut through the air behind her. She turned once more, wondering what the noise was, but as she did so she felt whatever it was slam into the small of her back. Her breath spilled out of her mouth in a gasp as her legs gave way. She tumbled to the floor, rolling over and over before coming to a halt.

Domi gazed, upside down, as twin figures rushed toward her. Brigid ran ahead, her lengthy strides eating up the distance between them, as the tattooed woman reached up and caught the whirling line of metal that cleaved the air. It was a boomerang, Domi realized—the woman had hit her with a boomerang.

Unable to move, Domi organized her thoughts as her enemies closed in on her.

LAKESH IGNORED the sounds of fighting as he continued working at the keyboard in the ops room. Ten paces behind him, Broken Ghost swung her leg high and kicked Shizuka beneath the jaw, knocking the samurai off her feet.

"Are you a warrior?" Broken Ghost asked in her strange voice.

Lying beneath her on the floor, Shizuka rolled as Broken Ghost stomped her heel at her face, avoiding the attack by less than an inch. Shizuka's hands reached forward, grasping for the assassin's ankle in the semidarkness of the room and yanking as hard as she could. Broken Ghost was pulled from her feet, and she reached out and swept at the surface of a desk as she fell. Computer equipment, files and papers crashed to the floor all around them as Shizuka pounced at the woman, shoving her head against the hard floor as the glass in the woman's hair tore at her hands.

Lakesh continued typing, trying to remember the structured coding that operated the mat-trans protocols. With a sense of satisfaction, he typed out the final sequence and watched the screen as the characters shifted and the mat-trans unit fired up.

THEY FOUND a wheelchair in which they placed Grant, and Brigid kept pace as Kane pushed his partner through the bland corridors of the Cobaltville medical hub.

"Where do you want to go?" Kane asked as Brigid stabbed the elevator button for the top floor.

"We're going to the top of the Administrative Monolith," Brigid answered. "I'll recognize the gateway when I see it."

"And then what?" Kane asked.

"Then we're going to flee this dream," Brigid told him with a mirthless smile.

Sitting in the wheelchair, Grant looked over his shoulder and offered his partner a look. "Hey, Kane—you remember when it was just the two of us and plans actually made some kind of fucking sense?"

"It was never that simple," Kane retorted, his expression grim.

# Chapter 19

Decimal River walked back into the cave, chewing at a cooked chicken leg, grease running down his fingers. He had worked himself up with stress, been unable to eat for the final days leading to the push against Cerberus. Now that he was finally able to eat once again, the chicken tasted like something magical as it touched his tongue. Satisfied, he sat before his computer screen and gazed at the data feed.

The three subjects were still there, but there was something wrong. A new line of code was running rampant through the system, fragmenting his virtual world, destroying the trap. Someone had discovered them.

Decimal River wiped his greasy fingers on the legs of his pants, leaned forward and began tapping out a rapid code to grant him back-door access to the system. Two words appeared on-screen: "Access denied."

"But that cannot be," he cried as he ran through his code again.

THE ELEVATOR DOORS opened onto Alpha Level, and a well-dressed guard rushed over to greet the trio, a stern look on his face.

"I'm sorry," he began, "but this level is closed to—"

Kane's right arm lashed out and the Sin Eater rocketed into his palm from its wrist holster, extending to its full length in a fraction of a second. Kane's finger was crooked as it met the trigger, pushing the trigger down and blasting a stream of steel-jacketed bullets into the guard's face.

"No time left to argue," Kane told the unfortunate guard as he fell to the floor, his face now just a bloody smear.

"Let's go," Kane told Brigid as the Sin Eater retracted into its holster and he maneuvered Grant's wheelchair.

"This way," she directed, relying on the vague memory of a gateway that someone called Lakesh had described.

LAKESH HELD HIS BREATH as the information on the monitor flickered, and his fingers darted forward to adjust the code. Someone was trying to break through the Cerberus firewall, the same person who had originally manipulated the data. With a swift tap on the keyboard, Lakesh added a further level of encryption to his data stream, blocking his unseen opponent's access.

He looked up from the screen, watching with nervous anticipation as howling began and the familiar mist began to fill the mat-trans chamber itself, billowing from the vents and fogging up the glass.

As he watched, Lakesh became aware of a presence behind him, and he turned just in time to duck a powerful punch aimed straight at the back of his head. Kane stood there, a bloody streak across his chest and torso, blood oozing down the casual clothing he wore. Not Kane, Lakesh reminded himself—something other.

Lakesh spun from his chair and leaped out of the way as the false Kane swung another pile-driver punch in the older man's direction.

"Time to die, you irritating little megalomaniac," Kane growled as he stalked toward the retreating scientist.

ON THE OTHER SIDE of the ops room, Broken Ghost was caught in a tangle on the floor with Shizuka lying on top of her. Broken Ghost tossed her head back until it crashed into Shizuka's forehead with a loud crack. Shizuka felt a wave of nausea flood through her with the impact, and her grip weakened on the assassin's agile body.

A moment later, a sharp elbow slammed into Shizuka's belly as Broken Ghost renewed her attack. The skull-faced assassin thrashed on the floor tiles, throwing Shizuka's battered body aside. A moment later, she stood over the samurai as Shizuka slumped to the floor, utterly exhausted.

As Broken Ghost flexed her muscles, preparing to put Shizuka out of her misery, the door beside her crashed open and Cloud Singer and Brigid Baptiste entered, dragging the unconscious form of Domi.

"Lakesh is gone," Cloud Singer explained hurriedly. "You promised me we'd—" She stopped, spying the ongoing skirmish on the far side of the room via her night lenses.

Lakesh was there, backing away as a bloody, wounded Kane closed in on him. As Cloud Singer watched, Lakesh stepped into a wall of smoked glass at the edge of the room, finding himself trapped with nowhere left to run.

"THIS IS IT," Brigid declared.

In front of them was the pewter-gray armaglass wall of the secret gateway that Lakesh had used to commute between Cobaltville and the Cerberus redoubt.

"How does it work?" Kane asked, clearly skeptical.

"Guess we'll find out," Grant rumbled.

Brigid entered the chamber and looked around, a puzzled expression on her face. She touched the control panel inside the armaglass-walled chamber, then examined the lock on the door. "We all have to be in here," she stated, and motioned for Kane to lift Grant out of the wheelchair and into the jump chamber.

Brigid closed her eyes, visualizing her fingers, touching the keypad and locking the door before her memory was overwhelmed with a rising howl and spark-shot mist. She opened her eyes and looked at Kane and Grant.

"This is it," she said, reaching for the keypad.

LAKESH FELT his heart pounding in his chest as he backed up against the armaglass wall of the mat-trans. Kane stood before him, fists clenched, his chest oozing blood over his torn shirt. Behind him, in the half-light cast by the computer screens, Lakesh saw three women stalking toward him—the fake Brigid Baptiste, the tattooed teenager called Cloud Singer and the skull-faced athlete who had introduced herself as Broken Ghost.

Lakesh peered into the darkness beyond them, trying to locate Domi and Shizuka, hoping against hope that they might yet come to his assistance.

"They're dead," Broken Ghost said, as though reading his thoughts.

"If it's me you want," Lakesh said, struggling to keep the tremor out of his voice, "then just kill me. Please, leave my people alone."

"You killed my friends," the teenager snarled.

"No," Lakesh began, shaking his head, "I didn't—"

"Liar!" Cloud Singer spat. "You ordered your people there, ordered them to kill my war brothers. They may have done your dirty work, Kane and his ilk, but the blood is on your hands, Lakesh of the Cerberus tribe."

The four figures had surrounded Lakesh now, where he stood backed against the tinted armaglass, the mists billowing within the cubicle behind him. There was nowhere left to go, nowhere left to run. He had done everything he could.

"It's over, Lakesh," Brigid said, her emerald eyes fixed on his. "Time to go."

Behind him, the mat-trans was powering down. Suddenly the mists swirled out of the opening.

As the door swung wide, three figures emerged and Grant's voice came through the open doorway of the mat-trans: "…where someone doesn't start shooting at us?"

# Chapter 20

Kane leaped through the open mat-trans door at his blood-drenched double, swinging his right fist at the jaw of his surprised opponent. "You don't really want me to answer that, do you?" he responded to Grant's question from a second before.

Wrong-footed, the tired, bloody clone of Kane fell to the tiled floor with a wet slap like so much meat, the energy leaving him instantly. He lay there, unable to move as the figure he had been based on surveyed the Cerberus ops room. Kane saw the familiar forms of Cloud Singer and—was that Baptiste?—as well as the skull-faced assassin who led them both in a charge at Lakesh.

Behind Kane, still at the open doorway of the mat-trans, Grant jumped forward, his left arm coming up to block Broken Ghost's attack as she swung a high kick at Lakesh's head.

"Not if it's going to depress me," Grant growled at Kane as he pushed Broken Ghost's leg back, forcing her to lose her balance and topple to the floor.

Furious, Cloud Singer's eyes fixed on Kane and his partners and she let loose a low growl. "Deal with these animals," she ordered the double of Brigid Baptiste, who remained in her thrall, "while I finish the leader." Broken

Ghost had taught her to tamp down her anger well, but she wanted to hurt Kane so much in that second that it took all her determination not to launch herself at him. Lakesh had to come first.

Beside her, the Brigid duplicate was already moving, arms cutting through the air as she clambered over a desk and pounced at the Kane in the faded denim jacket who had just stepped out of the mat-trans. Kane looked up, distracted by the semidarkness of the room, and grabbed for Brigid as she dropped onto him. Together, the pair fell backward, crashing into the busy desk of one of the Cerberus ops staff.

"What kind of foul trick are you?" Brigid spit as Kane wrestled with her atop the desk.

"Could ask the same question, Baptiste," Kane responded as he drove a punch into her breastbone, knocking her off him.

The Brigid Baptiste creature wasn't even fazed. She regained her balance in a split second and lunged at Kane before he could get up from the desk. She pinned him down with the weight of her body, a knee on his chest and her hands reaching around his throat. "I don't know what you are," she told him, "but it won't matter for much longer."

Kane felt her grip tighten around his neck, cutting off his air supply as he tried to take his next breath.

Meanwhile, just a few paces away, the true Brigid had emerged from the mat-trans wearing a suede jacket, a scarred leather satchel over her shoulder. She turned to Lakesh, her brow furrowed in confusion. "Lakesh, what on earth is going on here?"

"Mat-trans glitch," Lakesh explained briefly.

As Brigid looked at him, eyes wide in surprise, Lakesh

saw the dark form of Cloud Singer rushing at them both through the shadows.

"Brigid, watch your back!" Lakesh cried as the fierce, tattooed warrior started to attack.

In a flurry of movement, Cloud Singer vaulted over a desk, knocking the computer equipment from it in her haste. A moment later she was on Brigid's back, the razor-sharp boomerang in her hand, sweeping the shining blade down toward Brigid's face.

Brigid stumbled as she adjusted to Cloud Singer's weight, turned her head as the sharp edge of steel raced toward her. She felt the swish of air, and a handful of red-gold curls fell to the floor as the boomerang cut through her hair.

As the tattooed girl tried a second time, Brigid let her body go lax, dropping to the floor like so much dead weight. She landed hard on her back, with the struggling Cloud Singer taking the brunt of the impact.

Cloud Singer shrieked unintelligibly as the pain drove through her coccyx.

Driving herself off the fallen warrior, Brigid arched backward and angled a solid right cross at Cloud Singer's cheek.

A little way across the room, Grant was standing opposite Broken Ghost, sizing her up as she stalked left and right like a prowling jungle cat, head down, watching him. With the night-vision implants, the assassin who moved like a ghost could see Grant far better than he could her, and she was taking her time to settle on her best strategy. Still six paces from her, Grant appeared to swing a punch at the woman—too far away to hit her—and Broken Ghost saw the blaster appear in his hand.

As Grant pulled the trigger on the Sin Eater, Broken Ghost went into motion, running forward over Domi's prone body, into Grant's firing arc and bounding into the air. Grant tracked her, his finger holding down the Sin Eater's trigger, as she leaped before him. His bullets were just behind the skull-faced assassin, ripping through the air where she had been just a fraction of a second earlier.

At the apex of her jump, Broken Ghost's bare foot kicked out, the curled toes ramming into Grant's right eye like a fist. Grant's head snapped backward with the blow, and he fell toward the floor, his bullets spraying wildly about the room.

Grant hit the floor with the side of his head, knocking himself so hard that he saw stars for several seconds. His pressure on the trigger eased and the Sin Eater stopped firing. When his vision recovered, he found himself looking up at the pale-skinned assassin as she stood over him, the cord of the bull roarer coiled in her fists, poised to execute the killing blow.

LYING ON HIS BACK on the desk as the false Brigid strangled him, Kane felt the pressure increase on his throat, saw his vision blur. And his blurred vision was good, for it meant that he didn't have to see what it was he did next.

His right fist swept around, jabbing Brigid below the rib cage, pounding hard into her kidneys. He tensed his wrist tendons as he punched, calling the Sin Eater to hand, his finger immediately squeezing at the trigger.

Kane felt the recoil against his hand as the Sin Eater unleashed a volley of bullets, point-blank range, into the fake Brigid's guts. He shook as her body leaped in place, bouncing back and forth as the slugs drilled through her,

her gripping hands jarring against his neck as she tried to cling to him, cling to life.

It took just three seconds. Then her grip loosened and she fell from Kane, collapsing over the side of the desk in a lifeless heap, her bright red mane of hair flopping over to hide her face.

Kane lay still a moment, sucking at the glorious air as the pressure on his throat eased. "Baptiste is never going to let me live that down," he muttered as the Sin Eater returned to its holster at his wrist.

SPRAWLED ON THE FLOOR as the battle continued above her, Domi snapped back to consciousness just as Broken Ghost leaped over her, bullets from Grant's Sin Eater cutting through the air all around. There was something sharp digging into Domi's belly where Cloud Singer and the fake Brigid had tossed her on the floor like so much worthless trash. She reached beneath her to find out what it was. A glass shard from one of the damaged computer monitors was digging into her, its sharp edge pressing against her belly. As Broken Ghost snap-kicked Grant in the eye, knocking the larger man off his feet, Domi plucked the shard free.

Broken Ghost landed beside Domi, readying herself to execute Grant with the taut cord of the bull roarer as he struggled on the floor. As the assassin stepped forward, Domi lashed out with the glass shard, swinging it like a knife. With a spurt of blood, the glass cut through the tendons at the back of Broken Ghost's bare ankles, and the assassin cried in agony as she found herself toppling forward, no longer able to stand.

She crashed against the floor tiles and rolled into the mat-trans unit, unleashing a shrill cry as blood pumped from her ruined ankles. Domi was crawling across the floor then, the shank of glass glinting in her hand as it caught the lights of the monitors.

As she raised the shard above her head, preparing to plunge it into the assassin's breast, Domi felt a hand grasp her wrist, halting her attack. When she turned, she saw Grant there, a firm, no-nonsense look on his face.

"No, Domi" was all Grant said, but it was enough.

Domi's grip on the glass loosened and it dropped from her hand, clattering to the floor.

Across the room, Brigid Baptiste was using the flex from one of Skylar's broken computer units to bind Cloud Singer's hands. The young warrior was unconscious now, from equal parts exhaustion and the effort of a solid right cross from the feistiest archivist that Lakesh had ever seen.

"Put her in there," he directed, pointing to the jump chamber, "then close the door. We'll secure the redoubt, then decide what to do with them."

"We all okay?" Kane asked as he looked around the shadow-filled room.

"I believe that we are," Lakesh announced after swiftly eyeballing the room himself and counting heads.

Kane stepped toward the Cerberus leader, with Grant and Domi a few paces behind, making their way through the debris-strewed room.

Lakesh cleared his throat, relief evident on his features. "I believe that I owe you—all of you—my deepest thanks," he said.

Exhausted, her shoulders drooping, Domi pulled the rebreather from her face and passed it to Lakesh. "Save them until we're out of here. This place isn't safe."

Lakesh took the mask gratefully as Domi went to the equipment locker to find more gas masks for her companions.

Kane looked at his surroundings, almost as though he was seeing them for the first time, and then he extended his hand toward Lakesh, gripping the older man's hand tightly. "I think we all owe you some thanks of our own," he said. "For a moment there it was starting to look like we'd never get out of Cobaltville."

Lakesh had no idea what the man was referring to, but he nodded regardless, just relieved to still be alive.

As Domi passed around gas masks, Lakesh updated the others on everything that they had missed while they had been trapped in the digital limbo. As he spoke, Grant noticed a woman's leg sticking out from behind one of the desks, where it had been almost hidden by the shadows. He stepped over the fallen body of the false Kane and made his way over to the shapely ankle, crouching beside its owner.

"Shizuka?" he asked in a gentle voice.

Face spattered with trash and blood, sporting a fat lip and a darkening bruise on her forehead, Shizuka looked at him, eyes flickering as she struggled to regain consciousness. "Grant-*san?*" she asked timidly. "Is that really you?"

Grant shrugged. "Who else would it be?" he asked as he reached one arm gently behind her head and, rolling her toward him, lifted her from the ground.

Grant stood, holding the featherlight form of his lover in his arms. He looked at the dried blood on her face, the food and garbage stains that spotted the silk of her familiar dressing gown. "What happened to you?" he asked.

"I got trashed," Shizuka said and she began to giggle as Grant's expression turned from concern to bewilderment.

They filed out of the ops center to convene on the plateau outside the redoubt where the rest of the Cerberus personnel waited.

When the anteroom was empty, the emitter array beneath the mat-trans unit began to whine, and mist began to swirl as the gateway powered up.

# Chapter 21

Cloud Singer opened her eyes and peered around her. She was lying on a bed, the sheets tangled about her legs, sweat shining on her tattooed body. She reached out, fumbling in the darkness until her fingers found the switch that turned on the bedside lamp. It came to life, lighting the small bedroom with a warm, orange-hued glow.

She lay on a double bed in a box room barely large enough to accommodate it. Rolling, Cloud Singer kicked off the damp sheets and sat up on the bed, trying to get her thoughts in order.

She had come from somewhere, traveled here somehow, but she couldn't remember how or why.

Rubbing sleep from her eyes, the tattooed warrior stood up, barely taking in the weirdly familiar surroundings. She stepped through the doorway, out into a compact room that contained a sagging, dilapidated couch, a single shelf holding three books, one of them a hidebound tome labeled *The Law*. A simple kitchenette stood at the side of the spartan room.

Cloud Singer padded across the room on bare feet, switched on the kitchen light and splashed cool water on her face, trying to remember where she was. Opposite the kitchen, she saw three windows reaching from floor to ceiling, long, characterless brown drapes dangling before them. She made her way across the room toward the windows, groping for the pull that operated the drapes.

The drapes inched back on their rails, revealing the impressive view from the windows. It was nighttime, a sliver of moon peeking from the thick clouds that ambled across the sky. Beneath the sliver of moon, a forest of lights sparkled and glinted like jewels or stars. It was a human settlement, a ville dominated by a massive tower that strained toward the heavens, a perfectly ordered, self-contained society.

Cobaltville.

Cloud Singer blinked, fear worming its way up from deep in her belly. She was trapped.

A SUDDEN JOLT OF PAIN and Broken Ghost was awake.

She struggled to open her eyes, but they wouldn't open. She felt so lethargic and yet, strangely, she was utterly awake.

And the pain. The crazy pain.

It was so intense, so absolute, that it threatened to overwhelm her, consume her. She clenched her fists, holding on to her tenuous grip on wakefulness. Did her fists really clench? She couldn't tell, couldn't be sure. No matter now, what really counted was the pain. *All* that counted was the pain.

She calmed her mind, remembering the techniques that she had been taught by Bad Father years before. A wet worker is never ruffled, never swayed by emotion.

Pain assaulted her, high in her right leg, a rending, tearing, ripping pain.

She struggled once more to turn her head, to open her eyes. I'm awake, she told herself, but I can't wake up.

The pain worsened then, threatening to overwhelm Broken Ghost.

And suddenly her eyes were open, assaulted by lights so bright that it stung to look. She saw them as shadows first of all, shadows moving back and forth until they took proper form. She was lying on her back before them, these shadow people, dressed in their starched clothing, masks over their shadow mouths.

The air smelled of antibacterial wash, and from somewhere nearby she heard the regular beeping of machinery, the hissing of a pump.

Suddenly one of the doctors, a middle-aged man with a shaved head and vibrant blue eyes, wearing a cotton mask over the bottom half of his features, leaped back from where he stood at the foot of the gurney, and Broken Ghost watched as a fountain of blood flew up and splashed over the doctor and the other people there.

Her leg, she realized. They were cutting through her leg.

As the thought spun through her mind, Broken Ghost sank back against the gurney, feeling the darkness of sleep take hold once more.

THE COUNCIL OF ELDERS granted an audience to Decimal River within their cave. He brought his laptop with him under one arm, closed up like a clamshell until they agreed to look at the data that it contained. The programmer felt empty, drained, no longer able to engage with others as he powered up the computer, having failed in all of his attempts to change the information that showed there.

The councillors peered at the screen as Decimal River

brought up the information. Eight words glowed in a box on the screen as the data stream surged behind.

Subject: Singer. Status: Active.

Subject: Ghost. Status: Active.

ONCE THEY HAD PURGED the air vents, a service was held outside the Cerberus redoubt to honor the recently departed. The body of Michaels was recovered from the machine room and buried, while Lakesh led his people in tribute to Trent, whose body had been destroyed in the re-cycling processor. Skylar Hitch remained on the list of those missing in action, although the general consensus was that she was probably another victim of the savage assault on the redoubt. The fate of the two invaders was a mystery, as the jump chamber was empty when they returned to the ops center.

That afternoon, three more bodies were recovered and buried beside those who had died bravely defending Cerberus redoubt. These three graves, however, were unmarked. It was an onerous task, but Kane, Grant and Brigid felt it was somehow their responsibility. The corpses wore their faces, serene in death despite all that they had been through in those final hours.

"It's a lot like losing a brother, isn't it?" Kane observed as he leaned on his shovel beside the three freshly dug plots.

"Or a sister," Brigid said sadly, "one you never knew you had."

Kane peered at her then, hearing the emotion in her voice. "You okay, Baptiste?"

Brigid stood for a moment, gazing at the blanket-wrapped body that shared her form as sunlight played in the trees around them. "I'll be fine," she finally said, but it was clear to Kane that she had a great burden weighing on her mind.

Grant, the third member of the party, took the opportunity to lighten the mood, reminding them that they had survived, hale and hearty, despite trying odds. "Everything's getting back to normal," he assured his colleagues. "We should, too."

"If this even is 'normal,'" Kane said, sweeping their surroundings with his gaze. "What's to say we didn't walk out of one trick and into another?"

"You don't want to start thinking like that," Grant told him. "That's the road to madness, Kane. Let it go. Be damn thankful we all have two arms and two legs, my friend."

Kane nodded his agreement and, after a few moments of thought, Brigid did, too, thanking the ex-Mag for his concern.

"Before long," Kane said as he and Grant got to work filling the graves with soil, "all that happened will just be a bad, old memory."

As they replaced the topsoil over the mountain graves, Kane felt something tug at his senses. He glanced up and saw Shizuka standing at the edge of the clearing, watching the three of them work. He nudged Grant and pointed out Shizuka. "We'll finish up here," he assured his partner as Brigid placed flowers on the unmarked graves.

"Thanks, man," Grant said, resting his shovel against the trunk of a nearby tree.

Brushing dirt from his clothes, Grant made his way over to where Shizuka waited. "Hey, you," he said quietly.

"Hey, yourself," Shizuka replied tentatively. She had dressed once more in casual clothes, light cotton trousers and a blouse of warm peach. "You all done?"

"Yeah," Grant told her, and then his words began to tumble out in a rush. "Look, Shizuka, I'm really sorry for what happened, for what 'I' did. I mean, it wasn't me but it was, and I understand if maybe you feel uncomfortable with that just now. It's okay, really it is."

Expressionlessly, Shizuka looked up into Grant's dark eyes. "That monster attacked me, Grant-*san,* tried to rape me. It was horrible and it had your face."

"I know," Grant said. "It must be hard to—"

Shizuka stopped him, holding a finger to her lips as Grant watched. "Grant, that thing wasn't you. My eyes were deceived for a while, but never here, never in my heart." She clutched a hand against her chest, her expression sad.

Grant looked at the wonderful warrior woman who stood before him, trying to put into words things that could never really be said, and he nodded. "You're sure?" he asked eventually, not knowing what else to say.

Shizuka nodded. "I love you, Grant," she assured him, stepping forward and reaching her arms around him.

A moment later, Grant had his arms around her, holding her close, as if he would never let go.

"Grant?" Shizuka said quietly from within his enveloping arms. "I just had a call through. I'm expected back at New Edo this evening."

Still holding Shizuka tightly, Grant kissed her on the forehead. "Then we'd better make the most of our time together," he said.

"Always," she replied, her voice barely a whisper.

Arm in arm, Grant and Shizuka made their way to the redoubt's entrance.

Watching the couple walk off from where he stood beside the three fresh graves, Kane spoke quietly to Brigid. "What do you think they're talking about?"

She smiled. "Things that happened to other people, living other lives," she told him.

"Those things don't matter," Kane said firmly as he saw Grant and Shizuka disappear into the redoubt. "Not anymore."

AT THE END of the long day, Brigid found herself alone in her quarters, readying herself for sleep.

She stood there, staring into the bathroom mirror as water splashed from the faucet. Her eyes were so green in the sharp lights, so bright that they almost glowed. She turned off the faucet and looked at her reflection a moment longer, focusing on her emerald eyes as the water rushed down the drain. Her eyes were just like hers, just like the girl's.

Brigid switched off the bathroom light and padded across the room on bare feet. She climbed into her bed and leaned across for the book that waited on her bedside table before thinking better of it. She was tired and her body ached with the need for rest. She reached over and switched off the bedside lamp, plunging the room into darkness.

Lying in bed, gazing up at the ceiling, Brigid whispered words to her empty room: "Good-night, munchkin. Sleep tight."

# The Executioner®

## Don Pendleton's

## DARK ALLIANCE

**A power struggle has deadly consequences....**

From the lazy heat of Miami to the steamy Colombian jungles, Mack Bolan is on the trail of a missing American journalist. She was close to exposing the key players in a dangerous drug cartel and may have been kidnapped to protect their empire. Each step pulls him further into an unforgiving world of guns and violence until he himself is captured. Tortured and beaten, Bolan is only seconds away from escape... or death.

*Available September wherever books are sold.*

GOLD EAGLE®

GEX370

# Don Pendleton
# SKY SENTINELS

### A new spark in the Middle East could ignite the ultimate global conflagration....

Iran is flexing its military muscle, kidnapping
U.S. journalists and openly daring America to retaliate.
When Iranian intelligence officers kidnap three prominent
Americans from D.C., Stony Man gets involved.
Dispatched to free the hostages and get a handle on
the main event, Stony Man discovers the planning
stages of a radical multinational plot that could
ignite the next—and last—world war.

# STONY MAN®

*Available October
wherever books are sold.*

# JAMES AXLER
# DEATH LANDS®

## Alpha Wave

### A struggle for survival in a land of sudden death...

Across the flat plains of the Dakotas, an iron horse shrieks and rumbles across refurbished tracks. Inside the boxcars, Ryan Cawdor and his companions face trouble as never before. Jak is missing, Krysty is dying and the train is loaded with sec men, whitecoats and the horrifying experiment of a baron — whose aim it is to control every living soul in Deathlands.

*Available September wherever books are sold.*